MURDER IN MYSTIC HILLS

Mysteries of Mystic Hills

CHRIS CANNON

Chapter 1

There were days where I wondered if my life was a reality television show for some higher power.

My nosy neighbor smiled at me and held out my mail, which she'd pilfered from my mailbox, sorted by size, and decorated with stickers featuring bible verses. "I thought these might help you." Gladys passed me the stack of bills and a few random ads.

"Why do you have my mail?" seemed the politest way to phrase my question. Normal neighbors didn't steal other people's mail and use it for judgmental craft projects.

"It's my gift to my fellow tenants," Gladys said. "It warms my heart to know I've helped those who've gone astray."

I was offended on several fronts. First because she was judging me, and second because I hadn't had a chance to go astray in quite some time. "My life isn't that exciting, so I'm going to need a clue. What are you talking about?"

"I've seen the food deliveries to your apartment late at night. I know what that means."

I laughed. "It means I've been binge-watching or binge-reading something and I didn't feel like cooking dinner." If I'd been getting lucky every time the Dine & Dash guy knocked on my door, I'd be far less irritated with this odd woman. Wait a minute. Maybe I should date someone who worked for Dine & Dash. Not a bad idea. Back to the problem at hand. I smiled at the judgmental busybody. "I'm an adult and I can order pizza whenever I want." Even if my jeans said otherwise. "I'd appreciate it if you didn't touch my mail in the future."

She patted me on the shoulder. "Don't worry, dear. It's no trouble. Have a nice night." With those parting words she turned and walked away.

Once I was in my apartment, I dropped the mail on the kitchen table and wondered what there was to eat. I knew the answer, but I opened the refrigerator and stared inside like there might be some forgotten treasure. Nope. Nothing exciting. I had the necessities: coffee creamer, milk, apples, string cheese, and wine. Honestly, this was the only time I regretted breaking things off with Greg. He might have been a cheating jerk, but he'd kept the refrigerator fully stocked.

So…time to call Dine & Dash again? Maybe I should act like an adult and order groceries instead. I poured myself a glass of white wine and grabbed a piece of cheese. Fifteen minutes later, I'd ordered a cart full of groceries which wouldn't arrive until tomorrow evening. There. I'd behaved like a responsible grown-up so I could order pizza with a clear conscience.

While I waited for my double pepperoni to arrive, I sorted through the mail. I didn't recognize the law firm who'd sent me a legal sized envelope. Should I be concerned? Maybe they were trying to drum up business. I pried the flap open and pulled out a stack of papers. There was a handwritten letter on top.

. . .

DEAR BELINDA,

I hope this finds you well. If you're reading this, I'm dead. Sorry…couldn't resist the drama. I know we haven't spoken in a few years, but I always felt we were kindred spirits.

Now that I've passed on, I need someone to take my place at the tea house. If you're skeptical, know that if you accept this arrangement, you'll be taking over my business and my home in Mystic Hills. Both are paid off. They'd be yours free and clear if you agreed never to sell either property. You can rent them out, but Tea & Spirits and my home must remain in the Harbinger name. I hope you'll accept this gift and carry on the family tradition.

Love,

Aunt Teresa Harbinger

Okay…there were a few problems with this situation. My name was Linda James, not Belinda Harbinger. I didn't have an Aunt Teresa and I'd never been to Mystic Hills. Had the nosy neighbor given me someone else's mail?

I checked the name on the envelope. Nope. It was addressed to me. Weird.

I grabbed my cell and dialed mom.

"Hello, dear. Please tell me you're not eating pizza for dinner again."

I laughed. "Hi, Mom. I'm not eating pizza *yet*, but it should be here soon."

"I made lasagna for dinner. Come join us."

"Maybe I'll come over tomorrow for the second round." Even though we were a family of three, she always cooked enough to serve a dozen people.

"That would be lovely. What's up?"

"Something odd happened. I received a letter from someone who passed away. Her name was Teresa Harbinger. She claims we're related."

"That's impossible," my mom said.

"I figured it was a mistake. Too bad, she offered to leave me her business and her house. Could've been a sweet deal."

"No. I spoke to Teresa last month." Her voice shook. "She can't be dead." It sounded like her phone clattered onto the counter.

"Mom?"

I heard her crying and then my dad's voice came through the phone. "Linda, are you hurt? What's wrong?"

"It's not me, Dad. Teresa Harbinger died."

"What? How?"

"I don't know. I received a letter from her lawyers."

"There's so much you don't know. Hold on, I need to take care of your mother."

Did I really have an Aunt Teresa? If my mom's crying was any indication, I did. Mom had never mentioned a sister in the twenty-six years I'd been alive. Maybe they'd had some kind of falling out and recently reconnected?

While I waited for someone to come back on the line, I moved the letter to the side. Underneath there was a legal contract that was bunched up in the middle. I tried to flatten it out and felt something between the layers of paper. I flipped through the pages until I came to a crystal bracelet in a clear envelope.

"Linda, I've put you on speaker," my dad's voice came through the phone. "What does the letter say?"

I read it out loud and told them about the attached contract. "Please tell me what's going on."

"Not over the phone. Why don't you join us for dinner so we can talk."

My doorbell rang. "Hold on. My pizza is here."

I set the phone down and walked over to open the door. When my hand touched the doorknob, it sounded like a cat meowing behind me. I turned around to check. Yep. A huge black and gray tabby, was sitting on my end table.

"I don't own a cat," I said to the universe in general.

The universe did not respond.

The cat hopped down to wind around my ankles and then looked up at me and said, "You shouldn't leave him waiting in the hall. He's crabby on a good day."

What the heck? "I *definitely* don't own a talking cat."

The universe continued to ignore me.

The doorbell rang again. "Do you plan on letting me in?" a man asked.

"Your pizza is here," a different male voice said.

"Who else is out there?" I asked.

"Some dude dressed for cosplay. Not to be rude, but I have other deliveries."

I opened the door and stared at the two men who were polar opposites. The pizza guy was blond, tan, and probably working his way through college. The other guy wore some sort of old-fashioned suit. It emphasized his broad shoulders, but the inky black fabric made his skin look even paler than it was, and his eyes were so dark, they appeared black. He looked like he was auditioning to play a vampire.

I took the pizza from guy number one and handed him his tip. "Thank you."

He glanced at the other guy. "You sure it's okay to leave you alone with Vlad?"

I studied my strange visitor. He was intimidating but not threatening, if that made sense. "You're not here to kill me or anything, right?"

"I'm here to discuss the tearoom." He enunciated each word like he was biting at the air.

"We're good," I told pizza guy. "Thanks for asking."

He nodded and sprinted down the hall.

"May I come in?"

"Get in here before anyone else sees you," the cat said from behind me.

"You heard him, right?" I asked Vlad.

"I've listened to his incessant chatter for years."

"Rude," the cat pronounced from behind me.

"Who are you?" Did I really want to let

this guy into my house?

"I'm Victor. I worked with your aunt."

The smell of Italian spices made my mouth water. I needed food to figure this out. "Come in."

I set the pizza down and spotted my cell where I'd left it. "Crap." I reached for the phone. "Mom, Dad?"

"We're in the car, on our way," my mom said. "Don't sign anything until we get there." The call ended.

I flipped open the lid of the pizza box and grabbed a slice, before turning it toward my two strange guests. "Want some?"

"You show an alarming lack of self-preservation," the cat said.

"You worry too much," Victor said to the cat. He took a step toward the pizza and then frowned. "May I have a plate and perhaps some utensils?"

I took a giant bite of my pizza as I walked over to the cabinet to retrieve three plates and some utensils. I changed my mind and added two more of each for my parents and then I sat at the table and observed my strange guests. After I inhaled the first slice of pizza, I hoped this situation would make more sense. As I watched, Victor cut half of his pizza into dime sized bites and then set the plate on the floor.

"Thank you," the cat said.

"Are you friends?" I asked.

"No," they said in unison.

"We're house-mates," the cat explained.

"I should ask, but I won't." My brain had enough new information to roll around. I didn't need to hear about their relationship.

After a second piece of pizza, I cleared my throat. "Can you shed some light on this whole situation, like why you're here?"

"I could," Victor said, "but if you put on the bracelet, you'll understand everything."

"Don't do it," the cat said. "Wait for your parents."

Curious, I tilted the envelope so the bracelet slid out onto the table and then I picked it up. The blue and white crystals varied in shape and size and the hair on my arm stood up as something like static electricity shot up my arm. "What happens if I put it on?"

"Can't tell you," Victor said.

"He's baiting you," the cat said. "Ignore him."

Light reflected off the crystals casting

rainbows on the ceiling. "It's beautiful." The static electricity feeling increased to a hum. It warmed in my hand. I wanted, no needed, to put the bracelet on. The crystals pulsed with light drawing me in like a beacon.

A knock sounded on the door, I dropped the bracelet, hopped up, and ran to answer it. My parents stood in the doorway looking frazzled. I waved them inside.

"Victor?" My dad stopped short and froze for a second, before continuing into the room. "It's been a long time."

"It has," Victor responded.

No love lost there. "Pizza?" I pointed at the box hoping to break the tension.

"I left the lasagna in the car," my mom said. "We wanted to make sure you were okay before we brought it in."

"I'm extremely confused," I said. "Other than that, I'm fine."

"We'll explain everything," my dad said as he went back out to grab the lasagna.

"Tell me about the bracelet." I walked back to my kitchen table and picked up my new sparkly friend.

"Drop it," my mom commanded in the same tone she used to tell the cats to get off the kitchen counter.

I clutched the bracelet tighter. I was after all, an adult. "Excuse me?"

My mom's mouth fell open before she said, "Sorry. Please wait to put the bracelet on until we've talked."

I shoved the bracelet in the front pocket of my jeans. My dad came in with the pan of food. "It's still warm." He set it on the table next to the pizza box.

I grabbed a spatula and cut the lasagna into squares. "Help yourselves."

We crowded around my butcher block table and my mom said, "You need to know that we love you more than anything or anyone else in the world."

And there went my appetite. I set my fork down. "This is going to be bad, isn't it?"

"Not bad," my mother said. "Just sad in places. I grew up in Mystic Hills. It's a town situated above an intersection of ley lines, meaning it's a nexus for magical energy. Most of the population has some sort of gift or magical power. I didn't. Citizens without magic are encouraged to leave, so I went to college and met your father. When you were born, we knew there was a chance you'd inherited the Harbinger family gift. I took you home to be baptized as Belinda Harbinger.

In the rest of the world, you're Linda James. Every year, on your birthday we took you to visit my family."

"No, we had birthday parties at home." I'd been there, I should know.

"You have two birthdays. The date of your birth we celebrate here, and the date of your Christening in Mystic Hills which is the anniversary of when you turned six months old."

"Like a half birthday?" That would fall in the summer. "You're saying every June, you took me to a town called Mystic Hills to stay with an Aunt I can't remember, who you never told me about until after she died?"

"The bracelet contains your memories," my mom said. "Teresa collected them at the end of each visit and stored them away in case you ever wanted them."

"I need more wine." I went to the fridge and filled my glass before offering it to my guests. "Anyone else?"

My mom smiled. "Yes, please."

I poured a glass for my mom and grabbed a beer for my dad. "Victor? Cat? Any beverages?"

"I'll take a beer," Victor said.

"Do you have any flavored creamer?" the cat asked hopefully.

"You mean like French vanilla coffee creamer?"

"Yes. In a bowl if you don't mind."

"Wouldn't you rather have milk?"

"I'm lactose intolerant," the cat said.

"Creamer it is." After passing out drinks in various forms, I said, "Okay, go."

"First," my mom said, "I need to know how Teresa died."

Victor scowled. "It was labeled an accident. But Teresa did not fall and break her neck in her own house. Someone or something pushed her. No one will help us. They are all frightened. Afraid something might happen to them. We need Belinda to come home with us so she can speak to Teresa and find out what happened."

Wait. What? "If Teresa is dead, how am I supposed to talk to her?"

"That's your gift," Victor said. "You see spirits and speak to the dead."

"Nope." I pushed my chair back from the table. "I'm a teacher. My gift is teaching preschoolers that they have to share and take turns. I do not talk to dead people."

"It's in our blood," my mom said. "Believe me there are worse gifts."

"Put on the bracelet," Victor said. "You'll understand your duty."

I pulled the bracelet out of my pocket. "Mom?"

"It might help with the transition. Please remember, we did what we did out of love and concern for you. If we let you remember your time in Mystic Hills, your gift would have blossomed. If you weren't prepared…well it's hard to explain to a six-year-old why ghosts are talking to her."

I'd been about to slide my hand through the bracelet but stopped. "Wait. Ghosts can just talk to me?" I thought I'd need to hold a seance or say a spell.

"Think of yourself as a ghost magnet," the cat said.

"I'd rather not," I shot back. "What do the ghosts want?"

"Some have unfinished business, problems they need to solve before they can move on," Victor explained. "The recently dead don't always realize what's happened. It's your job to help them accept their new reality."

"If what Teresa told me is true, it can be

overwhelming at first." Mom touched my arm. "You can learn to control it, but you'll have to do that in Mystic Hills."

This house and business no longer seemed like such a good deal. Seeing dead people hoping to settle a score didn't sound fun. "Can I just ignore all of this? Send Victor and the cat back to Mystic Hills with the bracelet?"

"You could," my mom said.

"But you shouldn't," Victor said. "Teresa has been knocking paintings off the walls trying to get our attention. No one will help her. The longer she's distressed the more vengeful and unstable she'll become. She won't be able to cross over if you don't help. She'll be stuck here, and all her humanity will drain away. She'll become a leech."

"She'll become a blood sucking bug?" That didn't make sense.

"No." Mom wiped at tears sliding down her cheeks. "A leech sucks the life force from its victims trying to gain power. The stronger it becomes the more dangerous it is. The Mystic Hills elders would hunt her down and damn her to hell for eternity."

Chapter 2

"Are you serious? Either I help Teresa or she's damned to hell? How is that fair to either of us?"

"It's not," my dad said. "I never wanted this for you."

"This was not on the list of how I wanted to spend my first week of summer vacation. I thought I'd sleep in. Go to the movies. But no. I'm going to put on a magical memory bracelet and maybe see ghosts and then try to save someone from damnation?"

"You won't be working alone," Victor said. "It's my job to help the deceased cross over."

Wait a minute. "Why can't you talk to Teresa?"

"I can't. Not on my own. My magic is symbiotic. Without you, or someone like you with your gift, my power is useless. Before, my powers complimented Teresa's and now they will compliment yours allowing me to see and talk to ghosts so can I ferry them across the river to the light."

"You what? No. Forget it. Doesn't matter. You do you. I'm going to put the bracelet on after I finish this." I picked up my wine glass and downed the last of it. Then I reached across the table and stole my mom's wine downing the rest of her glass. I still wasn't ready. "I'm going to the restroom first."

I all but sprinted ten paces down the hall to the bathroom. Once I was inside, I brushed my teeth just to stall for time and then I studied my reflection. I had the same chestnut brown hair, pale skin, and light brown eyes I'd had this morning. I didn't look like someone who'd forgotten about a secret life in a magical town. What were the odds this was some type of mass hallucination brought on by a gas leak or some other phenomenon? Maybe I'd put on the bracelet, and nothing would happen. There we go. That was my coping strategy. I'd put on the bracelet, and nothing would happen. Then I'd take a nap and wake up and everything would be back to normal.

Clutching denial to my chest like a warm blanket, I headed back out into the kitchen and refilled mom's wine glass before taking my seat.

"Okay. Here we go." I picked up the bracelet, slid it over my wrist and was hit by a wall of sound and light. It felt like I was being submerged by a tidal wave of emotion. A woman smiled at me with so much love, it hurt. She looked like my mom. Same chestnut hair and round cheeks. Her image was replaced by laughter and balloons and cake.

Then I was riding a new bike with a big pink basket on the front. Next there was a picnic and a swing set and a teddy bear and a paint set and cookies and cupcakes and all the images came at me out of sequence but there was one commonality. The love. Aunt Teresa had loved me like the child she never had. She loved me like her own baby, her own daughter.

Suddenly I saw myself through her eyes

at my graduation and the party in my back yard with my friends, and when I was trying on dresses for Christmas, and when I graduated from college, and those memories weren't mine. Those were Teresa's. There was so much love and pride and sadness and longing it made my chest ache. How could I have forgotten her?

When the images stopped coming, I heard myself sobbing…Hot tears streaked down my face…someone had their arm around my shoulders, but it wasn't my mom or my dad…it was Victor.

"Sorry," I blurted out.

"It's okay. Your memories hold much emotion." He squeezed my shoulder before removing his arm. "Can you stand?"

And that's when I realized I was on the floor.

"I think so." I scooted away from him. Feeling a little unsteady, I reached for the table to pull myself up and then I saw them. White wispy forms billowed through the room like curtains on a breezy day. I stayed crouched on the floor. "What are those?"

Victor stood and pulled me to my feet. He held my hand as he glanced around the room. "They are free floating spirits. Nothing to worry about. They are at peace."

"How do you know?"

He smiled. "When you see a ghost with unfinished business, you'll recognize the difference."

Not exactly something to look forward to.

"We should pack your bags and head back to Mystic Hills tonight," Victor said.

"You don't have to go." My mom sounded like she was on the verge of more tears.

"Doesn't she?" my dad asked.

Mom turned to him with a look of betrayal on her face.

He placed his hand on her shoulder. "You knew this day would come."

"Not now," she said. "Not yet. My sister should have lived another forty years."

"And she would have if someone hadn't murdered her," Victor chimed in. "If you ever loved your sister, then Belinda needs to take her place in Mystic Hills so she can help solve Teresa's death."

The sound of sirens off in the distance added to the ominous feeling of the moment. A cold breeze flowed through the apartment, even though all my windows were closed. Suddenly the guy who'd delivered my pizza was standing next to the kitchen table. His tan had faded and his outline was hazy. He clutched his right arm to his chest like it was injured and there was a wild look in his eyes.

"What's going on?" he turned in a circle. "Why am I here?" He stopped and tilted his head at me. "I delivered your pizza." He moved toward me. "I think…I think I was in an accident."

Holy Crap. Was he dead? I stumbled back a step. He floated closer, which kind of proved the whole dead theory since normal people didn't float. He tilted his head and looked at me like I could help him. Like it was my job to help. I took a calming breath. He needed my help.

What the heck should I say? I cleared my throat. "What's the last thing you remember?"

"I was driving. Some jerk veered into my lane. I thought he was going to hit me."

"I think he did hit you," I said.

Victor's skin became iridescent. He clasped my right hand and held his left hand out to the young man who'd been alive in my apartment less than an hour ago. "The string of your life has been cut short. I'm sorry, but it's time to move on."

Pizza guy shook his head. "No. No way man. My girl is coming to stay with me this weekend. I bought a ring. I'm gonna propose."

My eyes burned. This was so unfair.

Light filled my apartment as Victor glowed a bright bluish silver. "You'll see her again. It's time to go."

The young man glanced at me. "Do I have to?"

I nodded and swallowed over the lump in my throat. If I tried to speak, I'd cry and that wouldn't help the situation.

The young man took Victor's hand, and the light reached out to surround him. When the light faded, he was gone.

"Who was it?" my dad asked.

"The pizza guy." Funny, I didn't even know his name.

"Car accident," Victor said, back to his normal, non-glowy self.

"Well that sucked," I volunteered since no one else was commenting.

"It's another phase of life," Victor said.

"Where did you send him?"

"I can't tell you," he said. "Rest assured he's at peace. Teresa is not."

Dang it. "I'll pack a bag."

My mom sniffled. "We could go with you."

Did I want my parents to come with me? Moral support would be nice, but this felt like something I had to come to terms with on my own. I needed to understand why Teresa had included her own memories in the bracelet. She must have been trying to tell me something. "I'll call you when we get there."

"You'll need to put this on." Victor pulled a small leather box out of his pocket and flipped it open. A delicate sliver ring with a single black pearl lay inside.

"Why?" The last piece of jewelry I'd put on packed an emotional punch, so I felt the need to be cautious.

"It connects your powers to Victor's, so he won't have to touch you to see ghosts," the cat said.

"Is anything weird going to happen when I put it on?"

"You'll probably feel some warmth," Victor said. "Nothing distressing."

Hoping he was right, I slid the ring on

my right pointer finger. A warm breeze caressed my face. "That wasn't bad."

Wait a minute. I checked my wrist. The bracelet had changed from sparkling crystals to a thin silver chain. "What happened to my bracelet?"

"The crystals were imbued with memories. The chain is what's left. The spell is played out. You don't have to continue wearing it."

It felt warm against my skin and somehow comforting. "I like it."

———

FIFTEEN MINUTES LATER, I was riding in the back seat of a lilac Volkswagen Bug. "How long is the drive?"

The cat who'd been riding in the front passenger seat hopped into the back with me. "We're traveling by ley line. Once we reach the portal we'll be home in no time."

Ley lines and Portals? I read as much paranormal fiction as the next girl so I kind of knew what he meant, but a little clarification would be nice. "What's a ley line?"

"Lines of magical energy that connect

important places around the world," the cat said.

"And you use the magic to travel by portals?"

"Exactly. Look out the window." The cat sounded amused.

We drove past a local park. Victor turned down a side street and I could see a tunnel up ahead. It sparkled. Tunnels didn't usually do that.

"We travel through tunnels or under bridges. The path has to pass through an opening so the points can meet up."

Sure. That made sense. Victor slowed down as he turned into the tunnel. Blue light sparked all around the car, and then the car did a three-hundred-and-sixty-degree roll like the roller coaster I'd puked on in eighth grade. The pizza I'd eaten for dinner swished around but didn't come back up. Instinctively, I used my arm and legs to brace myself, and then we were driving right side up down a county road like nothing strange had happened.

"Fun, isn't it?" the cat said.

Not how I'd describe it but I didn't want to complain, so I nodded. Hopefully we wouldn't be doing that again any time soon.

Old fashioned streetlights lined either side of the road, and the car slowed. We passed a sign that said, "Welcome to Mystic Hills." No mention of what state we were in or the population. Did they not want to share that information?

"How many people live here?" The two-lane road we drove on which wound around a hill couldn't support much traffic.

"Do you mean how many humans or how many humans and shifters and other beings combined?" the cat asked.

"Total population." I didn't want to seem racist, or humanist or whatever the term might be.

"Eight to ten thousand depending on the season," Victor said. "We're coming up on Main Street."

We circled back around the hill. I would have sworn we'd end up right where we'd started. Instead, we entered the town proper. It resembled an old-fashioned village. Quaint shops and restaurants with outdoor seating lined the street. Some people sat at tables enjoying the cool evening air. Others wandered down the sidewalks. They didn't look magical. It could have been a scene in any small town.

As the car bumped up and down, I realized the streets were made of cobblestone. While it was pretty it did not make for a comfortable ride.

"Most of the side streets are paved," the cat said.

"What's your name?" He'd never volunteered the information.

Victor snorted.

"Shut it, or I'll shred your favorite sweater," the cat warned. He sat up straighter. "My previous owner allowed his five-year-old daughter to name me, so my official Mystic Hills name is Mr. Fluffy Bum. My actual name, which I'd prefer you to use is Dave Wainright."

No wonder Victor had laughed. "Dave it is. Not to be rude, but what type of magical creature are you?"

"I am a Familiar who is in between witches," he said. "Until I bond with someone else, I'm stuck in cat form."

"What happened to your previous witch?"

"He passed away from natural causes."

"I'm sorry."

"We were together for thirty years,"

Dave said. "I miss him but it's been ten years so I'm ready to move on."

I did some mental math. "You're forty?"

"I'll be forty-one in July," he said. "And before you ask, Familiars have the same life span as humans."

That made sense, I guess. We turned off onto a side road and the car stopped bumping up and down. Thank goodness. It felt like we were going up at a slight angle through the lush grass fields dotted with wildflowers. Two story houses were the norm along the road that steadily rose. The houses weren't close together like a normal subdivision, they all had double or triple lots. Did people here have more money or did they like their privacy?

I had no idea where the town was located and that bothered me. If and when I wanted to leave I'd like to be able to do so under my own power. "I feel completely turned around. What towns border Mystic Hills?"

"Mystic Hills exists at the nexus of multiple ley lines. If you aren't born here, or if you're not related to someone from the town, you'd never be able to find it."

"So, it's not on Google maps," I joked.

"No," Dave said. "And your phone won't work while you're here."

No cell phones? I could feel my neck muscles tightening. "Are there phones that work here?"

"Of course there are," Victor said.

"Cell phones?" I clarified because I wasn't sure Victor would make that distinction.

"Not the kind you're used to," Dave said. "But we do have computers that run on the Mystic Hills internet."

I wanted to ask about streaming networks but wasn't sure I was ready for the answer. There had to be some sort of magical Netflix or Hulu. As we drove the streetlights flickered on, casting a cold white light.

"Here we are." Victor pulled into the driveway of a two-story house. I could make out the wrap around porch but the details of structure were lost in the shadows.

Victor parked and then sighed. "I still expect her to be inside waiting to greet me."

I swallowed over the lump in my throat. "I'm sorry for your loss." How had I not thought to say that until now?

"Thank you." He cleared his throat. "Let's go inside and put on a kettle for tea.

I'd like to contact her tonight if possible, to put her spirit at ease."

I climbed out of the car and grabbed my duffle bag while Victor picked up my suitcase. A strange sense of Deja vu hit as I entered the side door and walked into the kitchen. The back wall was pale green and decorated with small reproductions of Van Gogh's Irises, Monet's Water Lilies, and other famous paintings I'd seen but didn't know by name.

The white cabinets and appliances seemed familiar. How many times had I been in this room? It gave off a warm, cozy vibe. I set my bag down and approached the cabinet next to the sink. Cookies and tea? I opened the door and saw a dozen types of tea and several bags of cookies. The memory of Aunt Teresa setting me on the soapstone counter while she put cookies on a plate and made earl gray tea washed over me, followed by a sense of loss and a spike of irritation. Why had my mother kept this from me?

I grabbed the electric kettle, filled it with water and then pushed the start button. My fingers grazed the chamomile tea. If I planned to contact a ghost, caffeine might be

a better idea. Black tea and a bag of chocolate chip cookies sounded like a good combination.

When I turned around, Victor stared at
me wide-eyed. Had I done something
wrong? Was he offended I'd made myself at
home?

"I wasn't able to see her before," he said.

I set the tea and cookies down as the hair
on the nape of my neck stood up. I followed
Victor's gaze. The hazy outline of a woman
floated a foot above the tile floor. Her clothes
were indistinct but her face I recognized
from the memories. "Aunt Teresa?"

Chapter 3

She floated toward me, smiling. Were those tears running down her face or just ghostly distortion? She held a hand out to me. It was instinct to reach for her. My hand passed through hers, but I felt some sort of energy.

"So happy you're here," she said.

"I wish I'd known about you," I said. "I would've come back."

Teresa turned from me and floated over to Victor. "I'm so sorry you found me like that."

"Who did this to you?" Victor demanded.

"I have no idea. One minute I was walking down the steps and then I was at the bottom of the stairs, floating above my body."

"Was someone else in the house?" Victor asked.

"No, but I did *not* trip and fall."

"The elders declared it an accident," Dave chimed in.

"I heard them when they were here. It made me so angry." Her image crackled like static on a television and then she settled down. "Sorry about the temper tantrums. I couldn't believe my so-call friends wouldn't help you contact me."

"Neither could I, after all you've done for this town," Victor said. "That's why we recruited Belinda."

"It's weird how that feels like my name now," I said.

Teresa floated over. "It's always been your name."

Tears burned my eyes.

Her image wavered and became indistinct. "Tired. Sorry. Talk soon." And then she blinked out of existence.

"Wait." There was so much I wanted to ask her, but she was gone. "Is that normal? Will she always disappear so fast?"

"I'm not sure," Dave said. "Hopefully she'll stick around longer next time."

I made myself busy with the tea while I tried not to cry. I sniffled like I was having an allergy attack, so I probably didn't fool anyone. Once the tea was ready, I grabbed the chocolate chip cookies and joined Victor at the farmhouse style kitchen table where he sat with his head in his hands.

"Thank you," he said without looking up.

"You're welcome." I didn't know what else to say, so I studied the paintings. They looked like oil paint on canvas. Whoever created the reproductions had talent.

"We need to figure out who killed her," Victor said.

"Agreed." How we'd do that, I had no clue, but I would find them and turn them over to the police. Aunt Teresa deserved justice.

"You need to sign the contract." Dave hopped up on the table and lapped at his cup of tea.

"I forgot about that." I was happy to see my aunt again, In a weird way it felt like she'd filled a blank spot in my life. Like I'd found something I hadn't known was missing. Sure she was a ghost, but I could still talk to her, still get to know her.

The letter she'd written explained if I signed the contract I'd own the house and her business. I wasn't ready to make that kind of commitment yet. I was still getting my bearings.

"You don't want to tie yourself to Mystic Hills," Dave stated in a judgmental tone.

"You must sign." Victor pulled the letter out of his inside jacket pocket. "The magic of Mystic Hills won't fully respond to you until your name is on the deed."

"What does that even mean?"

"You can't travel on your own using ley line portals or effectively use any of the everyday magic of Mystic Hills until you're legally signed in as a citizen." He shoved the pen across the table to me.

I shoved it back. "I need a day or two to think about it."

"You don't understand," Dave said. "Magic runs through the town, it's part of every house, it fuels the power grid and the utilities. Notice how the lights in here are a bit dim? That's because the house is between owners. It respects that Victor and I live here, but the magic is holding back because our names aren't on the deed."

I rubbed my temples hoping to stave off the headache I could feel coming on. "I came here to help. I'd like some time to think about it before I tie myself to a house and a business for the rest of my life."

The lights in the house slowly dimmed until we were sitting in pitch black darkness.

"Now you've done it," Dave muttered.

"Seriously?" I wasn't sure if I was talking to the house or the universe but either way I was ticked off. "I came here on good faith. I'd appreciate it if you acted on good faith too. A day to take all of this in isn't too much to ask. Is it?"

The lights came up almost as high as they were before. "Thank you."

A knock on the door almost made me spill my tea.

"Dad?" A man opened the door partway and stuck his head in before coming inside. "What's with the lights?"

"She hasn't signed for the house yet," Victor said. "Belinda, you might remember my son Reed."

"Sorry, I don't." And I would have re-membered him because Reed emanated his own light, which made him shine like some sort of dark haired, dark eyed angel, except angels probably didn't fill out black t-shirts and faded jeans to perfection.

"Are you doing that on purpose?" I asked.

"Doing what?" he asked.

"Glowing," I said, fighting off a sigh. Light and warmth radiated off of him like a summer day. My heart rate kicked up a notch. Was this some weird magical pheromone thing?

Victor sucked in a breath.

"Not a word, Dad." Reed's jaw tensed.

What had him so upset? Why did he have to be warm and attractive on the outside and crabby on the inside?

"Until she signs the deed she's an *outsider*," Reed said the word like it was an insult.

"I will give you all my earthly possessions if you sign the deed right now," Dave said like it was some sort of joke at Reed's expense.

"What's the big deal?" I tried to diffuse the situation. "I saw your dad glow when Pizza guy crossed over."

"Pizza guy?" Reed looked at me like I

had two heads. "You know what. Never mind. Dad, I set my laptop to alert me when you came home. I wanted to make sure you were all right."

"Teresa spoke to us," Victor said. "She doesn't know what happened, but she's calmed down."

"Could the house tell Belinda what happened?" Reed asked.

"I don't know," Victor said. "I never thought of that."

"The house is alive?" Creepy.

"It's imbued with magic," Dave said. "Which you could control if you signed the deed."

I was not a fan of the hard sell. "You all need to back off about the deed."

"Welcome back to Mystic Hills," Reed's voice was laced with irritation. "Maybe you should stop thinking about yourself and do right by your aunt."

Seriously? "Thanks for the insincere welcome. I'd appreciate it if you kept your judgmental comments to yourself."

The cat laughed. "This is going to be so much fun."

Reed pointed at Dave. "I will dose you

with catnip and drop you off at an outsider pet store if you say one more word."

"Okay" I stood up from the table. "I don't know why Reed is crabby and honestly I don't care. I'm tired. It's been an emotionally exhausting day. Dave, will you show me to a guest room, please?"

"Sure." Dave hopped off the table.

I walked over to my suitcase and duffle. When I reached for them, they disappeared…as in poof…they were gone.

"What just happened?" I asked.

"The house chose your room," Reed chuckled. "Good luck with that."

My neck muscles tensed, but I didn't bother responding. I was done engaging with his negativity. Instead, I followed Dave into the living room through to the front foyer and the grand staircase. The wooden banister was carved to look like it was wrapped in ivy. It was a work of art. I reached to touch the polished oak and then paused. "Is this where Teresa…"

"Yes," Victor said from behind us.

I made sure to hold onto the railing so history wouldn't repeat itself. The three of us headed up the steps and then down a hallway. Victor paused at the first door. "My room is here. Good night, Belinda."

"Good night."

Dave stopped at the next doorway. "This was Teresa's room. I doubt the house put you here."

I hoped not. I wasn't ready to see all of Teresa's personal belongings, so rather than investigating I kept walking. When we reached the third door, I pushed it open. There was a lovely four poster bed with a matching antique dresser and armoire. My bags were nowhere in sight.

"I planned to put you in this room," Dave said.

A door across the hall creaked open. Curious I walked over to investigate. My bags sat on a narrow bed with what resembled a panel from a white picket fence for a headboard. The dresser and armoire looked like antique thrift store purchases that had been painted blue and white. Of course, it was hard to tell what color they were since every surface was coated in a thick layer of dust.

Had the house made the room dusty on purpose or had no one been in here for a long time? Something in my head clicked. "I know this room."

"It's where you stayed when you came to visit," Dave said. "No one else used it."

This was all so frustrating. The room felt familiar, but I had no specific memories of my time here. "Why can't I remember everything?"

"It should come back over time. You'll have to be patient."

Speaking of patience. "I'd be happy to clean this room tomorrow but for tonight I'm going back to the other one."

I reached for my bags, and they disappeared again.

"House, what did you do?"

"Oh dear," Dave hopped up on the windowsill. "I believe your bags are in the street."

"Why should I sign the deed for a house that's being rude to me?" I tapped my foot and glared at the window because where was I supposed to look?

My bags appeared in mid-air and dropped to the floor with a thud barely missing my foot.

"Is there a hotel I can stay in?" I asked Dave.

"Tonight? No. I suggest you make peace

with the house." With that he turned and left.

I grabbed my bags and backtracked down the hall to the room with the four poster bed. Tired and emotionally wiped out I changed into the unicorn PJ's I'd purchased for pajama day at school and climbed into bed.

Something nagged at me. I'd forgotten something….something I was supposed to do. Something important.

Dang it. I was supposed to call my parents.

They'd be waiting by the phone. I grabbed my cell. The blank screen reminded me my phone didn't work here. Stupid magical town. Was there a phone in this room? I reached for the lamp on the nightstand and turned it on. No phone that I could see. Great.

Where would a land line be? I had a vague memory of sitting on the counter in the kitchen talking on a phone. How bad would it be if I waited until tomorrow to call them? My mom was already traumatized from Teresa's death, so I dragged my body out of bed and headed downstairs.

I heard voices in the living room. Victor

must've decided he wasn't ready for bed yet. Pretending I didn't care if anyone saw me in my unicorn pajamas, I entered the living room and said, "Don't mind me. I forgot to call my parents."

"What are you wearing?" a voice that was not Victor, or Dave's asked. I paused and turned back to find Reed, once again, looking at me like I was an idiot.

"Unicorn pajamas," I stated like it was obvious and he was the moron.

He tilted his head. "Do all outsiders where unicorn pajamas?"

"Unicorns, llamas, elephants, dogs whatever makes us smile." I pointed toward the kitchen. "Is the phone normal or do I have to ask it to call my *outsider* family?"

"Dial 1234 and then the number," Dave said.

"Thank you." The lilac phone was on the wall next to the back door. I dialed and was relieved when the call went through.

My dad answered on the second ring. "Thank God. I've been pacing a hole in the carpet. I'm putting you on speaker phone."

"Sorry it took me so long to call. It's been a busy night and my cell doesn't work here."

"Did you speak to her?" My mom's voice sounded like she was trying not to cry.

"I did. She's not panicked anymore."

"What did she say?"

"She doesn't know how she fell. We're going to investigate and see if we can figure it out."

"Once you help Teresa, you need to come home," my mom blurted out.

"Let's take one day at a time. Okay?"

"Mystic Hills isn't what it seems," my mom said. "Don't trust them."

"I'll call you again tomorrow," I said. "Love you guys."

"Love you too," My parents responded.

I hung up. What had my mom meant? Don't trust who?

"Everything okay?" Dave asked from the doorway where he stood next to Reed.

Had they been eavesdropping? "My mom is upset which is only natural given the circumstances." I walked over to the cookie cabinet and grabbed the box of vanilla sandwich cookies. I ate one as I filled the kettle with water. "I'm making chamomile. Anyone want a cup?"

"No," Reed said. "You're really not embarrassed about your pajamas?"

"Nope." I made my tea and took it to the kitchen table with the cookies. "Does no one here wear fun PJ's?"

"Depends on what you mean by fun," Reed said.

"Did Mr. Serious make a joke?" I checked to see if he was smiling. He was, and wow. He had a sexy smile and intense brown eyes and he was glowing. "You're doing it again."

"Doing what?"

"Glowing."

He muttered something under his breath that was not fit for polite company.

"Are you not supposed to be glowing, or am I not supposed to be able to see it?" Those seemed like two different problems.

"No point explaining unless you plan to stay," he said.

"I could always bribe Dave with creamer since he seems to know."

Reed shook his head. "Don't." His happy joking manner vanished. "You don't have a clue how things work around here. It would be best for everyone if you went back to your world. You don't belong here, and you'll never fit in."

Wow. No wonder my mom left. "I'm

here to help my aunt. I don't know how you fit into this equation, but I'd like to cordially invite you to go glow at someone else."

Dave laughed.

Reed's eyebrows slammed together. "I'd love to, but fate has a strange sense of humor. I never would've chosen you."

Ouch. I broke a cookie in half while I formulated a response. "If I knew what you were talking about, I might be insulted." I ate the icing side first and waited to see if he'd cave and fill me in.

He stood and stalked out.

"Well, that was fun." I finished my cookie and then went up to bed.

I was half asleep when a cool breeze blew through the room. I opened my eyes. Aunt Teresa stood next to my bed; her image was less fuzzy. I could see she was smiling. "Be patient with Reed. He's been through a lot."

"What's with the glowing?" I asked.

She grinned. "Not my secret to tell. Good night, dear."

"Good night."

THE SMELL of coffee and bacon woke me the next morning. Never a bad way to start the day. Since I'd already made one appearance in my pajamas, I threw on a pair of jeans and a t-shirt and then brushed my chestnut brown hair into a ponytail. I went down the main stairs and into the kitchen. Victor and Dave sat at the table eating. A quick glance didn't show any extra food on the stove. Looks like I'd be cooking for myself.

"Good morning." I headed for the coffee maker where there was still half a pot of coffee. That was the most important part of breakfast anyway.

"Good morning," they replied in unison.

I went to the refrigerator hoping for creamer. There was an entire shelf full of different flavors. "Dave, is this your creamer stash?"

"Yes, and I don't mind sharing…except for the peppermint mocha because that's seasonal."

"No worries. I'm a French vanilla girl." I poured a healthy dose into my cup and then drank half of it while checking the refrigerator for eggs or bacon or anything else that might work for breakfast. The shelves were bare. Weird. At least there were cookies. I headed back to the tea and cookie cabinet and grabbed the bag of oatmeal raisins thinking they were healthier than the other options.

"Is that all you want for breakfast?" Victor asked.

"It will do until I can run to the grocery store." Not like I had any other options.

"Either you don't know how to operate the refrigerator," Victor said, "or the house isn't responding to you."

"I'll bite. How is a Mystic Hills refrigerator different from a regular one?"

"You tell the refrigerator what you want, and the house will transport it from the grocery store to the refrigerator or the cabinets."

"Seriously?" That sounded awesome. I went to the refrigerator and said, "bacon and eggs". When I opened the door, there was one egg and one strip of bacon. That seemed a bit stingy. "Can I have two eggs and four strips of bacon?" Nothing changed.

"You have to shut the door to make it work," Victor said.

I closed and then opened the door to find two eggs and two strips of bacon. Good enough. Maybe the house was irritated that I hadn't signed the deed. Didn't matter. I had food to cook. Next step: find a pan.

"Stop," Dave said. "Put the food back in the refrigerator, go to the stove and tell it what you want. Open the oven door and your meal will be inside. If you want a cold dish you ask the refrigerator."

Oh. My. Gosh. "The house shops for groceries and cooks the food?"

"Yes," Dave said. "Ready to sign the deed yet?"

"Getting closer," I returned the eggs and bacon to the fridge and walked over to the oven. "Scrambled eggs and bacon, please."

When I opened the oven door my meal sat waiting on a plate. The bacon was extra crispy verging on burnt and the eggs looked suspiciously runny.

"House, I'd like some edible food or I may have to start knocking down walls to make an open floor plan."

My plate burst into flames. I jumped back. The smell of burnt eggs and bacon filled the room.

Oh, it was on.

I walked over to the knife block on the counter and grabbed the butcher knife. "I wonder if this will go through the wall. I'll have to try it and see." I waited to see if my threat would work.

The window opened by itself and fresh air filled the kitchen. The oven door closed and then popped open. I took the knife with me to peek inside. An unburnt plate of scrambled eggs and bacon sat on the rack. I almost reached for it and then paused. "Not that I don't trust her, but Victor would you grab my plate for me?"

"You could just sign the papers," Victor muttered as he retrieved my breakfast.

"Thank you." I took the plate, joined my not-quite-friends at the table, and dove into my food. When the house wasn't out to get you, magical meals just appearing was a cool feature. Guess there weren't any Dine & Dash people employed in Mystic Hills. Wait a minute. "I remember baking cupcakes with Aunt Teresa the normal way."

"The appliances have non-magical settings. You can cook if you want to," Dave said. "Teresa loved to bake."

Another memory popped into my brain. We made rice krispy treats with chocolate chips. A moment of joy was followed by a wave of sadness. "I hate that my parents kept this from me. If I'd remembered I could've spent more time here."

"Teresa wanted to permanently restore your memories on your eighteenth birthday," Victor said. "You could have stayed in Mystic Hills that summer and learned to control your gift. Your mother refused. She said it would ruin your life."

Chapter 4

"Knowing I could communicate with the dead wouldn't have ruined my life, but it might have changed it." Had my mom been afraid the lure of magic would be too strong? Speaking of magic. "Why doesn't my mother have any special power?"

"About a quarter of younger siblings don't receive the gift," Dave said. "Those without magic typically move to the outside world because they don't fit in here."

"That sucks." The idea of my mom being pushed aside ticked me off. "Shouldn't everyone be treated the same and made welcome in their community?"

"In a perfect world, yes," Victor said. "Like most places, Mystic Hills isn't perfect.

We have our powers struggles and infighting like any other town."

"Why don't I remember everything?" I asked.

"Teresa didn't include all your memories in the bracelet. It was imbued with specific memories so you'd remember special occasions and time spent with her," Dave said.

I understood now. "Love. The bracelet was meant to show me that she loved me and I'd loved her." I sniffled and wiped at my eyes. "What about the rest of my memories, the things I did, other people I knew?"

"Those may come back in time," Victor said. "If not, you'll see Mystic Hills with fresh eyes. That's not a bad thing."

"What about people I met and don't remember? How am I supposed to deal with that?"

"It's almost like a high-school reunion," Victor said. "Anyone who wants to say hello will, and the rest will smile and nod and go on with their day."

"I hated my high school reunion," Dave muttered.

AFTER BREAKFAST I went back up to the guest room and grabbed my toiletries. The idea of being naked in a shower where the house could control the water temperature made me nervous. Maybe it was time to make peace.

"House? I would like to take a pleasant shower. If you can play nice, I will sign the papers."

The bedroom door popped open. Was she leading me to the bathroom? I grabbed my bags and walked out into the hallway. The door to my old bedroom swung open. What was she trying to tell me? I entered the room and there wasn't a speck of dust in sight. The scent of lemon furniture polish floated in the air.

"Thank you." The room felt warm and homey.

A door I'd presumed was a closet creaked open to reveal a bathroom with a lilac pedestal sink, toilet, and shower. Purple, specifically lilac, must have been Aunt Teresa's favorite color. Growing up, I'd wanted to paint my room lilac purple and my mom refused. Maybe this was why. My mother must have loved her sister, but this entire situation was complicated.

I unpacked and hung my clothes in the armoire, hoping the house would see that as a commitment to stay, even though, if I did stay, I had no idea how to balance Mystic Hills with my real life.

I was a preschool teacher, not a ghost whisperer.

After a shower where the house didn't try to burn or freeze me, I stared into the armoire. What should I wear? I'd brought a little bit of everything because I wasn't sure what I'd need. What said, *I'm nice, but don't mess with me?* I grabbed my favorite black halter dress. It was a little bit dressy and a whole lot of comfortable. Plus, it had pockets which I usually felt compelled to tell people about if they commented on the dress. I'd try to rein that in today. Magical people probably didn't get excited about dresses with pockets.

I ran a brush through my hair which I'd been growing out since the hair-pocalypse a year and half ago when I'd naively believed a hair stylist who'd told me I'd look good with a pixie haircut. The woman had insisted it would make my eyes stand out. It had, but it also looked like someone had cut my hair with a weed whacker. After eighteen months my hair finally brushed my shoulders. I'd vowed never to cut it short again.

I pulled it back into a low ponytail and swiped on some mascara. That was good enough. I had no idea what Victor planned for the day, but I felt comfortable and confident.

I went downstairs, keeping a firm hold on the railing as I descended the steps. The carved Ivy leaves on the banister were beautiful, but they made it hard to hold onto. Given what happened to Aunt Teresa maybe I should change the railing. Could the house change things around if I asked? That might be worth looking into.

As I entered the living room I admired the floor to ceiling bookshelves, the fireplace, a cream colored couch and what appeared to be Dave's chair, since it was coated in a fine layer of cat fur. I'd expected to see Dave and Victor but was surprised to find my slightly sexy and definitely surly friend sitting on the couch. If Reed's frown was any indication, he was as happy to be there as I was to see him.

"What's on the agenda for today?" I stood by Dave's chair and reined in the impulse to pet him, because that might be awkward.

"A tour of downtown." Victor gestured to Reed who sat on the far end of the couch. "He'll introduce you to some of the local merchants. Hopefully some of them will talk to you about Teresa."

"Why Reed?" I asked. "Because the way his eyebrows are scrunched together tells me he didn't volunteer."

"I've questioned everyone already," Victor explained. "They might say something to you or Reed that they wouldn't say to me."

"It makes sense." Reed gave me the once over but didn't comment on my clothing. Since he was wearing jeans and a gray t-shirt, I didn't think he should criticize my style.

"So we're hunting for clues while you pretend to show me around town?"

"That's the plan." He pushed to his feet and sighed, like spending the day with me was some sort of punishment.

This should be loads of fun. We walked back through the kitchen and out the door. Behind the lilac Volkswagen sat a shiny black Mustang. "Nice car."

"Thanks."

Five minutes later I was gawking out the passenger window of the Mustang as we backed down the driveway. "The house is purple too?" It was lilac with pale green trim. It had been too dark for me to see it last night. The color scheme shouldn't have worked but it did.

"Purple was Teresa's favorite color," Reed smiled.

"I should have guessed based on her car and my bathroom."

"A few years ago, she crocheted purple scarves for all of us. They were the least manly color I'd ever seen, but we all wore them."

Awww. Reed's admission gave me a warm fuzzy. He had a heart after all. He'd obviously cared about Teresa. Maybe I'd judged him too quickly.

The other houses we drove past had interesting color schemes too: orange, pink, blue and yellow. The rarest color seemed to be white. Mystic Hills residents were a colorful bunch.

Main Street was tame by comparison. The quaint shops were all single-story buildings made of the same faded red and tan bricks. The doors and the windows varied, along with the signage which was a good thing or it might be hard to tell one from another. "What's with the matching shops?"

"Keeps everyone on equal footing. Decades ago, store owners tried to outdo each other by building taller more elaborate structures. It got out of hand, so the Mystic Hills Council of Elders created restrictions."

"Are there a lot of restrictions in Mystic Hills?"

"Depends on who you ask."

That was a nice non-answer. "Care to elaborate?"

"Magic is monitored. Some people don't like that."

There was so much I didn't understand. I needed a crash course in all things Mystic Hills. I wasn't sure the occasionally irritable male driving down the road with me was the best choice for the job, but he was all I had at the moment.

"Fill me on the local politics. Who's in charge? What's the political climate?"

Reed glanced at me. "What's with all the questions? I thought your memories would be back by now."

"Most of the memories Aunt Teresa

gave me were birthday parties or time we spent baking."

He frowned as we drove down Main Street. Was he figuring out how to explain life in Mystic Hills or was he annoyed by my lack of knowledge? I waited to see what he'd say as the car bumped up and down.

Tea & Spirits came up on the right side of the road. He pulled over, parallel parked in front the building I kind of owned and said, "So you don't remember the people you used to know, you know nothing about the Council of Elders, the different factions of magic, or the laws of sanctuary?"

"Nope."

He cursed and rammed his hand back through his thick, dark hair. "This is ridiculous. You're useless."

My heart pounded at the surprise attack. I was doing the best I could. He didn't have to be such a jerk. After a cleansing breath, I said, "Aunt Teresa told me to be patient with you because you've had a rough life but calling me useless is over the line. I never wanted any of this. I have a job I love and wonderful friends in the real world. I am sincerely trying to help solve Aunt Teresa's murder but we aren't going to get very far if you don't knock off the hostility. Either fill me in on all things Mystic Hills or point me in the direction of someone who can."

His eyes narrowed like I'd insulted him. "What else did Teresa tell you?"

"Nothing. Just that one line. Now can you be civil or should I hunt down a different tour guide?"

He turned off the ignition and stared out the window, like he was thinking about telling me something.

Whatever he was mulling over couldn't be worse than what he's already said.

He glanced at me. Anger and hurt evident in his face.

I reached over to touch his arm. "What's wrong? If you don't tell me I can't help you fix it."

He huffed out a breath. "There's no fixing it."

With that fun pronouncement he exited the vehicle. Okay. What did that mean? What was unfixable?

Reed opened the door to *Tea & Spirits* and gestured that I should join him.

What were the odds spirits referred to alcohol rather than ghosts?

I climbed out of the car into the early

morning sunshine and had to dodge past several free-floating spirits before I entered the building. If no one else could see them I probably looked drunk. Didn't matter. I did not want to walk through random ghosts. I opened the door of *Tea & Spirits* and gleaming hardwood floors greeted me. Round wooden tables were scattered about the room with mismatched chairs painted different colors of blue and green. There were a few gatherings of love seats and up-holstered chairs in various shades of brown. The eclectic furniture gave the place a homy vibe. An oak bar ran the length of the back wall. It appeared to be stocked with tea and alcohol. Thank goodness.

A blond woman popped up from behind the bar. Wait…not popped…floated. "Hello, you must be Belinda."

"Wings," was the only thing that came out of my mouth. The woman had wings sprouting from her back like a life-sized tinker bell.

"My name is Jezelle, and I'm a fairy…or half fairy."

My face heated as I crossed the room. "Nice to meet you. Sorry about the wings comment. This is new to me."

"You should work on your poker face," Jezelle said. "Because some people are offended when attention is drawn to their non-human traits."

"I'll do that." Now what could I say? "Is it too early for a drink?"

She grinned. "It's never too early for a drink, especially if you're dealing with that one." She nodded toward Reed who'd joined us at the bar while she poured two shots of whiskey.

Reed glared at both of us, which made me smile. "So his sunny disposition isn't just for me?" I picked up my whiskey and took a sip.

"He's grumpy on a good day." Jezelle downed her shot. "But he's dependable and he has a nice butt."

I almost spewed my whiskey onto the bar.

Jezelle laughed.

Reed wandered toward a door in the back of the room, and I noticed she was not wrong.

"When you're done bonding at my expense," he called back over his shoulder, "maybe we can get to work."

I sighed and downed the rest of my

drink. I loved the way whiskey warmed you from the inside out. "Jezelle, it was nice to meet you." A thought occurred to me. "How did you know what I wanted to drink?"

"It's my gift."

"No fair. Your gift is way better than mine."

"You have the whole I see dead people thing going on?"

I nodded.

"There are worse gifts," she said.

"So I've been told," I should probably get back to Reed before he became even grumpier. "How much for the whiskey?"

"It's on the house, but tips are always welcome."

I reached into my pocket, pulled out a five-dollar bill, and added it to her tip jar.

"Your dress has pockets?"

I nodded.

"I love a dress with pockets."

"Me too." Total female bonding moment.

As I walked toward the door where Reed disappeared, I thought about what I'd learned. Reed might be annoyed at the world rather than me. I'd feel better if it wasn't just me.

I found him seated behind an antique desk, flipping pages in a ledger.

I sat in the black leather chair facing him. "Was this Aunt Teresa's office?"

"Yes."

"Do you work here?"

"I've managed *Tea & Spirits* for a while. Teresa didn't want to be bothered with inventory and paying bills. She spent time with the customers. I guess that will be your job now."

"What do you mean?"

"You inherited the house and the business." Reed stated like I might have forgotten those facts.

"I'm aware, but I already have a job. I'm not sure I have time for another one."

"While you're here in Mystic Hills, you could fill in for her."

True. "What did she do?"

"People come here to drink and socialize. While they're here, they contact their relatives to ask questions."

I did not like where this was going. "She held seances?"

He snorted. "No. She summoned spirits of the dead."

"I thought she helped ghosts cross over."

"Ghosts and spirits are two different things."

"They are?"

"Yes. There's a major difference."

I put my head in my hands. "Keep talking. I'm going to have a minor existential crisis while you explain."

He chuckled and it was a warm happy sound, which made me like him more.

"Lesson number one. Ghosts are the souls of the recently deceased that need to cross over. Understand?"

I sat up and glared at him. "Yes. How are spirits different?"

"Spirits are souls who went to the light. They died and crossed over but are willing to come back and communicate with the living."

I tried to wrap my brain around this new information. "Ghosts need my help to cross over, and spirits are enjoying their afterlife but they're free to come back and visit?"

He nodded.

"How can people talk to spirits if I'm the only who can see them."

"You're the only one who can see ghosts. Once you call them, spirits can make themselves seen and heard whenever and to who- ever they want."

"So a spirit is like an upgraded ghost who can choose to be social and interact with people?"

"Yes," Reed said in a patronizing tone.

I leaned toward him. "If someone dropped you in a room full of preschoolers and told you to teach them pre-reading skills, would you know what to do?"

His eyes widened. "Point taken. What else do you want to know?"

"If I agree to take Teresa's place for a limited time, how am I supposed to contact spirits?"

"Not my area," Reed said. "You'll have to figure it out."

"Come on." I leaned toward him. "You worked with her for years, you had to pick up something."

"You're right. I did. I saw her call out to spirits by saying their names and the spirits would appear."

That was it? "That's not very helpful."

"Which is why I didn't tell you in the first place."

"Fine. Here's another question, what

happened to the people who died after Aunt Teresa passed away?"

"What do you mean?"

"If all the ghosts in Mystic Hills come to me and then your father helps them cross over, what happened to the ones who died when Teresa wasn't here?" Was there a backlog of ghosts I needed to worry about?

Reed reached up and rubbed his temples like he felt a headache coming on. "Not everyone who dies needs help crossing over. Some realize what's happened and they go to the light. Others who are unaware of their death or who have unfinished business seek you out and then my father crosses them over."

"Thank you for the straightforward answer. Was that so hard?"

"Yes." He grinned and started to glow and there was that warmth again. My stomach flipped.

Based on past experience I didn't mention the glowing. I returned his smile and said, "What do I need to know about Mystic Hills?"

He pointed at a giant map on the wall. "That is Mystic Hills."

It was shaped like an octagon but not all

the sides were the same length. Main street was dead center. The side streets didn't seem to follow a pattern. "Am I supposed to notice something significant?"

"The town is divided into areas for different types of magic users." He stood and walked over to the map. "Teresa's house is here. This entire area is full of people who have some sort of gift. He moved his finger over a few inches. "This area is where the witches live. Their magic is based on the elements and different witches have different powers. They create potions, spells, and hexes. They also keep the Mystic Hills grid and the internet up and running, which is why they have the most political power. Down here is where shifters and other creatures who wouldn't be accepted in the outside world congregate. Any type of magical being is allowed entrance into Mystic Hills by the Law of Sanctuary. Not everyone is happy about that. The fairies live mainly in this forested area. Then there are the half magical creatures like Jezelle. They blend between the communities."

"And you're all one big happy family?"

He laughed. "No. There's a reason your ability to speak to the dead is called a gift. It came to you freely. The ability cost you nothing."

"Except my sanity," I muttered.

"Witches magic isn't free. They pay for their power with their own life force, or blood. Some witches spill a little of their own blood for a spell or ask for donations. Others take blood without asking."

"Thus, the restrictions," I said. "So crazy witches don't randomly bleed people out for power."

"Exactly. Now witches have to rely on themselves or volunteers."

"I can't imagine there are many of those."

"You'd be surprised. Blood has always been currency in Mystic Hills. If you want a witch to create a spell or remove a hex it costs a pint of blood."

"Do people hex each other a lot around here?" That sounded like something I should avoid.

"It happens, but not as often as it used to. Teresa was part of a group that petitioned for stricter laws."

"Could someone have killed her for that?"

"Lots of people supported the restrictions, but she started the petitions which resulted in the laws."

"Did she tick off a certain group of people?" If I could narrow the suspects down to a certain species that would help.

"The witches said the new laws cut down on their business. Teresa instituted a waiting period on hexes. Someone could order a hex, but they had to wait forty-eight hours to finalize the order. The idea is that the cooling off period might make people change their mind."

"That makes sense. If I could have hexed Greg when I found out he was sleeping around, I would have. Forty-eight hours later I realized I was better off without him." Wait a minute. "Why did I say that out loud?"

He smiled and pointed toward the bar. "Jezelle likes to serve a little magic with her whiskey. You'll probably say whatever is on your mind for the next fifteen minutes."

"That's not good." I stood and stalked out to the bar. "Did you dose me with some blabbermouth whiskey?"

"I was wondering when it would kick in." Jezelle grinned and leaned against the bar exposing impressive cleavage. I smacked a hand over my mouth before I could comment on her boobs, because that would be awkward.

Once I had that impulse under control, I said, "Why?"

"You're here to poke around and ask questions about Teresa. You pry into our business; I figure we should know a little more about yours."

My feelings were oddly hurt. "I thought we bonded over pocket dresses. Reed doesn't want me here. Victor and Dave keep griping at me about the deed, but all they care about is having brighter lights. So far the only person I like in this town is a house."

"But you still haven't signed the deed," Reed said from behind me.

I turned to him. "No. I haven't, because I'm afraid of what it might mean." Right now I didn't want to talk to either of them, so I headed for the door.

"Belinda, wait," Jezelle called out.

I flipped her off without looking back as I exited the building and then stalked down the sidewalk. What was wrong with these people? Why should I stay here and help them if they were all rude and obnoxious? I'd come here to help Teresa, and I'd done that. She was at peace. If she'd known who'd killed her, we could have wrapped this up. It shouldn't be my job to figure it out. As Reed so rudely pointed out, I was useless.

I knew nothing of Mystic Hills and its inner workings and I wasn't sure I wanted to learn. Where did that leave me? I tuned back into my surroundings. Reed's Mustang was visible at the far end of the street. If I kept it in sight, I could find my way back. Now what? Maybe I'd talk to people like Victor asked. I didn't need Reed's help to meet new people. Where should I start?

I spotted a jewelry store two doors down. I had a vague memory of Aunt Teresa taking me there to look at earrings. If it was a store she frequented maybe they'd have an opinion on her death.

When I entered a lady with short silver hair and light blue eyes smiled at me from behind the counter. She wore a black sheath dress which was the perfect backdrop for the gold necklaces she wore. Each necklace was a different style chain, but somehow it worked.

"Feel free to browse. Some of the items are spelled and some are merely for decoration."

"I'm interested in the decorative kind."

"Then you should avoid the case by the cash register. Let me know if you want to try anything on."

"Thank you."

A blue opal ring caught my eye. I leaned closer trying to spot a price tag. "How much is this ring?"

"That depends on who's asking." She came towards me.

"I'm Belinda Harbinger, and you are?"

"I thought that might be you. Teresa used to bring you in when you visited over the summer. I'm Ann Seacourt. Your aunt and I were friends."

"Nice to meet you, or rather re-meet you." I leaned against the jewelry counter. "Can I ask you a question?"

She nodded.

"Do you think my aunt's death was an accident?"

Ann backed up a step and pointed at me like I was a child who'd done something naughty. "That is not the question I expected, nor is it one you should repeat to anyone else."

"Why not? You said you were her friend.

Wouldn't a friend want to find out what really happened?"

Ann clasped her hands together and shook her head. "In this town there are those with power and those without. The restrictions Teresa passed upset those in power. You don't want to make that same mistake."

"Do you think someone in power helped her down the stairs?" I asked.

Her eyes narrowed. "I will insist you to leave my store if you keep asking questions of this nature."

"It's not completely my fault," I said. "Jezelle put something in my drink which makes everything I'm thinking pop out of my mouth. I hope it wears off soon."

"Jezelle has been nothing but a nuisance since your aunt hired her."

"Why do you say that?"

"She amuses herself at her customer's expense."

"I'm surprised Reed hasn't spoken to her about it."

"I think he eggs her on." Ann adjusted her necklaces shifting them around a bit, so a rose gold necklace shone through. "Listen to me, going on like the town gossip."

I wanted to keep her talking. Time to

back off a bit. If I made her comfortable, maybe she'd share more information.

"Can I see the blue opal ring?"

She unlocked the case and pulled it out. I tried it on. The stone caught the light and gave off a rainbow of colors but it was too big. "Do you have it in a smaller size?

"I can size it after you buy it."

"How?"

"Magic," she said. "Before you decide on the ring, let me show you something your aunt was interested in the last time she came in."

"When was that?"

"About a month ago." She went to the case by the cash register and pulled out a silver bracelet with black pearls between the links.

"What does it do?" I asked.

"It goes on your wrist."

I laughed. "That's not what I meant. What magic does it possess?"

"It's imbued with a protection spell."

"Like a hex shield?"

She paused. "I never thought of it that way, but yes. And I may steal that phrase for a marketing campaign."

"Tell me more about the spell."

"You have to refresh it every three months. If you don't then it's just a normal piece of jewelry."

I connected the dots. "A person who considered buying this might have been afraid someone would try to hurt them?"

"Possibly. Would you like to try it on?"

"Yes." I put the bracelet on. It reminded me of the ring Victor gave me. Maybe they were part of a —

The bracelet tightened, biting into my wrist, piercing the skin, and driving razor sharp thorns into my flesh. Blood gushed. Searing pain took my breath away and I stumbled forward onto the glass case.

"Get it off." Blood dripped from my wrist, pooling on the glass.

Ann tried to undo the clasp. "It's not opening."

I cried out as the bracelet dug deeper and the black pearls swelled up like ticks. Blood no longer dripped onto the glass because the bracelet was collecting it like some sort of vampire.

"Hold on." Ann ran to the back room and returned with a small blue bottle. She pulled the stopper and poured a white powder over my wrist.

The pain lessened. The horrible sucking sensation slowed. Ann tugged at the clasp. "Come on." She poured more powder over it while I breathed through the pain and panic. Finally, the clasp came free.

I yanked my arm away from the bracelet and cradled it to my chest. Blood gushed from a dozen puncture wounds on my wrist. "What was that?"

"We need to bind your wrist," Ann said. "Let me help you, and I'll explain."

The door opened and Reed walked in. "I've been looking for you." He paled. "What happened?"

"Vampire bracelet."

Ann came out from behind the counter with a gold bracelet. "This will stop the bleeding."

"No." I backed away from her and lost my balance. The room went fuzzy around the edges. I turned to Reed. He glowed like the sun. "So pretty," I said, and then the world went dark.

Chapter 5

"Belinda, wake up," I knew that voice. It was Reed.

I was tired and he was perpetually crabby, so I yawned and rolled over. Or I tried to. Why couldn't I move?

"I'm not kidding. You need to wake up." The voice was much louder now.

I opened my mouth to tell him to go away, but what came out was a mumbled mess. Why couldn't I talk? Something bad must have happened.

"We've healed your wounds. Open your eyes."

He wasn't going to leave me alone, so I tried to open my eyes. Slowly my eyelids responded and the room came into view, or rather Reed did. He glowed like a star.

"Hi," he smiled down at me. An actual smile, like he was happy to see me. There was only one explanation. I must be dying.

"There's my girl," he said. "Stay with me."

His girl? There was a low buzzing sound in my head. I shook my head trying to make the sound go away.

"Belinda?" Concern bled through his words.

The buzzing faded away, thank goodness. I focused on forming coherent words. "What happened?"

"You had an accident."

I blinked and my vision cleared. Why was I on the floor? Why was Reed holding me? Not that I minded since he was smiling and glowing and warm.

"Let's try to stand up," he said.

"No." I turned my face into his chest and sighed. "Too tired."

"Do you want me to carry you down Main Street?" Amusement was clear in his voice.

Main street? What was he talking about? I opened my eyes and this time I saw more than Reed. Jewelry. There was jewelry everywhere. Wait a minute. I'd walked into a jewelry store and…what? It came back to me like a smack upside the head…the blood sucking bracelet. I sat up and examined my wrist. It had stopped bleeding and there were fresh scabs where the thorns had bitten into my skin. It ached like a giant bruise.

"You're back with us?" Reed asked.

I nodded and met his gaze. "What was that thing?"

"It should have been the protection bracelet your aunt wanted," Ann said. "But someone altered the spell to collect blood. I'm so sorry. The spell was probably meant for your aunt."

"Collect blood? More like steal it. That wasn't for a willing donor."

"It's the type of spell Teresa worked to ban," Reed said.

"I can see why." My voice had a shrill quality that sounded panicked. "Sorry. Didn't mean to yell. I'm not having a great day."

"No. You're not. Want to stand up?" Reed asked.

I nodded and he helped me to my feet.

"Thanks."

"Can you stand on your own?" he asked.

"Let's see." I stepped away from his warmth, even though I didn't want to. "I think I'm good."

Reed turned to Ann. "Who does your spell work?"

"I'll give you her card." She opened the cash register and pulled out a blue business card. "We've done business for years. I don't think she would have done this. She supported Teresa."

"Has anyone else looked at the bracelet or tried it on?" I asked.

"I'm not sure." Ann set the business card on the counter and pushed it towards me. "It's our busy season."

I glanced around the store which was empty except for me and Reed. "Seriously?"

"You should probably go home and rest," she said.

That I believed.

"Let's go," Reed said.

Ann cleared her throat. "The mayor's wife was in recently. She asked about the same pieces you were interested in." Her hand touched the bracelet.

Was she telling me the mayor's wife

might have put the blood sucking spell on the bracelet?

"We should take the bracelet," Reed said.

"What? Why would I want that evil thing?"

"It has your blood." He looked at Ann. "Unless you had other plans for it."

"I don't appreciate the insinuation," Ann said. "I planned to incinerate it."

"We'll take it," Reed said. "Just to be on the safe side."

"Will you be paying in blood or cash?" Ann asked.

"You want me to pay for the creepy bracelet that attacked me?" That was wrong. "You just said you were going to burn it, so you weren't going to get paid anyway."

Ann pointed at Reed. "I want him to pay for it because he always believes the worst in people. I wouldn't want to disappoint him. That will be one hundred dollars, or you could trust me to do the right thing."

Reed pulled out his wallet and slapped five twenty-dollar bills on the counter.

She picked up the bracelet by one end and dropped it in a tiny gift bag which she stapled shut with the receipt. He took the bag and exited the store.

Once he'd cleared the doorway I said, "Thank you for saving me from the evil bracelet." I didn't wait for a response. Instead, I caught up with Reed. I had no idea why he was so mistrusting, but from what I'd seen so far, Mystic Hills was not a warm and fuzzy place.

"It's important no one knows about this attack." Reed headed down the sidewalk back towards his car.

The blood didn't show on my black dress, but my wrist was mottled with bruises and scabs. Whatever healing magic they'd performed had stopped the bleeding but it hadn't done much for the plum colored bruises.

"Pretty sure the scabs will give it away."

He stopped and checked my arm. "That should have healed by now."

"It still hurts." I wrapped my arms around myself like I was cold to hide the marks.

I must've fallen asleep on the ride back to the house because I woke up on the couch in Teresa's living room.

Dave sat in his chair by the fire, watching

me. "Thank goodness. I was about to call a healer."

I yawned and pushed myself up to a seated position. "Ouch." My arm throbbed when I moved. My wrist was swollen and dark red streaks linked the puncture wounds. "A healer might be a good idea."

"Reed should have known better." Dave hopped down and went to do…what…could a cat use the phone?

Five minutes later footsteps pounded down the stairs and into the living room. Victor took one look at me and headed into the kitchen. I heard him speaking to someone on the phone.

This day kept getting better and better. My stomach growled. I had no idea what time it was, but my body was telling me it had been a long time since breakfast. I stood, which was harder than it should've been. Not a good sign.

One foot in front of the other. I could make it to the kitchen and then I'd throw myself on the mercy of the house.

Victor hung up the phone as I crossed the threshold into the kitchen. "Why are you up and moving?"

"Thirst and hunger."

"Sit. I'll bring you some tea and toast. You don't want anything that will upset your stomach."

"Thank you."

A minute later, he set the items in front of me. The toast was dry, but rather than complaining I washed it down with the tea.

By the time I finished my food, a man with bronze skin, brown eyes, and wings came in the door. Good thing I'd already met Jezelle or I might have commented.

"I'm Healer Bram. Tell me how this came to be."

I explained about the bracelet. "I have no idea what Reed did to heal my arm."

"It appears an infection has set in, or the bracelet could have been coated in poison. Where is it?"

Good question. "I guess Reed took it."

"I'll scan you and see what I can find. We might not need the bracelet." He pulled several cut crystal bottles from what looked like an old-fashioned black leather medicine bag. He picked up the blue bottle and removed the stopper.

"Smell this." He thrust the bottle under my nose.

"Why?"

"It's how I do my job. Tell me what you smell and if it changes."

Weird but okay. I inhaled. At first it smelled like fresh cut grass but then it turned to something rotten. "Grass and then garbage."

He picked up a pink bottle. I inhaled and my mouth watered. "Fresh bread and then Italian food."

"One more," he held up an orange bottle. I inhaled and sighed. "Oranges and vanilla."

"You have an aggressive infection."

He stated this like I should be happy about the diagnosis.

"Better than poison," he said. "Not all of them have antidotes."

"Good point. I'm team infection."

He poured different colored powders into a copper bowl and then he pulled out a small silver knife. "I'll need a few drops of your blood from the non-infected hand."

Great. I held out my hand and he neatly sliced the tip of my pointer finger. Oddly enough, I didn't feel it.

He must have seen the confusion on my face. "The blade is charmed with an anesthetic."

Interesting.

My blood dripped into the bowl, puddling in the middle of the powder. After a minute the wound closed on its own. Slowly the contents of the bowl began to swirl around like a miniature whirlpool. Once combined it turned bright pink. He picked the bowl up and handed it to me.

"Drink."

Drinking my own blood wasn't something I normally did. "I don't suppose I can have some antibiotics instead?"

"You could, but your arm would balloon up overnight and you'd have to consider amputation at the elbow." He said this with a straight face.

"Okay." I accepted the pink potion and sipped a tiny amount. It tasted like strawberries so I downed the rest.

"This is going to be uncomfortable."

"What is?" Heat rushed down my arm, and green goo broke through the scabs.

"Gross."

Victor hurried over with a kitchen towel which he slid under my wrist. It felt like my arm was in a blood pressure cuff and someone had pumped it up way too tight. The green goo turned yellow and then clear and the pain and pressure disappeared.

"Is that it?" I was almost afraid to ask.

"Now I'll wrap your arm in a fresh bandage. Tomorrow morning when you take it off, the swelling and pain should be gone. If it's not, soak your arm in salt water and call me."

"Thank you. I don't suppose you take outsider insurance cards?"

He laughed. "I'm employed by Mystic Hills health. They pay me quite well. You don't owe me anything."

Wow. Talk about a perk. Free health care. Of course, in the real world bracelets didn't drink your blood and give you nasty infections.

After the healer left, Victor sat at the table with me. "Are you all right?"

"Physically, yes. Mentally, no. I can't believe someone would make such an evil spell."

"Teresa worked for years to pass restrictions against blood gathering without consent."

"Do you think that's why someone killed her?"

He nodded. "I imagine they'll figure out

a way to bring the restrictions up for a new vote."

I did not like where this was going. "People who voted for them might be afraid of having their own accident if they vote yes again?"

"Exactly. I sent you out today to gather information and look what happened." He gestured at my arm.

Wait a minute. "You don't think this was an accident?"

"No."

"Do you think it was Ann Seacrest?"

"I hope not. If anyone heard her say the bracelet was for Teresa, they could have added the blood collecting spell."

"The moral of the story is don't touch anything a shopkeeper associates with Aunt Teresa." This town kept getting crazier and crazier.

"That would be wise. I'm going up to my room to read. I suggest you rest and let your body recover." He stood and touched my shoulder. "It might be best if you didn't tell Teresa about this incident."

After he left, I laid my head on the table. Mystic Hills was emotionally and physically exhausting. The savory scent of chicken noodle soup filled the air. I lifted my head to investigate. A bowl of soup sat in front of me with a sleeve of saltine crackers.

"Who did this?" I asked.

The kitchen lights blinked.

"House? Did you give me soup because I don't feel good? Blink twice if the answer is yes."

The lights blinked twice.

"You're my favorite person in this town."

The deed appeared on the table with an old-fashioned fountain pen. Okay, maybe the house had an ulterior motive but it was trying to take care of me.

I ate the soup and read through the contract. No surprises. Upon signing, the house and any and all possessions including Aunt Teresa's bank account and the tearoom were mine. Renting the property was allowed, but the deed must remain in the Harbinger name.

I picked up the pen, which was heavier than a modern-day ink pen. It felt substantial in my hand. I signed the bottom of each page. The lights brightened and a cupcake appeared on the table.

"Thank you." I picked up the cupcake, peeled back the wrapper, and took a bite. It

was chocolate, coffee, vanilla bean yummi-
ness. The house should have a name. "You
seem like a Lilly? Does that work for you?"
The lights blinked twice. "Lilly it is."

Dave padded into the room and jumped
onto the kitchen table. "You signed."

"I did."

"Thank goodness. Now the house can
shine again."

"Shine?"

"Yes. See how much brighter everything
is?"

Now that he mentioned it, the cabinets
gleamed like they'd just been polished.

"The house couldn't access it's normal
amount of magic while it was between
owners so it left some things undone, like
dusting your room."

Had I heard him right? "The house is
self-cleaning?"

"Of course."

"Lilly, I should have signed sooner."

The lights blinked twice.

"Can I be here when you tell Reed?" he
asked.

"No but you can explain why you are
amused at his expense."

"I can't, actually," he said. "And just so

you know, I'm amused at your expense too." With that he hopped off the table and went back into the living room.

Given the events of the day, I figured it was time for a nap. The only question was couch or bed. Bed sounded better, so I went upstairs into my room and crawled under the covers.

⸻

IT WAS dark when I woke. What time was it? I grabbed my cell phone. Still didn't work. Dang it. How many times was I going to make that mistake? I checked the clock on the dresser. It was eight. I'd slept for hours but didn't feel refreshed. A yawn overcame me. Should I stay in bed? If I did, I'd probably be wide awake at four in the morning. I rolled out of bed, headed to the bathroom, and splashed water on my face. When I opened my eyes to dry off Aunt Teresa was floating behind me. I sucked in a breath because I wasn't expecting anyone else in the room.

"Hello, dear." She smiled at me. "Sorry to startle you."

"That's okay."

"How did things go today with Reed?"

Did she listen in on our activities every day? That would be creepy. "Reed is moody."

"Men can be hard to read," she said.

"Since I signed for the house, I hope he'll calm down."

"I doubt your relationship will ever be calm."

What was she talking about? "We don't have a relationship. He thinks I'm useless."

"Why would you say that?"

"Because he told me, to my face."

"Oh, dear," she floated closer. "That is rude. Males are sometimes awkward about expressing affection, but it's almost like he's trying to push you away."

The memory of waking in his arms at the jewelry store flowed through my mind. I wanted to ask her about the bracelet without bringing up the evil spell.

"I met Ann Seacrest today. She showed me a black pearl bracelet that you'd been interested in, something about a protection spell."

"I don't remember any bracelet."

Had Ann lied to ambush me? That didn't make sense since she'd also saved me. "You didn't talk to her about a bracelet?"

"No..." Her image frayed at the edges. "I don't think I did. Sometimes it's hard to pull my thoughts together." She held her hand up. Her fingers drifted apart so her hand resembled a mitten. "Much like holding together this form. I need to rest now. Goodbye."

I backed away from the drifting pieces of my aunt. I wasn't sure if I could accidentally inhale part of a ghost, and I didn't want to find out. I walked downstairs into the kitchen and rooted around in a drawer until I found a notepad and pen.

Making lists helped me straighten out my thoughts, and since my phone wasn't working, I resorted to the old-fashioned paper route. What did I know? Someone, probably a witch who didn't like the new restrictions, pushed Aunt Teresa down the stairs. Ann Seacrest might have lied about the bracelet or Teresa might not remember. Were ghost's memories faulty? Could Lilly help? She couldn't talk, but maybe she could lead me to a specific room to figure out what Teresa had been doing on her last day in the house. It was worth a try.

"Lilly, what's the last room Teresa was in?"

A door which I'd assumed was the pantry creaked open. I went to investigate, pulling the string to turn on the bare light bulb hanging from the ceiling. It was the pantry, but on the back wall there was a door which was bolted from this side. I undid the dead bolt and opened the door. Narrow stairs went up to a landing. I'd read once that back kitchen stairs were for live-in cooks or maids. They could enter and exit the kitchen and head up to their rooms in the attic without crossing paths with the family who lived in the house.

During the day there might be an exterior window to light the stairwell, but now it was dark. I backtracked into the kitchen for a flashlight I'd noticed in the drawer when I was rooting around for the notepad. I stood at the bottom of the stairs, biting my lip. Nothing to be afraid of, right? Except someone closing the deadbolt and locking me in the attic. If they did, I could probably ask Lilly for help.

Not feeling reassured, I shone the beam of my flashlight all around the stairwell to make sure nothing was going to jump out at me. Here we go. I went up the steps at a normal pace. No need to run. No reason for this feeling of dread to hit me. I kept going until I came to a landing where the stairs split. I went to the right first, up a dozen stairs to a door that opened easily. I reached around inside the doorway hoping for a light switch. No such luck. "Lilly if there's a light in here, can you turn it on?"

Two bare bulbs flared to life momentarily blinding me. When the spots cleared from my vision, I saw a table covered with books and photos. Newspaper articles were taped to the walls. There was a map of Mystic Hills with certain streets highlighted in orange and others in pink. This must have been Aunt Teresa's office. The books were all about Mystic Hills Law. Not exactly light reading. There was a leather satchel draped across the table. Curious, I opened it to find a laptop. Maybe I could figure out what Aunt Teresa had been working on. I opened it, but the screen remained blank. Must need to be charged. I checked the bag for a power cord but didn't find one. There had to be one around here somewhere. I'd ask Victor. He'd know.

I back tracked down the stairs to the

landing and went up to the other room where I found a normal bedroom with a double bed, a dresser, and an armoire. The only thing out of place, was my aunt's body floating above the bed.

Chapter 6

My aunt's body was in the house...like her actual freaking body. Not the ghostly apparition I'd seen several times, but her physical body. I was caught between fight or flight. Part of me wanted to run screaming down the stairs while part of me wanted to know what the heck was going on. Was she dead or in a coma? Had Victor and Dave lied to me?

"Aunt Teresa?" I called out, like she might sit up and talk to me. That would have been too easy. Her expression didn't change. Her body didn't move. She just floated in place, like she was taking a nap about a foot above the comforter.

Crap. Crap. Crap. I inched toward the

bed until I hit some sort of barrier that shimmered. Victor never mentioned that he'd kept Teresa's body as a souvenir. Then again, he'd never mentioned a funeral.

I heard footsteps on the stairs. Should I hide or confront whoever it was? What if they had a weapon? My flashlight wouldn't do much to protect me.

"Belinda, are you upstairs?" Victor called out.

"Yes."

Victor came into the room acting like everything was normal. "Did you need something?"

I pointed at Aunt Teresa. "How about an explanation? Why is her body still here?"

"Where else would it be?" he seemed confused.

"Buried," I said. "Isn't that the normal thing to do?"

He blinked. "No. Not if her soul is still tied to this plane. Bodies aren't buried until the soul crosses over."

"Really?"

He nodded. "I presume outsiders bury their loved ones shortly after death because they don't know if the soul has crossed over or not."

"Within a few days." I headed for the stairs. "Lilly, can you have a bottle of whiskey waiting for me on the kitchen table, please."

Victor paused mid-step and then continued down the stairs. "You don't need to talk to the house. Just tell the refrigerator or the pantry."

"That's faulty logic," I said. "The entire house is Lilly. Why not talk directly to her?"

"Your logic is sound, but your behavior will seem odd to everyone else."

"I'm not sure I care."

We walked through the pantry and emerged in the kitchen to find a bottle of whiskey and four short tumblers on the table. When Reed came into the kitchen with Dave, I figured out who the fourth glass was for.

"I came back to check on you, since you were out like a light when I dropped you off," Reed said. "How's the arm?"

He came back to check on me. That was refreshing.

His dark eyes shone with concern and he had some sexy five-o'clock shadow going on and I should probably answer his question rather than staring at him. I cleared my throat. "It's better. Thanks for taking care of me." I didn't tell him about the healer because I didn't want it to sound like I blamed him for the infection. "Drink?" I sat and poured myself a whiskey, neat.

"No, thank you," Dave padded off. Victor shook his head and followed the cat.

"I'll take one." Reed joined me at the table. "Any particular reason we're drinking?"

I poured his drink while I tried to figure out how to explain. I went with the simplest explanation. "Outsiders don't keep dead relatives in the house until they cross over. It was a disturbing discovery."

He leaned back in his chair. "I imagine there are a lot of differences."

I sipped my whiskey and sighed. "So many differences."

He picked up his glass and downed half of it. "Since the lights are bright and the house is taking your requests, I guess you signed the deed."

"I did and I'm pretty sure Lilly is my new best friend."

The lights blinked twice.

Reed shook his head. "I could tell you no one names their house, but you'd just ignore me."

I nodded.

"Did you know signing the deed means you have to file your citizenship papers tomorrow?"

I smacked my glass down onto the table. "What?"

Reed finished his drink and poured himself another. "You can only own property if you're a full citizen."

"Why didn't anyone tell me?" I yelled loud enough for Dave and Victor to hear. I waited to see if they'd come weigh in on the conversation. "Chickens," I hollered.

Reed laughed. "That's the Mystic Hills way. No one tells you everything, and everyone has their own agenda. You signed and they get their house back up to full power."

A cold ache settled in my stomach. Was that all they'd wanted? I know we'd just met, but Aunt Teresa had trusted them. Both Victor and Dave had come to my aid when I was ill. Maybe this was Reed's cynicism coming out again. "You're saying I shouldn't trust anyone?"

"I didn't say that." He grabbed the bottle. "Come on. This isn't a conversation to have in a kitchen." He headed out the door.

"What?"

"Come with me if you want answers," he called back over his shoulder.

I followed him outside. "Where are we going?"

"To the widow's walk."

"That doesn't sound like a place I want to go." It implied someone had died.

"Wrong," he said. "It was one of your favorite places."

Now I had to follow him. Was it a favorite place I went by myself? Did he and I spend time there together?

He headed around the back of the house to the fire escape. We went up the metal steps that zig-zagged back and forth until we reached a wooden platform on top of the roof.

"Oh, It's like a terrace," I said. "A terrace with a terrible name that implies death." It was at least twenty feet wide. The railing meant to keep people from falling several stories to the ground was barely three feet high.

"It's a term from coastal towns. Back in the day women used to walk their terraces at night when their husband were out to sea, watching for ships and waiting for their husbands to come home. If their husbands never returned they became widows."

"There are neither ships nor any bodies of water close to this house," I said. "From now on, we're calling it the rooftop terrace. Sounds much more user friendly."

Reed sat on the whitewashed wooden surface and patted the spot next to him. "Doesn't matter what you call it, just don't get too close to the edge."

I joined him and looked at the city spread out below us. Lights sparkled in windows and trees swayed in the evening breeze. "It's beautiful."

"Up here you can't see all the backstabbing and political drama," he said. "Just the light."

"Do you know what I do for a living?"

"Teresa mentioned you were a teacher."

"I'm a preschool teacher. In preschool we teach kids to be nice and play fair. I'm always surprised at all the adults who forgot those basic rules. Adults mostly suck."

He laughed. "They kind of do."

He was glowing again, and I wanted to ask why, but I was relaxed, and Reed was sitting so close his shoulder brushed up against mine. Some type of warmth or connection pulsed between us. Did he glow when he was happy or relaxed? I hadn't figured it out yet, and asking would probably make him crabby, so for now I'd enjoy being near him.

"Why are you looking at me like that?" His voice was low and quiet.

Very smooth on my part. I cleared my throat and went with the truth. "I'm trying to figure you out. You're a bit of a puzzle."

"No. I'm not," he bit out. "I'm the guy who is angry at the world because his mom died and his dad moved in with some other woman and never came back home."

I tried to connect the dots. "You mean Teresa?"

He nodded. "My mom's death was sudden, unexpected. She had an aneurysm when she was standing right next to my dad. One minute she was there. The next minute she was gone."

"That's terrible."

"She was always so happy and full of life." He glanced at me. "She used to sing songs while she gardened or did the dishes." He looked away like he'd shared too much. "Anyway, my dad fell apart. He brought her here so Teresa could help him communicate with her ghost. The ring my dad gave you was the one Teresa used to combine magic with him. We moved in here so we could have time to speak with my mom before she crossed over. After a month, mom decided to move on. My dad never came home, said he couldn't live in the house without her, and he signed the deed over to me."

"So, you lost both your parents."

He paused and then nodded. "I never thought about it like that, but yes, I did."

"Which is why you aren't big on trust."

He nodded. "Growing up here, you learn no one does anything to be nice. If someone gives you something, it's because they expect something in return. Either a future favor from you or some sort of benefit from what they set in motion."

My heart ached for him. Had he never known unconditional love or true friendship? Surely everyone in Mystic Hills didn't think this way.

"What about Victor and Dave? Don't you think they have your best interests at heart?

"Maybe when I was a child," Reed's glow faded. "Once you're legally a grown up, you're on your own."

I didn't like his logic. Still..."Your dad

and Dave could have told me what signing the deed meant. Do you think they left that detail out on purpose?"

He nodded. "I'm sure they did and they'll see nothing wrong with their actions."

"Maybe I should threaten to kick them out of the house," I said in a teasing tone. "Just to see the looks on their faces."

"That would be funny," he said. "But it could set a chain of events in motion you don't intend. If Dave doesn't have an official residence, he must become the Familiar for whatever witch will take him. There are some bloodthirsty witches out there."

"This town in insane."

"Do you wish you'd never come back?" he asked.

"I don't know. I hate that my mom kept this from me, but I understand why. On the surface magic seems too tempting."

"Beneath the surface it's a constant battle for power. My mom used to say some magic users seek to create chaos and fear so they can control things. Others want to control people to keep the chaos and fear at bay. The two sides are always butting heads."

"Tell me more about this citizenship thing. What do I have to do?"

"Go to the mayor's office and sign a letter of intent."

That cleared everything up. "Saying I intend to do what?"

"Stick around. Keep the house. Become a full time citizen."

That didn't work for me. "I can't stay here forever. I have a job to get back to, family, friends."

"If you don't claim full citizenship, they'll take the deed and put Teresa's house up for bid. If you sign, you can leave for vacations in the outside world for as long as you want because Victor and Dave are here to take care of the house."

"I just have to bend the truth a bit."

"Now you're thinking like one of us."

"That is frightening." The wind picked up. A chill slid across my shoulders and goosebumps pebbled my arms.

"Want to head down?" Reed asked.

"No." What I really wanted was for him to put his arm around me. I waited to see if he'd move toward me or start glowing or do anything that hinted he wanted to be nearer to me or wanted to touch me. He didn't move in my direction one tiny bit, so I guess the attraction I felt wasn't mutual.

"You have that look on your face again," he said.

I really needed to work on my poker face. "I keep hoping you'll say something to make this place seem not so crazy."

He leaned back on his elbows and stretched his legs out in front of him. "There are perks. Look up."

I followed his maneuver and saw dancing light, like the aurora borealis. Green and purple and pink shimmered in the sky. "What is that?"

"It's a side effect of so many ley lines converging in one spot."

"It's beautiful." The colors swirled in the sky like a choreographed dance.

"Are you going to stick around until we figure out who killed Teresa?" he asked.

"I know I should, but as you so *kindly* pointed out earlier today, I probably won't be much help."

"I shouldn't have said that. When I saw you wearing the memory bracelet, I figured you remembered…everything."

He sounded sad like he wanted me to remember something. Was he just concerned about helping Aunt Teresa? An odd thought occurred to me. "Did we know each other?"

"Sort of." He seemed to be measuring his words, like he didn't want to give me too much information.

"I guess one day a year wouldn't be a lot of time to get to know a person."

"What the he—" Reed sat up abruptly. "They didn't tell you?"

"Tell me what?"

"You lived here for a week or a month each summer."

I sat forward so quickly I gave myself a head rush. "Are you freaking kidding me? I didn't just come here one day a year for my birthday?" I could barely wrap my brain around this. "Months? My parents stole months of my life from me?"

Reed didn't respond.

"Hello," I poked his shoulder. "I could use a little help here."

"What do you want me to say?"

"I don't know. Maybe tell me it's not a big deal or that you know where my memories are. Where in the heck are my memories, Reed?"

He grabbed both my hands in his. "You need to calm down."

If ever there was a wrong thing to say. "Don't tell me to calm down. Your parents didn't lie to you. They didn't steal months of your life."

"You're not the only one who lost something." Reed glowed and heat enveloped me. He was holding my hands and staring into my eyes and yet there was this gulf between us.

"What did you lose?" My gaze drifted to his mouth and back up to his eyes.

He dropped my hands and scooted away from me. "Maybe you're better off without your memories."

"Why would you say that?"

He cleared his throat. "You can have a fresh start…figure out what you really want."

What did he mean? What was there to figure out? "I don't understand."

"You can see Mystic Hills as an adult, not through some rose colored glasses based on what happened when you were a kid."

Okay. I'd go with that for now. "Right now, I see dishonest housemates, lying parents, and power-hungry, blood-stealing witches. Not sure how much help that's going to be."

"You just described the mayor and his

wife. I mean the power hungry blood stealing part."

"Great. Can't wait to meet them." I hated walking into a situation blind. "Can you go with me tomorrow for backup, just to keep me from saying or doing something that would make things worse?"

He was quiet for so long, I wondered if he'd heard me.

"What time did you want to go?" he asked.

Thank goodness. I did not want to face the mayor alone. "I have no plans, so whatever is convenient for you."

"We should go down to the mayor's office first thing in the morning because your signature will have shown up in the Land and Deeds department."

"What time do they open?"

"Seven."

I frowned. My summer plans for sleeping in and finding my Zen were not working out. "I'll be ready at six fifty."

"Afterwards, we could meet a few more people on Main Street," he said. "Maybe grab breakfast and see who approaches you."

"In my world I'm fairly anonymous. Does everyone here know everyone else?"

"For the most part, and I'd bet most of them will know who you are or at least recognize your name."

"Great." I couldn't shake the feeling that Reed was holding something back. "Is there something you want to get off your chest?"

"Yes and no."

"That clears everything up." I poked his shoulder. "Talk to me."

"It's hard to explain." He rubbed the back of his neck. "I knew you before, but not *this* you. It's weird. You're a different version of the girl I knew."

Was he saying we'd been involved? That would be unbelievably awkward if we'd dated and I completely forgot. Then again it would explain his initial hostility. And I could totally see my younger self falling for him. That brought up another question. "How long has it been since I visited Mystic Hills?"

"Four years." The warmth I heard in his voice was gone, replaced by regret or maybe anger. "Right after you graduated college you stayed for two months. You talked about looking for a job here and becoming a permanent citizen. Your aunt was thrilled. Then your mom came and insisted Teresa remove your memory again. You fought with her but in the end, she wore you down. You left."

My stomach clenched. I'd planned to stay in Mystic Hills? What could my mother have said or done to change my mind? I needed to find those memories. It felt like there was something else I needed to do. I took a deep breath and then blew it out before meeting Reed's gaze. "I'm sorry."

He froze for a second and then said, "For what?"

That was the funny part. "I don't know why, but it feels like I'm one of the people who disappointed you."

Sadness and anger flitted across his face before a mask of indifference settled on his features. "Doesn't matter. Water under the bridge." He pushed to his feet. "I need to go."

My mind reeled as his footsteps rang out on the metal fire escape as he practically ran away. The strange burning sensation in my stomach told me he had a right to be upset with me. If only I could remember what I'd done. Were we friends, or something more?

Had we dated the last time I was here? How weird would that be?

If I had dated him and believed we had a future together, wouldn't I have fought my mother to keep my memories? If Teresa had taken them, wouldn't she have saved them for me? I wasn't going to find any answers up here, so I headed down the fire escape and went back inside. I put the bottle of whiskey in the tea and cookie cabinet and then headed up to Aunt Teresa's room. My memories had to be somewhere, and I needed them back so I could understand what happened with Reed and find out if there was any way to fix it.

I entered Aunt Teresa's room and the sight of her four-poster bed draped in a lilac comforter made me smile. The dresser, chest of drawers, and one nightstand were painted white with purple accents. Her other night-stand was natural wood, devoid of any decoration. It seemed out of place. Maybe she planned to paint it but never had the chance. I investigated the plain piece of furniture. Inside the top drawer I found a deck of cards, a flashlight, and a bottle of lilac scented room spray.

"What are you doing in here?" Teresa popped up, in ghostly form right beside me.

Startled, I jerked backwards pulling the drawer off its track and spilling its contents on the floor.

"Sorry about that. I was looking for my memories."

"I gave them to you," she said.

"No. The bracelet had birthday parties and us baking together. Nothing else. I need to know what happened the last time I was here."

"Your mother," Teresa frowned. "She didn't want you here. Refused to let you stay."

"Where did you put the rest of my memories?" With her propensity for drifting apart, I didn't have long to get the information. "Are they in more jewelry?"

"No." Teresa turned in a circle. "I hid them."

Finally, I was on the right track. "Where did you hide them?"

She started to fade. "Somewhere with faces."

"Don't go." I reached for her, which was stupid even if it was instinct. My hand passed through her. "I need my memories."

"They're with the faces," she said, her voice faded on the last word and she popped out of existence.

What the heck did that mean? Whose faces? I picked up the drawer and tried to slide it back into place. It caught on something, so I pulled it out and investigated the opening where it should go. There was a piece of paper. I reached in to pull it out and the moment I touched the paper a wave of sound and light flowed over me.

A dark-haired boy laughed and threw a handful of popcorn at me. We were watching cartoons. Sitting on the carpet. I giggled and dumped my entire bowl of popcorn on his head. Spots danced before my eyes. I was standing in Teresa's bedroom again, clutching a picture of Reed and me smiling at a camera holding bags of popcorn.

Faces…the memories were in the faces… meaning they were in the pictures. "Aunt Teresa?"

She didn't respond. Maybe it took ghosts a while to build up their strength so they could communicate longer. Didn't matter. I had pictures to find.

I reached into the nightstand again, but

the space was empty. I put the drawer back in place and then turned in a circle surveying the room. There were photographs on her dresser. I picked up a picture of Teresa and Victor. Nothing happened. I grabbed a picture of Victor and Dave. Nope. No memories. She must have put them in photographs of me. I needed to find them.

When was the last time I'd printed a picture? I couldn't remember. Photos were images on my phone. In Mystic Hills people must still print photographs. I worked my way around the room, searching through drawers of clothes and sheets and came up empty handed.

Maybe the house could help. "Lilly, did Aunt Teresa keep photos in a certain room?"

The bedroom door, which I'd shut behind me when I came in, creaked open and then closed. What did that mean? Did she mean the pictures were in here? Where hadn't I looked?

Under the bed.

I shifted the bedspread and got down on my hands and knees. Nothing under there. I'd seen movies where people hid things under their mattresses, so I slid my hands between the mattress and the box springs. No luck.

I crossed the room, opened the door, and stepped into the hallway. "Where to now?" Hopefully she'd redirect me.

"Who are you talking to?" Victor asked as he came out of his room next door.

"Partly the house and partly myself," I admitted. Maybe he could help. "Did Teresa keep any photo albums? I thought they might jog my memory."

"She had several photo albums. I think she kept them in the living room on the bookshelf."

"Thank you." I headed downstairs and made a beeline to the bookshelves on either side of the fireplace. Dave was curled up in his chair. I checked the clock on the mantle. It was quarter til ten. The bookshelf to the right of the fireplace held an eclectic mix of books and artwork but no photo albums. The bookshelf to the left was much the same.

"What are you looking for?" Dave asked.

"Photo albums."

He stretched on his side. "Try the shelf with the cookbooks in the kitchen."

"Thanks." Last I remembered, the

kitchen didn't have bookshelves. Maybe I'd overlooked them. I walked into the kitchen and nope…no bookshelves.

The pantry door creaked open. "Lilly, did you do that?"

The kitchen light flashed twice.

Was she trying to tell me the photo albums were on a shelf in the pantry? I entered the pantry and searched each shelf. Lots of flour, sugar, and a few cookbooks, but no photo albums.

"Lilly, I don't understand."

The back door of the pantry opened. "The photo albums are upstairs?"

The pantry light flashed twice. I had my foot on the first step but paused when I heard raised voices.

"It will be your fault if this ends badly," Dave said.

Victor laughed. "It's Mystic Hills. Everything ends badly here, or hadn't you noticed."

"That's not true. Think about Reed."

"I am," Victor said. "We can't trust her. We never could. Reed would be better off with someone else."

Chapter 7

Were they talking about me or someone Reed was dating?

Footsteps came toward the pantry door. Crap. I didn't want to get caught eavesdropping, so I dashed up the steps as quietly as I could. What if they followed me up here? I reached the landing and bolted to the room with the desk. I sat at the table and opened a random book, flipping through the pages.

"Belinda? Are you upstairs?"

"Yes," I called back without getting up.

Slow footsteps approached behind me. I pretended to be engrossed with the book on Mystic Hills law. If I met Victor's gaze, I was afraid he'd somehow know I'd overheard his conversation.

"What are you looking for?" he asked.

"I thought the photo albums might be up here, but I couldn't find them so I figured I'd learn about Mystic Hills law. This stuff is clear as mud." Would he believe my partial truth?

"You've had a trying day. Why not go to sleep and we'll help you find the photo albums tomorrow."

Dang it. Guess I wasn't finding the photo albums tonight.

"You're probably right." I stood and brushed past him walking at a slow pace, pretending I didn't have a concern in the world.

The next morning, instead of searching for the photo albums like I wanted, I sat at the kitchen table and waited for Reed at the agreed upon time for my trip to the mayor's office so I could officially become a citizen and hold onto Lilly. Even if I didn't want to live here full time, I wouldn't let some stranger take Lilly from Dave and Victor. Plus, she felt like a friend now. And that was an odd thought even if it was true. I was friends with a house. Could the world get any stranger? Probably best not to ask that question. The minutes ticked by. Had Reed forgotten? Should I call him, or just take care of this myself?

The keys to Aunt Teresa's Volkswagen hung on a hook next to the phone. I checked the clock. He was fifteen minutes late. Should I give him more time or go by myself? Ten more minutes ticked by. I finished my coffee and grabbed the car keys. Wait a minute. I didn't know where I was going. It had to be on Main Street, right? Why not take care of two things at once? I picked up the lilac phone and called my parent's house to check in with them.

"Linda, is that you?" my mom asked.

"It's me. Good morning."

"Good morning, sweetie. How are things going?"

"Mystic Hills is interesting."

She laughed. "That's one way to put it."

We made small talk for a few minutes before I said, "Where's the mayor's office?"

"Why do you ask?" Her voice faltered.

"I have to take care of some paperwork for Aunt Teresa."

"It's on Main Street. It's the only building with marble columns. You can't miss it. When are you coming home?"

"I'm not sure. There are some loose ends to tie up here. Tell dad I said, hello."

After I hung up, I caught sight of Victor and Dave standing in the kitchen doorway. "Why didn't you tell me I'd have to claim full citizenship if I signed the deed?"

Victor tilted his head. "I'm sorry, I thought it was understood."

"The good news," Dave said. "Is we can take care of the house so you can visit your parents whenever you want."

The knot in my chest eased. They hadn't tried to trick me. "Okay then, I'm off to the mayors to sign paperwork." I showed them the keys I was holding. "I'm taking the car."

I stepped out the kitchen door and saw Reed's shiny black Mustang turning into the driveway. He came to a stop behind the Volkswagen and rolled down his window. "Sorry I'm late."

I pocketed the keys and walked around to the passenger side of the car. Once I was seated with my seatbelt fastened, I said, "I didn't think you were coming. I was about to drive myself."

"Jezelle insisted on us having breakfast together this morning. It's like she wanted to make me late."

So…he and Jezelle had woken up together. Jealousy jabbed at me like a dull knife to the ribs. I had no right to be jealous. Envious maybe but not jealous.

"You ready to become a Mystic Hills resident?" he asked.

"Honestly no. I spoke to my mom. She wants me to come home."

"Do you plan on leaving before you find out who killed Teresa?" he asked.

Apparently, Mr. Judgmental was back. "No. I want to bring her killer to justice," I snapped. "For now, she's at peace."

"Wrong. If she was at peace she'd cross over. The fact that she's hanging around as a ghost means she has unfinished business."

"Has anyone ever told you that you're really annoying when you're right?"

He chuckled. "I'll rephrase the question. After Teresa has moved on, do you plan to stay?"

I threw my hands up in the air. "I don't know. Part of me wants to run back to my normal life. Another part wants to stay here and give this place a chance."

"Mystic Hills can be great, but you need to be aware of the every man for himself mentality. Around here we're taught that there is only so much power in the world, so you better grab your share and hold onto it."

"That's a terrible way to look at life."

"It's how we think."

I couldn't help wondering if it was the way Reed saw the world due to his personal history. "I choose to believe people are better than that."

"Preschool logic?"

"Yes," I smiled. "I like preschool logic and rules. They make much more sense than adult chaos. Plus, we sing songs and play with blocks."

He laughed.

We drove in comfortable silence, which was nice because it gave me time to take in the green lawns and colorful houses we drove past. Hopefully Lilly took care of the lawn too, because while I liked planting flowers, I'd never touched a lawn mower and had no real desire to do so. When we hit Main Street, the mustang bounced down the cobblestone streets like a bucking bronco.

"Good thing I put on my seatbelt."

"We've all complained about the cobble-stone streets. The mayor claims he is big on preserving history. I think he's big on selling new suspension systems out of his brothers auto shop."

"Is the mayor elected by the entire town?" Who knew? Maybe it was an inherited position.

"The witches control almost everything. We all vote, but whoever they want to win, always does."

"And you're okay with that?"

"Those of us with gifts can't compete with the witches. Those with the power make the rules. You can't tell me everything is fair in your world."

"No. It's not. In my world, it's the people with the most money who have the power."

"The mayor's office is coming up on the right." He pointed out the window.

A pale marble building complete with pillars seemed to be impossibly wedged between a coffee shop and an art gallery.

"When you're done, you can meet me at *Tea & Spirits.*"

Crap. I'd thought he was coming in with me. Not that I needed him to hold my hand, but a little moral support would be nice. No worries. I could do this. "Any words of pessimistic wisdom before I go inside?"

"Keep your answers as short and truthful

as possible. Never volunteer any information or give an opinion."

"I can't have an opinion?" Was he serious?

"Until they figure out who you're siding with, you need to keep your conversation to a minimum."

"Who I'm siding with on what?" I asked.

"The new restrictions," he said. "Although they'll assume you're following in your aunt's footsteps."

"I probably will." Okay I could do this. I took a deep breath and exited the vehicle. When I reached the door there was no handle, just a doorbell. With no other option, I pushed the button.

"State your name and your business." A disembodied voice announced.

"I'm Belinda Harbinger. I signed the deed to my aunt Teresa's house. I've been told there's additional paperwork I need to take care of."

The sound of a buzzer filled the air and then the door popped open. I entered a white marble lobby. A brunette in a navy suit sat at a marble topped desk applying blood red lipstick that did not compliment her pale complexion.

"Do you like my new lipstick?" she asked.

Reed told me to keep my opinions to myself, but he couldn't have meant this. I decided to be diplomatic. "It's a lovely shade of red."

She put her lipstick away and smiled. "Why are you visiting the mayor today?"

"I'm applying for citizenship."

"Not to stick my nose in where it doesn't belong, but you do realize you'd be better off selling the house and going back to your own kind."

"Maybe, but I still need to file the paperwork."

She pushed a button on her desk. "Have a seat. He'll be out shortly."

I sat on the small velvet sofa, trying not to appear anxious. If I was in the normal world, I could've pulled out my phone or read a book on my kindle app or played a game. I really needed to look into purchasing a cell phone that worked on the Mystic Hills system. Maybe I could rent one.

A door off to my left opened and a tall thin man in a brown suit stepped out and scanned the room. I was the only occupant in the lobby besides the secretary, so I wasn't sure what he was looking for. When his gaze landed on me he frowned like I was an unpleasant discovery. "You must be Belinda."

"I am. And you are?" He didn't seem like the type of man who'd be elected mayor.

"Kyle Carter, I'm in charge of the Lands and Deeds department. You signed illegally for your aunt's house last night. I assume you're here to turn the property over to the city."

"No. I'm not." Was this guy trying to intimidate me? I stayed seated on the couch and kept my mouth shut. Volunteering information to this odd man didn't seem like a good idea.

"You can't own property," Kyle said. "You're not a citizen."

"I'm here to fix that," I said.

Another door opened and a man wearing a charcoal gray suit filled the doorway. He had silver hair and shrewd blue eyes, and looked like the type of man who'd be elected to office. "Miss Harbinger?"

"Yes." I stood and went over to meet him.

"I'm Mayor Charles Castor. Please come

in." He glanced at Kyle. "I'll handle this situation."

The mayor stepped back. I entered his office and my breath caught. Highly polished mahogany panels covered the walls and appeared to glow in the light from the wall sconces. An antique desk and couch sat in the center of the room. What caught my eye the most was the atrium filled with lush green plants and colorful flowers.

"Your office is amazing," I said.

"Thank you," he sounded genuinely pleased. "My wife designed it. Allow me to express my condolences about your aunt. We may not have seen eye to eye, but she was an asset to this community."

"Thank you."

"How can I help you today?" He walked over and sat behind his desk.

Obviously, he knew why I was here and was just being polite. I took a seat on the couch, which was not as comfortable as it looked. I shifted around trying to find a non-lumpy spot. "I need to fill out my citizenship papers."

"Is this because of the house?" he asked.

"Yes."

"Kyle mentioned that to me this morning. I'm a bit surprised you signed the deed. You've never expressed an interest in Mystic Hills before."

I could explain about my mom talking me out of staying but I didn't understand how she'd done that and I didn't owe this man an explanation. Reed had warned me against volunteering information, so I said, "Now I'm curious."

"I see." He steepled his fingers under his chin. "Do you plan to cut ties with the outside world?"

"I'm still figuring everything out."

"Well," he leaned back in his chair. "Maybe you should wait to sign."

"I already signed the deed, so I might as well sign for citizenship." He probably wanted the same thing Kyle did, but he was more subtle in his approach. A true politician.

"You should sign a temporary citizenship contract. That way you won't be tied to the house. It will give you room to maneuver."

Nope. "I own the house. Correct?"

"Yes, ma'am."

"To keep ownership of the house, I need to sign citizenship papers, so I'd prefer to sign now. I could always sell the house later."

"I was trying to save you some paper-work." He sat forward and tapped his fingers on the desk. "But if you insist." He paused like was giving me time to change my mind.

"I do."

He pulled his laptop closer and pecked one-fingered at the keys. A printer on the corner of his desk spit out a piece of paper without making a sound.

He set the page in front of me. "Sign on the bottom."

I read the contract that stated I was applying for citizenship. It also said I wasn't allowed to leave Mystic Hills for the next twelve months. "What's this?" I pointed at the section.

"It's a standard contract."

I doubted that. "Please remove that section and reprint it."

"I don't understand the problem, I thought you were staying."

Time to lie for the greater good. "I made plans for a vacation and the tickets are non-refundable, so you'll need to remove the time stipulation from the contract."

He went back to his keyboard and hit a few keys. A moment later another paper soundlessly appeared from the printer. He offered it to me. I read it over, carefully, making sure he hadn't added anything strange. It all looked in order. "I sign this and I'm a full citizen?"

"Yes. With all the rights, privileges, and duties of a true citizen of Mystic Hills."

I signed but didn't hand it over. "I'll need a copy of this for my records."

"Of course." He plucked the paper from my hand, signed his name below mine, and then the paper doubled itself...on its own. No copier needed.

I accepted the paper he offered me. "Thank you for your help with this matter."

"You're welcome. Now there's the matter of paying your taxes."

Really? "When are they due?"

"Now." He gestured at the lumpy couch. "We'll only take half a pint today. You can pay again in a few months."

"You want my blood?" He couldn't be serious. The memory of the vampire bracelet biting into my wrist made my stomach twist.

"Every citizen pays taxes in blood." He went to his desk and pulled out a syringe, some tubing, and a blood bag.

"I'm busy today. Why don't I schedule

an appointment for later this week?" When I knew if this was a real thing or if he was trying to take advantage of me.

"This must seem strange to you. Perhaps you should call Victor. He'll tell you this is a perfectly normal procedure in Mystic Hills."

"May I use your phone?" I asked.

"Of course."

I dialed. When Victor came on the line, I explained the situation. "Is this normal?"

"We usually pay July first. Make sure you get a receipt, or they'll ask you to give again."

I thanked him and hung up. "I don't suppose you have a Welcome to town brochure which explains how everything around here works."

"Never needed one since most residents are born here." He gestured toward the couch.

I sat back down. He joined me, sitting to my right. He pulled the cap off of the needle and reached for my arm. Jerking my arm away was my first instinct, but I managed to hold still as he slid the needle into the vein on my right elbow with alarming efficiency. Once it was in, he attached the tubing and the bag. "This should only take a few minutes."

While I'd given blood before, it had always been in a clinical setting. This felt wrong…just sitting on a couch watching my blood flow through the tubing into the bag. No alcohol swabs. No gloves. I needed to keep my mind off of what was happening before I freaked myself out. "Where do you store the blood?"

The mayor stood and then resumed his seat behind his desk. "Every business and office has a refrigerator for blood collections, even the tea shop you inherited."

"Can I ask you questions while I'm here?"

"I may choose not to answer, but you can ask."

Okay. "From what I've heard, witches have more power than the gifted."

He smiled and nodded. "That's true."

"How do you learn to create spells and hexes?"

"Knowledge is passed down within families. We trade in spells and hexes the way you trade in blood and money."

Maybe I could get on his good side.

"That's fascinating. Can a gifted person learn to create spells?"

"No. You can purchase and use any number of spells, but you could never create one," he said. "Are you interested in purchasing a spell?"

"At the moment, no." I glanced at the blood bag which was half full. Seeing my blood on the outside of my body always made me a little queasy. "We should probably stop, don't you think?"

"In a minute." The mayor tilted his head and studied me. "Why are you really here?"

"To find out what happened to my aunt," I blurted out. What the heck? I hadn't meant to say that. "Did you put a spell on me?"

"The needle is coated in an honesty spell. It takes a moment to kick in."

Son of a… "Do you do this to everyone, or am I receiving special treatment?"

"It's something we use when warranted, to make sure certain citizens have the town's best interests at heart. Do you plan to live here full time?"

The words flowed out of me. "I don't know." I tried to stop talking, but it was like a floodgate had opened. "I have no clue how to balance my other life with this one."

"Do you have any ill intent toward Mystic Hills?" he asked.

"No, but I'm mad at my mother for keeping this from me, and I'm mad at you for this stupid spell."

He grinned and then stood, adjusting his tie. "Sometimes deception is necessary for the greater good. And there's no real harm done. Right?"

"Physically no, mentally yes. How long will this last?"

"The spell will wear off before you exit the building." He came over to the couch and removed the needle. Rather than applying a cotton ball and a bandaid, he placed his finger on the wound. When he removed his finger, the bleeding stopped.

"Miss Harbinger, I suggest you accept that your aunt's death was an accident. Move on with your life. Enjoy your time in our beautiful town."

That sounded like I was dismissed. Time to leave before I shared anything else. I stood, taking a moment to see if I felt lightheaded. No. I was good. I headed back out into the lobby, where the receptionist smiled at me like she knew a secret.

"Have an orange juice." She set a small bottle on the counter.

"Is there a spell on it?" I asked.

"No." She shook her head. "Have a nice day."

I took the juice and headed for the door. Her eyes tracked my progress across the room. Outside, I spotted Reed's car parked down by *Tea & Spirits*. Now what? I wasn't sure.

Yesterday Reed had mentioned having breakfast but he'd already eaten with Jezelle this morning. Maybe I'd grab a cup of coffee myself and do the see and be seen thing. Where should I eat breakfast?

As I walked down Main Street, I people watched. When I made eye contact some people smiled in greeting while others looked at me with suspicion. I shouldn't let anyone's behavior bother me. It was a beautiful warm sunny day. Orange and yellow marigolds bloomed in terra cotta planters on the sidewalk. The aroma of fresh baked bread drifted through the air making my mouth water.

Where was the fresh bread smell coming

from? The most likely place was *The Bakers Dozen* which was three stores down from the tearoom. The outside dining area was packed, so the food must be good. I crossed the street and headed for the bakery. I dropped the bottle of orange juice in the trash bin outside the bakery.

When I pushed the door open, the scent of cinnamon and vanilla made my stomach growl. I wove between the tables of people toward the baked goods which were dis-played in a glass case that took up one corner of the store. A cashier worked at a counter next to the case taking orders.

I ignored the patrons who openly stared at me and waited in line behind a couple ar-guing over what muffins they should purchase for their brunch. Once they had their order taken care of I stepped up to the cashier. She looked me up and down. "With that chestnut brown hair and the I don't care if people stare at me attitude, you must be a Harbinger."

I laughed. "I'm Belinda Harbinger. Teresa was my aunt."

"I'm Grace Stewart. Don't let all these busy bodies bother you." She turned toward the women already seated and spoke in a voice that carried through the room. "In case you weren't sitting close enough to eavesdrop, this is Belinda Harbinger."

"Hello," a lady in a flowered dress called out.

"Hello," I responded.

"Welcome to town," another lady said.

"Thank you."

"Now what can I get for you?" Grace asked.

I scanned the chalk board menu behind her. "I'll have a cup of coffee and a cinnamon scone."

"For here or to go?"

"Here." Maybe I could meet a few people and find out something about my aunt.

Order in hand, I scanned the room for an empty table. There was one near the door and one dead center of the room. I headed for the one where I could talk to more people. I'd barely stirred the sugar into my coffee when a white-haired woman turned from her table and said, "I'm sorry about your aunt. She was a wonderful woman."

"Thank you. I wish I knew more about

what happened to her. The police aren't sharing any details."

She leaned in. "They won't. If you ask me, it was someone opposed to the restrictions."

"Which means it could be any witch in town," another woman said.

"Don't go lumping all the witches together," a woman with steel gray hair snapped. "I voted for those restrictions."

"I don't really understand how everything works in Mystic Hills. Are there different political parties within the witch community?" I took a bite of my scone and waited for someone to respond.

The woman with the steel gray hair picked up her coffee and came to join me. "There are different factions of witches who care about different things. Some want power and have political aspirations. Others put all of their energy into creating new spells and couldn't care less about politics."

"Should I ask which camp you fall into…I'm sorry I didn't catch your name." I sipped my coffee and waited.

"Yelena. For me, creating spells is like making art. I want to be left alone to pursue my craft, but I pay attention to politics and speak up for things I believe in."

"Do you think my aunt's death was an accident?"

"No one in this town believes it was an accident, but the fact that it wasn't investigated means the police were warned off. The best thing you can do for your aunt is honor her memory by communicating with spirits and ghosts. Attempting to avenge her death will only get you or your housemates killed."

I almost choked on my scone. After washing it down with a sip of coffee, I said, "You truly believe that."

She nodded. "Mystic Hills is not like the outside world. Whoever is in power controls the town. Be careful whose toes you step on."

"What about my Aunt? She's not at peace and she's not crossing over. How can I help her?"

She pursed her lips. "It would be best if she passed over. She'd be stronger in spirit form. But she always was a stubborn thing, so I'll bring something by the house that will help her focus and be at peace while she's on this plane."

"Thank you, Yelena. I'd appreciate that."

"You're welcome." With those words, she stood and went back to her table. I ate the rest of my scone while I considered where this left me. Hopefully whatever Yelena brought would help Teresa hold her form longer. Maybe she could help me find my memories. The fact that no one believed Teresa's death was an accident, yet they weren't going to do anything about it didn't work for me.

Chapter 8

After I finished my food, I exited the store and headed to *Tea & Spirits*. Maybe Reed could help me make sense of this.

I stepped out onto the sidewalk and squinted against the bright sunlight. Had I packed my sunglasses? I couldn't remember. If not, I'd have to buy a new pair. I was almost to the tearoom, when a twister of some cloudy mist whooshed around me and then stopped, coalescing into a ghostly version of tiny woman with her hair pulled back into a severe bun.

"Hello? Can you see me?"

The hair on my arms stood up. "Yes. Can I help you?"

"I'm dead. I've been waiting to cross

over."

Nervous energy zinged through my body. A dead woman was talking to me. A ghost had tracked me down on Main Street. Was this my life now? Why did she need me if she knew she was dead? "I can take you to Victor. Is that what you want?"

Her form flickered. "I won't go until someone takes care of my cat, Sadie. I need to know she's safe."

Aww. How sweet. "Where's your cat?"

"At my house. Where else?"

Okay. Maybe that was a dumb question. What should I do next? I needed some advice. Reed would have to do. "Come with me to the tearoom and we'll figure everything out."

"It's a cat. How hard is that to figure out?"

I bit my lip to keep from responding. The woman was dead after all and worried about her pet. She had a right to be crabby.

"This way." I entered the establishment and headed for Reed's office trying to appear calm, even though I was freaking out on the inside.

He glanced up at me. "What's wrong?"

Apparently, I wasn't covering my emotions as well as I thought. "Someone died."

"Who?"

"What's your name?" I asked the ghost.

"Mrs. Tate."

I relayed her name to Reed.

"Genevieve Tate?" he asked.

She nodded and I repeated the gesture. Remembering how Victor had needed to touch me to see and hear the ghost, I lightly placed my hand on top of Reed's. "Mrs. Tate, can you tell us what happened?"

Her form became staticky and then solidified. "I fell down my stairs and Sadie is beside herself. Please help her."

Death by stairs? Goosebumps skittered down my spine. That couldn't be a coincidence. "We'll help her, but first… how did you fall?"

"I don't know. One minute I was heading downstairs to make breakfast and then I was floating through town but no one could see me."

Interesting.

"Sadie is waiting," Mrs. Tate snapped.

"Reed, do you know where she lives?"

He nodded.

"Should we call the police?" I wasn't sure how accidental death was handled in

Mystic Hills. Just because they didn't investigate deaths, didn't mean we shouldn't report them.

Reed blinked like he was coming out of a fog. "Yes." He picked up the phone on his desk and dialed, jabbing at the numbers with force. He mustn't be as unaffected as he appeared. After explaining the situation to someone, he hung up. "They said," his voice cracked. He cleared throat. "We can retrieve the cat, but they don't want us to touch the body."

"Okay, we're going to get your cat."

Mrs. Tate disappeared.

Reed stood. I followed him to his Mustang. Once we were in the car I said, "Do we need your dad to help Mrs. Tate cross over?"

"No. I can do it." He pulled out of his parking spot and onto the road. If the frown on his face was any indication, he wasn't happy about this situation.

"Have you helped people cross over before?"

"Just my mom."

Dang it. "I'm so sorry."

"For what?"

"That shouldn't have been your job."

He shrugged and put on his blinker.

"Someone had to do it. My dad couldn't."

Poor Reed. There was nothing I could say that he would appreciate. I'd just try to be more patient with him in the future like Aunt Teresa had suggested. On that note, there was no way a second death caused by falling down stairs could be a coincidence. Someone was doing this. I needed to figure out who. I needed to learn how this town worked. I needed to pay more attention to people and my surroundings.

Flowering trees lined the side street. We went up the hill, around a bend, and drove past four houses before pulling up to a yellow house with orange trim. Such a happy house, and such a sad reason to be here.

Reed parked in the driveway, took a deep breath, and then blew it out. He climbed out of the car and I followed him down the walkway and up the porch steps.

Not sure what to do next, I tried the door. It was open. When I stepped across the threshold Mrs. Tate appeared. "This way."

We followed her through the front room and down a hallway to the main stairs. Mrs. Tate's body lay sprawled across the bottom few steps. Her neck bent at an unnatural angle. I clutched at my stomach and backed up a step. Logically I knew a ghost meant a dead person, but a dead person and a freshly dead body seemed like two different things.

Mrs. Tate floated into my peripheral vision. "Don't wimp out on me now. Sadie needs you."

I could do this. I could. I really didn't want to, but the cat needed me. That was it. I would focus on the cat and not the body. Sure. That would work. I turned, holding my breath and focused on the feline. The orange and white cat lay curled up next to her owner. When the cat saw us, she hissed.

"It's okay, Sadie," Mrs. Tate pointed at me. "This nice lady is going to take you home."

I was? Sure Mrs. Tate had asked me to help her cat, but I didn't realize she wanted me to keep Sadie. Not that I minded. I'd grown up with cats, but there was probably a family member who would want her. I could take care of Sadie until Mrs. Tate's children decided who would keep her. I sat down on the floor where I was, because I didn't want to go any closer to the body. "Hey, Sadie. Come here." I held out my hand. The cat yowled.

"I know you're sad, but I promise I'll take good care of you."

Reed's eyebrows came together. "You should probably clear that with Dave."

I ignored his comment and turned to the ghost. "Is there someone in the family she'd be more comfortable with?"

"I have a good feeling about you," Mrs. Tate said. "Sadie has a cat bed in the living room and a carrier in the pantry." She floated over to Sadie and tried to pet her. Her fingers appeared to touch the cat, or maybe they went through the fur. Either way, the cat purred. "Go with this nice lady. She'll take care of you."

Sadie assessed me with her feline gaze and then she stood and crossed the floor. Stopping next to my knee, she meowed. Slowly, I reached out and stroked the top of her head. She leaned into my touch. Once I was fairly certain she wouldn't bolt, I picked her up and then stood.

I heard footsteps coming from the front room. "Is Mrs. Tate still here?" A man in police uniform asked.

"Yes," I said.

"I'd like to take her statement before she passes over." He asked questions rapid fire. I repeated Mrs. Tate's answers. Nothing strange had happened lately and she hadn't been in power struggles with anyone.

"My balance has been off lately. I think I just fell." Mrs. Tate frowned. "Stupid way to die."

I relayed the first part of the message and left out the commentary.

"We're all done here," the policeman said. "I'll notify her family to make arrangements."

"Is there anyone you want to speak to before you cross over?" I asked.

Mrs. Tate sighed. "I think that would only make it worse for them."

"Your turn," I told Reed.

"I need to touch you so I can see her."

I nodded that I understood. His warm fingers rested on my forearm. "Mrs. Tate, are you ready?"

"Since Belinda agreed to take care of my Sadie, I'm ready to cross over."

Reed glowed. It was a glimmer at first and then it increased until I could barely keep my eyes open. It was like looking into the sun. Warmth flowed between us. I felt connected to him, like we were one. After the light faded, Mrs. Tate was gone.

Chapter 9

Once Reed tuned back into his surroundings, he released my arm. The warmth and connection I'd felt drifted away, which was a shame.

He helped me gather all the cat paraphernalia and we headed out to his car. Sadie yowled from the cat carrier in the back seat as we drove. "It won't be long," I said.

Reed snorted but didn't say anything.

"You don't talk to your pets?" I asked.

"I talk to familiars because they're people, but cats are just cats. She can't understand you."

Sadie hissed from the back seat, which made me smile. "That was Sadie calling your bluff."

"That didn't mean anything," Reed scoffed.

Sadie let out a long yowl and another hiss.

"You were saying?"

Reed glanced in the rear view mirror. "If you can understand me, meow three times."

The cat remained quiet.

"See," Reed said. "Just a coincidence."

"Growing up, my cat would hock up furballs in my dad's shoes when he fed her low calorie cat food."

"First off, gross. Second, the two things probably didn't have anything to do with each other."

"He was the one who kept trying to put her on a diet, and his shoes were the only ones full of furballs."

"If you want to know what an animal is thinking, there are families who can talk to them."

Families. Plural. Interesting. "Multiple families have the same gift?"

"No. Some families hear birds, others hear mammals. It varies."

"So each family has its own gift?"

"Yes. Gifts are passed on by lineage.

Sometimes gifts are symbiotic like my family and yours."

"Are there other families that can talk to ghosts?" Harbingers couldn't be the only ones tasked with talking to the recently deceased.

"There's a family who can hear ghosts, but they can't see them. There's a family that can allow ghosts to speak through them."

Goose bumps pebbled my arms. "Like possession?"

He nodded.

"That's worse than mine. Is there a list of gifts somewhere?"

"Probably."

"Speaking of gifts, are you okay, after what you did for Mrs. Tate?" He didn't appear upset, but I had to ask.

"Yes. The process of crossing someone over is surprisingly peaceful."

Odds were it hadn't been peaceful with his mom. "It's funny. When I see a ghost, I feel compelled to help them. They seem nicer than some of the live residents of Mystic Hills."

Reed laughed. "Mrs. Tate gave everyone hell for years. She was a force to be reckoned with. Now that she's gone, they'll have to promote another citizen to be on the Council of Elders."

"Maybe that's what someone wanted," I said. "To shake up the Council."

Reed didn't respond.

"Both Aunt Teresa and Mrs. Tate taking fatal falls down their stairs can't be a coincidence."

"We don't know that." Reed tapped the steering wheel with his index finger. "But my gut says you're not wrong."

"Did they have a common enemy?"

"It's possible. Politics in Mystic Hills are cut throat, literally. If a witch saw an opportunity to take them both out, he might do it."

"We need a way to narrow down the list of suspects," I said.

Sadie yowled from the back seat, like she agreed with me.

"Who did Mrs. Tate side with when she voted? Was she on Teresa's side for the restrictions?"

"I'm not sure."

I had another question. "Why was Mrs. Tate's ghost so clear, but Aunt Teresa seems to have trouble holding her form and sticking around."

"I'd guess it's either because Mrs. Tate was recently deceased or she was at peace with the situation because she believed her death was an accident. The higher the ghosts emotions, the harder it is for them to maintain their shape. The longer a ghost stays here the more they unravel."

That reminded me. "I spoke to a witch named Yelena today. She's going to drop something off at the house which should help calm Aunt Teresa and make it easier for her to hold her shape and communicate with us.

"Yelena is powerful. She's a good ally to have."

When we pulled into the driveway the Volkswagen was gone. The keys were still in my pocket. Huh…Victor must have a spare set.

Sadie meowed. Time to focus on the newest member of my Mystic Hills family. "I'll take the cat carrier if you grab everything else."

Once we had the cat inside, I spoke to the house, "Lilly, this is Sadie. She's come to live with us."

The lights blinked twice.

I opened the wire door of the cat carrier so Sadie could come out and explore. She poked her head out and sniffed the air. I heard water running and I turned to see Reed filling her water bowl. He set it on the floor against the back kitchen wall and then added her food bowl with some dry food.

A black rubber placement decorated with feline paw prints appeared underneath the bowls.

"Thanks, Lilly," I whispered.

Sadie eased out of the carrier. I took her cat bed into the living room, a large oval shaped pillow, and set it on the couch.

"Isn't that supposed to go on the floor?" Reed asked.

"It could, but I'd rather Sadie feel at home." Growing up my cats had free range of the furniture. There was nothing quite as relaxing as a cat sitting on your lap while you read a book. Sadie would probably take a while to warm up, but that was okay.

The cat in question wandered into the living room and headed straight for the chair Dave normally slept in. I'd swear she winked at me before she hopped up and made herself comfortable.

Where was Dave? He must have left with Victor.

"Can you call for Teresa while I'm here," Reed asked. "I have some questions about how our symbiotic relationship works."

"Sure." I sat on the couch. Reed joined me, placing his hand on my forearm.

"Aunt Teresa, are you here?"

She popped into existence in front of us. "Hello, darlings. What's up?"

"We helped Mrs. Tate crossover," I said. "And we adopted Sadie."

Her form went staticky and then solidified. "Genevieve is dead? How did she die?"

"She fell down her stairs," I said.

"She was murdered just like me?" Her form grew and stretched.

"We're investigating," I tried to reassure her.

Her form buzzed and then popped out of existence.

"We should have anticipated that," Reed removed his hand from my arm.

"Yes, we should have." Now what? What else did I need help with? I remembered. "Where can I get a cell phone that works here?"

He frowned. "Teresa's has to be around here somewhere. You could use hers."

That would work for now. Wait a minute. I shot up from the couch. This could be big. "We should check her voicemail. Maybe it will give us a clue about who killed her." I scanned the living room. No phone. Where would her cell be? Where did I leave my phone when I wasn't using it? Charging on the nightstand.

"I bet it's in her room." I dashed up the stairs to Aunt Teresa's bedroom. The phone sat charging on her dresser. I picked it up and flipped it open. As in, it was a flip phone. Hello outdated technology. The screen was similar to the land line my parents insisted on keeping. I punched a few buttons and found her incoming and outgoing calls.

Reed's footsteps on the hardwood floor announced that he was headed my way.

"What are you looking for?" he said from the doorway.

I scanned down the recent calls list. "The jewelry store called twice the week she died. Teresa called the mayor's office three times and they called her back twice. Other than that, it's just your father." I punched another button and frowned. "Where's voicemail on this thing?"

Reed joined me and pointed at a button on the side of the phone, "Press speaker phone so I can hear too."

I hit the correct buttons.

"We need to discuss the restriction on hexes." The mayor's voice said. "The waiting period is impacting local businesses which is not good for the town."

That was it. "So, the mayor wasn't happy about the new laws."

"Honestly, I'm surprised they passed. The Elders sided with Teresa."

"Who are they, again?"

"They advise the mayor and most of the time they side with him, but they didn't on this. They voted seven to three to make waiting times on hexes a law and to restrict taking blood. The mayor was furious."

Interesting. The mayor or someone from his side seemed like the number one suspect in Aunt Teresa's murder.

"Before you say it, the mayor would never go after Teresa. He'd have one of his associates do it." Reed frowned. "Mrs. Tate was an Elder. They'll have to fill her spot before they can vote on anything else."

"How do they choose who'll take her place?"

"It's done by age. They start with the oldest residents and work their way down. A lot of people refuse the position because they don't want to be involved with politics."

That reminded me. "Speaking of the mayor and his friends, they added a section to the official citizen contract stating I wasn't allowed to leave for a year."

Reed's eyebrows went up. "That's new."

"I made them take it out before I signed."

"Smart move." Reed chuckled. "I bet they put it in there, hoping you wouldn't notice. Then when you left town, they could revoke your citizenship and take the house."

"This house is amazing, but why would they want it?"

"Power. Owning more real estate means you have access to more power through the grid."

"Who will Mrs. Tate's house go to?"

"I'm sure she has a will drawn up, like Teresa did."

I turned the phone over hoping a magical screen might pop out of the phone somewhere. "There's really no internet?"

"Not on the phone. You need a special laptop. Teresa had one." He glanced around the room. "I don't know where she kept it."

A memory tickled my brain. Where had I seen a laptop? "I found it right before I discovered Aunt Teresa's body, so I forgot to ask about a power cord."

"It doesn't need a cord. There's a charging station."

"I want a manual on how to operate everything in this town. Do you have one of those?"

"No, but there might be some books at the library."

And since I was an official citizen, I could apply for a library card. My inner bookworm did a happy dance. "I'll visit the library another day. For now let's check on Sadie. I don't want her to feel abandoned."

"We should change the phone over to you. Just hit the settings button, delete Teresa's name and type in yours. Since the address is the same it shouldn't be a big deal."

I did as he'd said and then we went to check on Sadie. The cat in question was curled up right where we left her.

I heard the kitchen door open. "Who is that I smell? What is going on here?" Dave called out as soon as he entered the house. He dashed into the living room and froze when he saw Sadie in his chair. "Who is that and why is she in my chair?"

"Her name is Sadie and she's come to live with us."

"Absolutely not," Dave said.

Who knew Dave was so territorial? "I promised Mrs. Tate I'd take care of her, so you're going to have to make peace with the situation."

Victor came in with a small smile on his face. He walked over and squatted down by Sadie holding out his hand so she could sniff him. "Hello, Sadie."

The cat didn't move away from him, so he reached out and scratched her ears. Sadie purred in appreciation. "She's a lovely cat, Dave. You'll adjust to her presence. Maybe even make a new friend."

"Where's Mrs. Tate?" Dave asked.

"She died." I told them about Mrs. Tate coming to find me on the street and how Reed helped her cross over.

"Do you think her dying in that manner is a coincidence?" Victor asked.

"She didn't suspect foul play," Reed said. "But we agree it seems suspicious."

"When she crossed over?" Victor looked down at the floor as he spoke. "How was it?"

"Peaceful," Reed said.

I'd expected there to be some type of accusation in his tone, but there was none.

"Good," Victor sighed. "Can we talk?" He looked up at Reed. Conflict shone in his eyes.

"Sure." Reed stood. "Let's go for a drive."

They left to have what I hoped was a heartfelt moment. My stomach growled. "Time for a snack."

Sadie rolled over and stretched before closing her eyes. I walked into the kitchen. "Lilly, can I have pretzels, peanut butter, and a glass of iced tea?"

The food appeared on the table. "Thank you."

I crunched my way through one of my favorite snacks while I played with the phone. It seemed straight forward. You could call or text. That was it. I missed my reading apps and games. I could hear Dave talking to Sadie. Reed and his dad were still out. Now that I was fueled up and had the house to myself it was time to hunt for my memories.

Someone knocked on the kitchen door.

Maybe that was Yelena. When I opened the door, I found the gray haired woman standing there with a purple pillar candle the size of a coffee can. "Light this in her room. It will help center her."

"Thank you." I took the candle which must have weighed five pounds. "Would you like to come in?"

She smiled. "Another time, but thank you for asking."

I shut the door and walked into the living room where I picked up a matchbook from the jar on the fireplace, and then headed up to Aunt's Teresa's room. Where should I put the candle? The dresser seemed like the best place. I struck a match and lit the wick. "Aunt Teresa, this is supposed to help you."

I exited the bedroom and said, "Lilly, do you know where the photo albums are?"

The light over the stairs blinked twice. "I need to go downstairs?"

Two more blinks.

"Okay." I went downstairs and waited. The kitchen light blinked. Once I was in the kitchen, the pantry door popped open and then the back stair door opened too. I headed up the steps to continue my search and stopped on the landing. "Right or left?" I hoped they weren't in the room on the left with Aunt Teresa's body. No matter how normal that was for Mystic Hills, my brain couldn't deal with it.

The lights in the room on the right blinked. I went back up to the office and checked all the books on the table and desk and came up with nothing. A search of the drawers didn't yield any results.

"Can you give me a hint?"

A paper taped to the wall fluttered like there was a breeze. I investigated. The paper was a page from a calendar. My birthday, January sixth, was highlighted. What did Lilly mean by showing me this? I checked the other items hanging nearby. They were recipes and a receipt for a nightstand. I pressed my palms against the wall thinking there might be a hidden panel. No such luck.

"Lilly, I don't understand."

Apparently, she didn't have any more clues to give. "Aunt Teresa?" I called out.

She didn't appear.

I pulled all three pieces of paper off the wall and checked the front and the back of each one. No clues popped out at me. What about the nightstand? The only item that looked new in the house was the one in Teresa's room. I'd found one picture in there, stuck behind the drawer. Maybe there were more that I'd missed in my search.

I grabbed the satchel with the laptop and headed back down to the kitchen and then upstairs to my aunt's room. I pulled the top drawer from the unfinished nightstand, and then pulled out the bottom drawer which held sheets. Just in case, I removed the sheets to check for a false bottom. Nothing.

I pulled the nightstand away from the wall. This plain piece of furniture stood out compared to all her shabby chic painted antiques. It's not like she needed a nightstand. She had one on the other side of her bed, so she must've bought this for a reason.

Maybe there was a secret panel. I ran my hands down the sides but didn't feel anything odd. I scooted the nightstand out further and studied the back. It looked normal. I ran my hands across it and felt it give a little on the right side. Hope bounced around in my chest as I pushed and pulled the back panel from every angle. When I pressed the top right corner, something released, and the back panel came off. Inside, there was a small photo album, the kind where there was only one picture per page.

Energy emanated from the pale green cover. I retrieved the album and opened it. The first page was a picture of me when I was a toddler hugging a teddy bear. If past experience taught me anything, I probably needed to sit down for this, so I sat on the bed and touched the photo. Happiness flowed over me like a warm breeze. I played outside in the grass with the sun shining down. There was a wading pool and lots of toys and hugs. Toddler me was completely in love with Aunt Teresa.

Turning the page I found a photo of me blowing out a candle shaped like a number 5. Laughter and cupcakes and running barefoot in the grass filled my mind. I loved coming to Mystic Hills. I always asked my mom if we could stay longer. She couldn't wait to leave.

I ran through the pictures of my childhood. Every photo I touched held happy memories. My mom started leaving me with Aunt Teresa while she and my dad went on their own vacations. I had a glorious childhood in Mystic Hills, playing board games, running around outside, and baking cup-cakes with Aunt Teresa.

When I hit my teen years, the tone of my memories changed. I'd wanted to stay the whole summer with Aunt Teresa. I wanted to learn how to use my gift. My mom refused on both counts. I felt like she resented the time I spent with Aunt Teresa, maybe even resented me because I had a gift and she didn't. I never said that to her because I knew it wasn't far from the truth.

Reed filled my memories when I was sixteen. I'd had a huge crush on him. He showed zero interest, but he'd made a good friend, so I went with it. Besides, a romance in Mystic Hills was doomed from the start if my mom kept making Aunt Teresa remove my memories. I didn't understand why I couldn't keep them. I'd train to use my gift, learn how to block ghosts in the real world, and I'd be good to go. My mom didn't see it that way.

My seventeenth summer was one long backyard party and barbecue. I'd wondered if Aunt Teresa went all out for the rest of the year or just the time I was there. Either way, I hadn't wanted to go home when my parents showed up a few days early. They'd purchased a new house and we were moving. I was mad they only told me after the fact. Not that I expected to have much input, but a little warning so I could've packed my room would've been nice.

My eighteenth summer in Mystic Hills was cut short because we were going on a family vacation. Aunt Teresa fought with my mom about giving me my memories. I could train to keep my gift in check. I wanted my memories. At the start of every summer, my aunt restored them and as I grew older and had more memories it felt like emotional whiplash. I'd argued that I was legally an adult and I wanted what was mine. Nothing could persuade my mother. My dad never intervened. He always sat off to the side. I asked if he'd talk to mom for me, and he said he would never interfere in Mystic Hills business. It was my mom's choice because she'd grown up here. She knew what was best for me and I should listen to her.

Next, I came to a picture of my aunt looking like she was about to cry. I touched the photo. Sadness and darkness flowed over me. Aunt Teresa was disappointed and angry that my mom refused to let me stay and keep my memories. Images of me arguing with my mom and crying filled my head. I dropped the photo and swiped at the tears running down my face.

In the next photo Aunt Teresa toasted me with her wine glass. The summers during college were different. Aunt Teresa treated me like an adult, whereas my parents did not. She never said a bad word about my mom, but I knew she thought my mother was wrong about the memories.

I flipped to another photo and my breath caught. Reed sat on the couch next to me. He smiled at me like I was his world. I knew it. We'd been in a relationship. What had I done to ruin it? Did I really want to know? I probably couldn't change it.

Mentally bracing myself, I touched the photo. Happiness and light surrounded me. I'd told Reed I planned to stay in Mystic Hills, and he'd kissed me. Turned out he'd had a crush on me but didn't want to act on it if I was going to disappear and forget about him again. We'd had a blissful two months before my mom arrived and ruined everything.

I dropped the photo as heartache crashed down on me like it was brand new. My mom had given me an ultimatum. I had to choose her or Mystic Hills. If I stayed, she'd cut all ties with me.

How could she have done that?

She argued that she didn't want me to throw away the degree I'd spent four years of my life achieving. She'd promised if I went home, I could come back to Mystic Hills after I worked for one year. But she didn't keep her word. She didn't bring me back. She didn't tell me about this other life I had. A life where I had loved Reed. A life where he'd loved me. A life where I'd sworn to Reed I'd come back to him.

My gut twisted. Reed had trusted me, and he thought I'd betrayed him...that I'd known about him and chosen to stay in the outside world. No wonder he'd been so obnoxious at first.

We'd been in love and he felt abandoned. He had every right to push me away. If I decided to stay, was there any way he'd trust me again?

A knock sounded on the door. "Belinda?" It was Victor.

"Just a minute." I used my shirt to wipe at my face. "Come in."

He entered and I stood, holding onto the photo album.

"Oh," he said. "You found your memories."

I sniffled and nodded.

"Remember that memories are seen through one person's eyes. Sometimes that person can be an unreliable witness. Even if it's us."

Chapter 10

After Victor left, I collapsed back on the bed and stared up at the ceiling trying to figure out how not to be furious at my mom. I loved her and I understood she felt rejected by Mystic Hills. There were some mean, power-hungry people here and the politics seemed cutthroat. She probably wasn't made to feel welcome and didn't want me to be part of the system that shunned her. However, she should have let me make my own choice. The whole thing about my degree seemed suspicious. I could've taught in Mystic Hills or online and then I could have been with Reed. Instead, I'd taught at a preschool I loved but somehow managed to waste two years of my life with someone who cheated on me.

Of course there was no way of knowing if Reed and I would've ended up together forever, but I wish I'd had the chance to find out. My mom had stolen that from me. Even thinking such a thing made me feel like a terrible daughter. She'd wanted what she thought was best for me. She still did. I knew that. One question remained. Why didn't she bring me back in a year like she'd promised? That part I was angry about. She'd lied to me.

Ugh. I sat up and gathered the pictures. Now that the memories were in my head, I didn't have a reaction to the photos. There were half a dozen I hadn't touched, but I couldn't take any more right now. What else could they show me?

Maybe I should look at them. Just get all the drama over with. I turned the pages without touching the photos. The images were older and faded. There was a house I didn't recognize, a cake that said Congratulations, a crib, a church, and a much younger Aunt Teresa with a man I didn't know.

Had she been married? I touched the

photo of the couple and happiness flowed over me. Aunt Teresa loved Johnathon. They'd just announced their engagement. The cake held memories of her wedding shower. The house was his and they planned to move into it after the wedding. I touched the church expecting to see the wedding. Anguish and pain poured over me and dragged me down to where I could barely breath. It wasn't a wedding. It was a funeral for the man she loved. I dropped the picture and laid there trying to catch my breath. Poor Aunt Teresa. She'd had her entire life in front of her with a man she loved and then he died. How? The memory didn't include that. Maybe I should be grateful.

There was one picture left…the crib.

Aunt Teresa materialized in front of me.

"I'm so sorry about your fiancé," I blurted out.

"He was my husband. We had five years together before someone bled him out."

"What?"

She flickered but stayed visible. "That's why I worked to pass those laws. Johnathon was a wonderful man. He didn't deserve to die that way. No one does."

"Did they catch who did it?"

"No."

My head pounded as a terrible realization hit. "Did you find out he died when he came to you as a ghost?"

She nodded. "He was late for dinner, and then he appeared in the kitchen. The last thing he remembered was walking out to his car after work."

"Tell me about the crib." If she'd lost a baby, I didn't want to experience the emotional devastation.

"The crib was for you. I was in a deep depression when I found out that I was going to be an aunt. It was something for me to hold onto. Your visits were the highlight of each summer. There was comfort in knowing that you'd continue the Harbinger line."

"I'm glad I could help." But it didn't sound like enough. "Did you ever move on and have a relationship with anyone else?"

"Victor," she said with a small smile. "After his wife passed, of course."

"Why didn't he tell me?"

"Due to gifts that are overwhelming, some residents are very private people. They don't share each other's secrets or pry into each other's business or talk much about their own lives. Victor and Reed both fall in that category, and you have to respect their nature."

"Is that why you didn't tell me about my relationship with Reed?"

"I think he would have told you in time."

Anger brewed inside of me. "Why did my mom make me leave?"

"You'd have to ask her."

"I don't see that conversation going well." I sighed. "Will you tell me about Reed's life these last four years?"

"He was angry for months after you left. Little by little he moved on. He's managed *Tea & Spirits* for me and dated a few different girls."

"Next awkward question, do I tell him I remember, or do I go with the ignorance is bliss program?"

"That's up to you."

This was one of those times where I wish there was a hotline where you could call an adult who had their life together and ask for advice.

"I feel much more myself." She floated over to the candle. "Who did this?"

"Yelena brought it by."

"Thank her for me."

"I will. Now that you're calm, is there anything you can tell me that might help us bring your killer to justice?"

Her image shimmered, but she held together. "No. Rather than focus on the past, let's talk about your gift."

"Now?" At this point all I wanted was a nap.

"Your gift has been brewing under the surface for so long it came out at full power. If you were able to see and communicate with Mrs. Tate, then the only other thing you need to learn is how to block ghosts."

"What? Why?"

"Not all ghosts and spirits are as non-threatening as Mrs. Tate. You don't want them to have access to you twenty-four hours a day, so you need to come up with a mental waiting room where they can stay until you're ready to see them."

"Okay." That didn't sound easy.

"Stop doubting yourself and try," she said.

I had no idea where to start. "Explain the waiting room to me. How does it work?"

"It helps if you visualize a room that floats near you, like something in another dimension. Imagine you can hold onto a ghost or a spirit and send them to your room."

I was about to see if my years of reading and watching all things paranormal and science fiction would pay off. Eyes closed, I visualized a room with a couch and a coffee table. The image wasn't clear, so I pictured the living room of my apartment, minus the doors and windows. "Now what?"

"Feel my energy and guide me to that place."

Keeping my eyes closed, I imagined that I could grab her hand and pull her through a passageway to the waiting room.

Aunt Teresa laughed. "I can feel what you're trying to do, but you need to think bigger, be stronger."

Fine. I opened my eyes and reached for her with two hands. I could feel her energy tickling my palms "I think I've got you. Now what?"

"Instead of trying to pull me into something, get a firm hold and then push. Push me into the room."

I took a breath, and the tingling sensation on my palms increased. It felt like I was trying to hold onto something that was ice cold. I shoved as hard as I could. An ache started at the base of my skull. I took a deep breath and gave one final push and Aunt Teresa blinked out of existence and appeared in my waiting room.

"You did it," she said.

"I did." And I had the headache to prove it.

She moved around the room touching the couch and the walls. "Well done. I can't detect an exit, which means ghosts and spirits will have to wait until you're ready to work with them."

"How do I let you out?"

"Add a locked door. Then visualize unlocking it."

I did as she suggested, and she popped out in front of me.

"I think it's time for both of us to rest. You should practice more. Call out to Ida Smith at the tearoom." She disappeared.

━━━

I WENT to the bathroom off Aunt Teresa's room and splashed water on my face. What a weird day. I searched her cabinet for Tylenol but didn't find any. There were some crystal bottles with different colored powders and liquids. One was labeled pain reliever, but I wasn't about to take something magical when normal medicine would work. "Lilly, I have a headache. Can I have a bottle of Advil or Tylenol please?"

A crystal bottle filled with green liquid appeared on the vanity.

I picked it up. "Is this for my headache?"

The lights blinked twice.

Should I trust the house? She hadn't steered me wrong yet. Still, I wasn't sure. "Can I have normal medicine like I'm used to?"

Two Tylenol caplets appeared on the counter next to a glass of water.

"Thank you." I took the medicine and then headed to my room for an afternoon nap. I was drifting off to sleep when I felt the mattress shift. I opened my eyes to see Sadie laying at the foot of the bed. "Nap time for you too?"

She meowed in response.

⸻

WHEN I WOKE UP, Sadie was still on the bed.

"Hey, there." I sat near her and she

yowled at me. "I know. I'm sorry you miss Mrs. Tate." I ran my hand from her head to her tail, repeatedly. She gave a quiet purr.

My phone rang, startling me. I'd forgotten it was in my pocket. I retrieved it and answered. "Hello?"

"Is this Belinda Harbinger?" a male voice asked.

"Yes." Who was calling me? Why didn't a magical town have caller ID?

"This is Mrs. Tate's lawyer. I need to speak to you about her estate."

"Why?" She'd already passed over. What could I do?

"Did you agree to take care of Sadie?"

"Yes."

"Mrs. Tate and her family were sometimes at odds. After last Christmas, she changed her will so the cat was her sole beneficiary."

"I…what does that mean?"

"It means whoever has the cat receives a monthly stipend for Sadie's care."

"Okay. Does that mean you send me a check for cat food?"

"No." He laughed. "It means you need to hire a lawyer."

"Why?"

"Her children will not be pleased to find they've been cut out of the will."

"Oh."

"We're doing a reading of the will tomorrow at noon. I suggest your secure representation before coming to the mayor's office. We'll set up the account at the bank after everything is settled."

"Why are we meeting with the mayor?"

"He oversees all legal proceedings."

"I didn't know that. Thank you for calling."

I hung up and looked at Sadie. "Should I ask Mrs. Tate's children if they want to adopt you?"

"No," Sadie said. "They're entitled brats."

I blinked. "You spoke to me, like Dave does."

"That's because I'm a Familiar, and you're my new witch."

"I don't think it works that way. I'm gifted, but I'm not a witch."

Sadie shimmered and shifted into a woman with a platinum blond bob, bright blue eyes, and a fluffy orange bath robe. "This is my other form."

I stifled a giggle.

"You're shocked. I can tell."

She laughed, so I assumed it was okay to join in.

"When I offered to take care of you, I didn't know you were a person. You're welcome to one of the spare bedrooms."

Sadie smiled. "Thank you, but I prefer my cat form. Occasionally I like to walk around on two legs. Being feline is so much less bothersome. A cat nap in a sunbeam fixes everything."

"That sounds nice, actually." There was something that didn't make sense. "How can you be my Familiar if I'm not a witch?"

"People are so stuck on labels. Anyone with magic is technically a witch. Familiars normally prefer full-fledged witches, but you're kind and you won't ask me to catch bats for you, or cut up spell ingredients, or perform spells at midnight. Right?"

"I definitely will not."

"Good. I'd appreciate it if you didn't tell anyone about me."

"Her children don't know about you?"

"No. Genevieve let them believe I was a normal cat because she liked to keep her magic to herself. Honestly, I can't wait to see her kids lose their minds when they discover what my Genevieve did." She leaned close and touched my arm. "Don't bother feeling sorry for them. They aren't nice people. The only time they visited their mother was when they wanted something. I found them stealing from Genevieve on more than one occasion."

"That's awful."

"Ask the nice young man who helped Genevieve cross over about a lawyer. He'll know someone."

"Can I tell him about you? I'd hate for him to find out and think I kept something from him."

"You must swear him to secrecy."

"I will." There was one other thing. "Dave lives here, and he's his own man, or cat…I mean he's not assigned to a witch. He's just free. Would you prefer that?"

"That's not an option because Mrs. Tate gave me to you. She passed on ownership."

Uhm… "I'm not comfortable with that terminology."

"To put it another way, she passed on care taking duties to you, so we are contracted to each other."

"That sounds much better. Is there anything I need to know about having a Familiar?"

"We're linked. If you're in danger, I'll know, and vice versa. I could help you with spell work if that was your thing, but it's not, so I'm basically retired now, which sounds heavenly. You have no idea how many spells Genevieve produced in a week. It was exhausting."

"Should I still pet you?"

"Of course. It's time for me to change back. Dave is sleeping in his chair. I'm going to see if I can cozy up to him. It's been a long time since I had another cat to snuggle." The air around her shimmered and grew hazy and then Sadie the cat stretched and jumped off the bed.

I dialed Reed's number. When he answered the phone, I blurted out the news about the estate being left to Sadie.

"That's odd," was his only response.

"Welcome to my life where odd happens on a daily basis. Do you know a lawyer I can hire? I have a feeling her children will not be pleased."

"No. They won't. Let me make some calls."

I wanted to tell him I'd found my memories, but that wasn't a conversation to be had over the phone.

———

REED CALLED BACK AN HOUR LATER. "I found someone. He wants to meet tonight to go over everything. He'll work for a percentage of the monthly stipend."

"Is that normal? I've never worked with a lawyer before."

"I went to school with Nathan and he helped Teresa draft the restrictions. He charges three hundred dollars an hour."

"Yikes. A percentage of the stipend sounds like a great idea."

"He wants to meet Sadie, so he can attest that she's being taken care of. He wants me there to confirm Mrs. Tate gave you the cat. We'll be over at seven."

"Can you come a little early? There's something about Sadie I need to tell you."

"Tell me now," he said.

"Not over the phone."

"Okay."

He hung up before I could thank him. I should tell Victor and Dave that we were going to have company. Dave was curled up with Sadie in his chair. He opened his eyes as I entered the room.

"Reed and a lawyer are coming over at seven to talk about Sadie."

"You can't give her away," Dave blurted out.

"I won't. I'm glad you like her. Do you know where Victor is?"

"No." He closed his eyes and snuggled closer to his new friend.

I walked into the kitchen just as Victor came in the back door. I told him about Sadie and Reed and the lawyer.

"You get yourself into the most interesting situations." The corners of his mouth turned up. "Teresa was the same way."

━━━

SINCE I WAS MEETING with a lawyer, I should change into something nicer. Maybe I'd just take a shower and start over. Due to the memories, it had been an emotional day and showers were good for washing away stress.

When Reed walked into the kitchen at 6:45 I was sitting at the table drinking a glass of white wine and wearing a blue maxi dress that looked nice but was as comfortable as my pajamas.

"Wine?" I asked as a greeting.

"No. Thanks. What did you need to tell me?"

"You can't tell anyone because I was sworn to secrecy."

"Now I'm worried." He joined me at the table.

I leaned close and whispered. "Sadie is my Familiar."

He jerked away from me. "That's impossible."

"Apparently not. Mrs. Tate must not have minded. So here we are."

Before Reed could respond someone knocked on the door. I went to open it. The auburn haired, pale complected man on the porch wore an expensive suit and a serious expression.

"Hello, I'm Belinda. Please come in."

"Nathan Gunn, nice to meet you." He entered the kitchen and glanced around like it amused him. I didn't like the vibe coming off him. Maybe it was a lawyer thing.

"Would you like something to drink?"

"No. Thank you. Let's get down to business. How did you come into possession of Mrs. Tate's cat?"

I told him the story.

"Were you aware the cat was the sole beneficiary of Mrs. Tate's estate?"

"No."

"Did you have any previous contact with Mrs. Tate?"

I shook my head no. "Not that I'm aware of. I'm not in possession of all my memories. Maybe we met when I visited in the past."

Nathan's brow furrowed. "We won't muddy the waters with that. Since you returned, this time, did you speak with her while she was alive?"

I shook my head no.

"Tomorrow, her children will try to say you stole the cat to steal their inheritance so be prepared and remain calm. I'll handle everything. Now where is Sadie? I need to confirm her condition."

"She's napping in the living room with Dave."

Reed snorted. "That didn't take long."

We all went to the living room. Dave and Sadie were cuddled up in his chair.

"She looks happy and healthy," Nathan

said. "I'll have you sign a few forms and we'll be ready for tomorrow." He retrieved a business card from his pocket and handed it to me. "If any of the Tate's try to contact you about the will before the reading, call me."

I pulled out my phone and added his number to my contact list.

After Nathan left, Reed said, "Explain about Sadie."

"I'm not sure this is a kitchen conversation," I said. "Want to head up to the roof?"

"No." He stood and shoved his hands into his front pockets. "Can't. I'm meeting friends for a drink."

I waited a few seconds to see if he'd invite me along. Apparently that wasn't happening, so I paraphrased what Sadie told me about us being contracted together through Mrs. Tate.

"Don't tell anyone about this," Reed said. "Not even Dave. Whatever you do tomorrow, don't offer to share the estate with Mrs. Tate's family. In your world that might be the nice thing to do but in Mystic Hills it would be seen as an act of weakness."

"Seriously?"

"Yes. Mystic Hills isn't preschool. The

faster you learn that, the better off you'll be." With those mildly insulting words he left.

Annoyance tinged with regret settled over me as I watched him walk away. If I'd stayed four years ago, would we still be to-gether? There was no way to know. We'd only dated a few months. We were probably in the infatuation stage and would have broken up when we started to get on each other's nerves. At least that's what I was telling myself. Besides, he was involved with Jezelle.

Nervous energy zinged around inside of me; I needed some sort of stress reliever. Plus, I was hungry…so it was time to make a salad.

Chopping vegetables with gusto was something my mom taught me to do when life wasn't going my way. I went to the refrig-erator. "Lilly, can I have a bag of carrots, some celery, a yellow bell pepper and some romaine lettuce?"

I opened the refrigerator and the items I requested were inside. After washing every-thing, I found a cutting board and a sharp knife and whacked my way through enough vegetables to make a family sized salad.

Victor came into the kitchen. "I wondered what all the noise was. You know Lilly would make you a salad."

"I'm aware." It made me smile that he'd called the house by name. "This is culinary frustration management. Want some?"

"Sure." Victor went into the pantry and came out with a cruet of vinegar and olive oil. "Is this okay?"

"Yes."

Dave wandered into the kitchen followed by Sadie. "You're eating," he said. "But nothing smells good." He hopped up onto the table. "I remember eating salad as a human, but as a cat it has no appeal."

"What would you like?" Victor asked.

"Baked chicken in bite sized pieces, please."

Victor went over to the stove, made the request, and then brought the food back to the table. Sadie hopped up on the table and joined us. Together we ate dinner and made small talk. Even without Reed in my corner I still had people here I liked. If I'd missed my shot with him that was okay, somewhat sad, and depressing, but okay.

THE NEXT DAY, I sat in the mayor's office with two furious witches named Tim and Tina Tate, two smug lawyers, Reed, and the mayor himself. Their lawyer presented the Tate's case. My lawyer presented the story of how this came to be, and then we sat and waited. Apparently, the mayor had final say in this matter. How had he ended up being judge and jury?

"Reed, you've been a solid citizen for years," Mayor Castor said. "Did Mrs. Tate ask Belinda to take care of Sadie?"

"Yes."

"And how did you hear this?" he asked. "Your gift is to cross people over."

"My magic is symbiotic with Belinda's in the same way my father's was with Teresa Harbinger's."

"A match made in hell," Tim muttered.

I ignored him.

"Belinda, did you know about the estate?" Mayor Castor asked.

"Not until her lawyer called me last night."

"Liar," Tina said. "You probably refused to cross my mother over until she agreed to give you our inheritance."

"Two things." I raised two fingers.

"Name calling is childish, and I asked your mother if she wanted Sadie to go to a family member and she said no."

"She isn't even a full citizen," Tim complained.

"Signed the papers yesterday," the mayor tapped his fingers on his chin. "Which makes the timing a little suspicious."

I clamped my mouth shut and hoped Nathan would step in. Thankfully he did. "If you look at the timeline Belinda never spoke to Mrs. Tate when she was alive. Belinda is the sole owner of Sadie at the request of Mrs. Tate."

"There is the matter of the house," the mayor said. "I think we'll auction it off."

I didn't care about the house, but maybe I should.

"I believe the house is part of the assessed value of the estate which the stipend is based on, so it also belongs to Sadie."

"We'll see," he said. "For now, I find in favor of Belinda. She'll receive the stipend monthly to be used however she sees fit."

The Tate siblings exited the room muttering unkind things about me. I pretended not to hear them.

"Let's go to the bank and take care of this," Nathan said.

"I'm going to work," Reed announced to no one in particular. Maybe that was his way of telling me that I could find him there if I needed a ride home.

Both lawyers accompanied me out the door, turned right, and walked down the street.

"The bank is on Main Street?" I asked.

"Yes," they said in tandem.

We walked for two blocks. I may have imagined it, but it felt like everyone was staring at us.

The bank was a grand structure made of polished granite. It sat back from the road. White roses lined the walkway up to the door and their fragrant scent drifted through the air. When I entered the lobby, I came to an abrupt halt. The floor was tiled to look like the night sky and the lawyers walked across it like it was invisible. They'd probably been here hundreds of times and didn't even notice it anymore. That was sad. I followed behind them at a slower pace, admiring the floor which gleamed with the sun shining down through the skylight.

A security guard caught my eye and smiled. "Beautiful, isn't it?"

"It's amazing."

"I've worked here twenty years and that floor makes me happy every day."

"Belinda." Nathan's voice was sharp.

I hurried into an office where a blond woman with green eyes glared at Nathan like she wanted to set his hair on fire. He didn't seem to notice or care.

"Sorry, the tile floor is a work of art. I stopped to enjoy it for a moment."

The blonde's expression changed into something much friendlier as she turned her gaze to me. "Miss Harbinger, I'm Lisa Laddow, the president of the bank. It's nice to meet you. What can we do for you today?"

"It's nice to meet you too. I need to open an account."

"She needs a private stipend account which will receive deposits monthly. Fifteen percent of each deposit will be transferred to my account for services rendered as legal counsel," Nathan stated, still without any eye contact.

Mrs. Tate's lawyer smiled. "I'll be taking fifteen percent before the money goes into her account. Nathan's share will come from the reduced amount."

I'd never seen lawyers flex before. It was amusing.

Papers were drawn up. Nathan passed me a pen. "Just sign. It's all in order."

"I'll read it first, if you don't mind." I scanned the pages trying to make sense of the legal wording until I came to the monthly figure. I had to stop myself from commenting on the amount. I was going to receive five thousand dollars a month to spend on myself and on Sadie. The money was a thank you for whoever became care taker of her beloved cat. There were no stipulations on how it should be spent. Wow. Five thousand dollars…that was more than my monthly paycheck as a teacher. I almost felt bad taking the money until I remembered how obnoxious the Tate siblings were. I signed and then the lawyers signed and passed the paperwork back to Lisa.

"You're all set up," Lisa said. "Here's your debit card. Feel free to call if you have any questions." She passed me the debit card and her business card.

"Thank you. I will."

The lawyers left the room without another word.

Lisa glared after Nathan's retreating form. "If your aunt hadn't passed the waiting period on hexes, Nathan would be bald."

Chapter 11

I smiled at Lisa's confession. "I noticed he avoided eye contact with you."

"We dated for a month and then he stopped returning my calls. No reason given. Just moved on to another woman. Jerk."

"I'm sorry. He seems like the type who will always like himself more than anyone else so you're probably better off without him."

"I like you," she said. "I was about to take my lunch break at Carson's Cafe across the street. Do you want to join me?"

"I'd love to." What were the odds Lisa was a good person, not just someone who wanted something from me? I'd choose to believe she was nice until she proved otherwise.

Walking into Carson's made my mouth water. The savory scent of Italian spices, barbecue, and Mexican food mingled together and flowed through the air. "Please tell me their food tastes as good as it smells."

"It does. Want to eat outside on the back patio?"

"Sure."

After the hostess seated us, I scanned the menu. When the waitress came, I ordered the lunch sized portion of lasagna with a salad and garlic bread.

Lisa paused. "I was going to order a salad, but I think I'll copy your order instead. You're a bad influence."

After the waitress left, Lisa said, "I told you about my man troubles, you should share yours."

"Before I came to Mystic Hills, I walked in on my boyfriend of two years having sex with an extremely flexible yoga instructor."

"Oh, no." Lisa laughed. "That's horrible."

"Back then I was traumatized. Now I think it's kind of funny. He tried to tell me they weren't having sex."

"After you caught him in the act?"

I nodded. "He claimed it was naked yoga."

"Wow," she sipped her water. "That's ridiculous."

"Men," I muttered. "Not sure they're worth it sometimes."

"My mother keeps telling me when I find the right one, I'll know, but she married her high school sweetheart so I'm not sure she understands dating as an adult."

"I'm guessing you only date other Mystic Hills residents."

She nodded. "You had a much wider pool of fish in the outside world."

"Didn't do me much good."

"Here everyone interacts within their own magical communities, so the pool is even smaller."

"Do witches and the gifted date each other?"

"That's tricky. If a witch chooses the gifted person, it can work. Gifted people never go after witches. It's frowned upon."

That seemed elitist. "Does everyone know who is who?"

"Pretty much."

"What about shifters or other types of creatures?"

"Shifters and hybrids do what they please. They aren't as constrained by the social standards."

Our food arrived and my first bite of lasagna was cheese-covered spiced-to-perfection, Italian heaven on a plate and made me think I might not need a man in my life after all. "This is delicious."

"I know. The chef is gifted."

"Meaning he is talented, or his gift is cooking amazing food?"

"Both."

I almost asked if he was single but refrained.

"Tell me about Reed," Lisa said.

I sipped my water while I tried to figure out what to say, "I think he's dating Jezelle."

"Really?"

"That's the impression I got from a conversation, but I could be wrong."

"I heard you're symbiotic with him."

"Just like my aunt and Victor. What's your gift?"

"Math, which is why I'm in banking. I can look at a spreadsheet and see the errors almost instantly. The numbers that aren't supposed to be there look wrong."

"What other types of gifts are there?"

"They are varied and strange," she said. "I think there's a book at the library that attempts to catalog them all."

"It would be nice if you could choose your gift." I hoped that didn't offend her.

"They say all gifts are necessary, but some are harder to deal with. My closest friend growing up could see the best way to kill a person at any given moment."

"That is horrific. How did she deal with it?"

"She lives a secluded life raising bees. We talk on the phone, but she keeps to herself to avoid all the images."

"Does anyone know where the gifts came from?"

"Supposedly the magic of the ley lines converging created the gifts and assigned them to different bloodlines."

She finished her lasagna and checked her watch. "Time flies when you're having fun. I need to go back to work. I'm having people over for a barbecue this weekend if you want to come."

"I'd like that."

"Why don't you call my phone so I have your number."

I pulled out my cell and typed in the number she recited. Her phone rang.

"We're all set. I'll contact you later in the week with the details."

She waived the waitress down and we paid for our lunches separately.

Since I didn't have any plans for the rest of the afternoon, I decided to investigate the shops on Main Street. Maybe I could find some more information about my aunt. Next door to Carson's was a clothing store called *The Perfect Fit*. Did they tailor the clothes they sold? That would be handy.

I entered the store and headed toward a rack of summer dresses.

"Oh, I have the perfect maxi dress to camouflage your hips," a man said as he came toward me.

"Excuse me?" There was nothing wrong with my hips.

He pushed his glasses up on his nose. "You're not that out of proportion but your hourglass is a bit fuller on the bottom. Don't worry, I have just the thing."

He grabbed a dress with an asymmetrical hemline. "This will distract the eye from your— "

"If you make one more comment about my hips, I'm walking out that door."

He smacked his hand over his mouth, and then slowly lowered it. "It's my gift. I find the perfect outfit to cover everyone's imperfections. I don't mean to be rude. It's how I see the world. Just so you know, no one is perfect. And you can barely tell that your left breast is larger than your right."

I considered calling him some very rude names but decided to be passive aggressive instead. "Do you sell a lot of clothes with this approach?" I was torn between being angry and wanting to try on the amazing dress he'd chosen.

"On their first visit most people are annoyed, but then they understand what I bring to the table. Plus, it's always buy one get one half off in the entire store." He held the dress out to me. "Would you like to try it on?"

"Yes. I would. No more comments about my imperfections. Okay?"

"I'll try." He seemed sincere.

I took the dress. "Where are the dressing rooms?"

"This way." He led me to the back corner of the store where there were small curtained off areas. I put the dress on, and I'd never looked better. Rather than stepping out and risking him critiquing my figure again, I hollered. "I'm buying this dress; can you pick out another one for me?"

"Yes."

I poked my head out from behind the curtain and waited for him to return. He came back with an asymmetrical short black dress I wouldn't have chosen in a million years.

"I have leggings to go under this dress if you prefer more modesty or you don't like your thighs. Statistically speaking most women's thighs lose a percentage of muscle tone every year after their eighteenth birthday."

"Thank you for the dress." I nabbed it from him and tried it on facing away from the mirror because I did not want to check my muscle tone at the moment. When I turned back around, I smiled. The dress was sophisticated yet sexy.

I changed back into my clothes and then stepped out. "I'll take both of them."

"Good." He led me to a counter with an

old fashioned brass cash register with a wooden cash drawer. I panicked for a moment until I saw the card reader set off to the side.

I pulled out my normal debit card. "This is from a bank outside of Mystic Hills. If it doesn't work, I can pay with a different card."

"It should be fine. Our banking system is tapped into the Outsider network because we travel."

"You do?" I had no idea.

"Yes. I buy fabrics from all over the world."

"Do you make the dresses?"

"No. My husband does. That's his gift."

"Which makes you the perfect couple."

"It took me years to convince him of that fact," he smiled.

"Did you comment on his imperfections?" That would make for a rough start.

He nodded. "After a while he understood what I was really saying."

"I'm glad it worked out for you."

"Thank you." He ran my card and printed out my receipt. "My name is Ethan Brandt. Feel free to stop by any time, Belinda. I'll try to keep my commentary to myself."

"Did you know my aunt, Teresa Harbinger?"

He nodded, but his friendly nature vanished.

"Did she shop here?"

"Sometimes."

Maybe I should just go with honesty. "If I was going to look into her death, do you know where I should start?"

He reached across the counter and touched my hand. "You shouldn't ask anyone else about your aunt. Someone might take it the wrong way."

"I appreciate your honesty, but if I was compelled to find answers what would you suggest?"

He frowned. "It's a universally accepted truth that the mayor and those closest to him are the most dangerous people in town, because they have all the power on their side which is why you should drop this."

Not what I wanted to hear. I nodded and left the shop, mulling over the day's events. On the negative side, no one wanted to talk to me about Aunt Teresa's death. On the positive side, some people around here could have pleasant conversations and talk about their families. That was a nice discovery. If everyone was as closed off as Reed and his father my time here would be lonely. So much had happened and I hadn't even been here a week.

"Did you decide to go shopping with my mother's money?" Tim Tate asked as he came toward me on the sidewalk. He weaved a bit. Had he been drinking?

"No. I used my money."

"It's not your money." As he spoke his face flushed red.

"I used the money I made teaching, so back off."

He kept walking until he was in my face. "You're a thief, and I'll prove it."

The alcohol fumes coming off his breath confirmed my suspicion. It was on the tip of my tongue to apologize for the strange circumstances that led to him being cut out of the will.

"It would be a shame if something happened to Sadie, and our family fortune reverted to me."

Anger boiled up inside of me. "If you harm one hair on that cat's head—"

"You'll what?" He leaned even closer invading my space. "You have no real power, no allies. If you disappeared would anyone even notice?"

I would not let him know he'd rattled me. "I have no idea. If you're done trying to intimidate me, I have things to do." I turned my back on him and walked away. It was a calculated risk. He didn't seem above stabbing someone in the back, but we were on Main Street. Hopefully that would keep him from coming after me. I went to the tearoom figuring there would be safety in numbers. Plus I needed a ride home from Reed.

The tables were mostly empty, which worked for me. I'd been stared at enough today. I avoided eye contact with Jezelle even though I could feel her looking at me and made a beeline for Reed's office. When I entered the room, he glanced up and frowned.

"That's how every woman wants to be greeted," I said.

His eyebrows came together. "I didn't say anything."

"Your frowny face made it clear you weren't pleased to see me."

"It's not you," he said. "That was my, who is interrupting me now face."

"That makes me feel better."' I sat in the

black leather chair. Should I tell him about Tim? The best plan was probably to ignore him and get back to work finding clues about my Aunt's death. And I knew just who I needed to talk to. "I'll keep the interruption short. Is there another office where I can work to contact spirits that isn't in the middle of the tearoom?"

Reed pointed at a door on the wall behind his desk. "That is my old office. Knock yourself out."

"Thanks."

"Don't even think about trying to take over my new office," he muttered.

"Wouldn't dream of it." I opened the door on a ten-by-ten room with a desk, a chair and a brass floor lamp. There wasn't a hint of personality in the place. "This is one sad room."

"The spirits won't mind," Reed responded.

"Someone is a smarty pants." I entered the room and shut the door before sitting at the desk. It was time to get down to work. "Ida Smith, can I talk to you?" Nothing happened. "Ida Smith, my Aunt Teresa suggested I summon you."

A spirit appeared in front of me.

"Someone new in town, I'd love to find out all about you dear."

"It's nice to meet you, Ida. Thanks for coming when I called."

She chuckled. "You make me sound like a golden retriever. I always wanted a dog, but my Familiar said he'd never forgive me if I brought another animal into the house."

We talked about her Familiar and the cats I had growing up. She asked all about the Outsider world and seemed fascinated with the idea of Dine & Dash. After fifteen minutes, I said, "I don't suppose you or any of your spirit friends know anything about how Aunt Teresa's died?"

"Sorry, dear. We never visited Teresa at home."

It was a long shot, but I had to ask. On to my next concern. "Can you help me practice with my waiting room? I used it once with my Aunt Teresa. I'm not sure if it would feel the same with someone else."

Ida shimmered. "You promise to let me out?"

"I do."

"Okay."

"Thank you." I pictured my old living room, minus the windows and doors and reached for Ida. I felt the tingling sensation. "Ready?" I asked.

"Yes."

I grabbed more firmly onto her spirit, and it felt like I was trying to hold onto a swarm of bees while a few of them were stinging me. Was she doing that on purpose? I ignored the pain and shoved Ida into the room. She blinked out of the office and appeared in the waiting room.

She turned in a circle. "This is nice. I wouldn't mind waiting here."

I imagined a door, which I unlocked. Ida opened the door and popped back into the room. "You did it," she said. "Want to practice with some of my friends?"

"Sure."

I sent ten spirits into the waiting room. Holding onto each of them felt different, but they were all mildly painful and by the time it was done it felt like my arms were sunburnt and I had a base drum beating in my skull. After the last spirit departed, I leaned back in my chair.

A knock sounded on the door before Jezelle opened it. "I think someone needs a headache potion and a glass of sweet tea."

"Thank you," I sat forward and accepted the drink and the potion she offered me.

"You're welcome." She turned and left without another word.

———

THAT EVENING AT DINNER, I told Victor, Dave, and Sadie about my run in with Tim. "Should I report him for threatening me and Sadie?"

"You could," Victor said, "but I'm not sure anything would come of it."

"We could hire someone to hex him," Dave suggested.

"As appealing as that idea may seem," Victor said. "It isn't wise. He's a witch and you're gifted. Everyone in power would be on his side."

That sucked. Maybe I should focus on something else. "I called out to Ida Smith. She visited with me and let me practice on sending her to my waiting room."

Victor made a sound of distress. "That woman never stopped talking when she was alive and she had no understanding of social cues. I backed out the door once, trying to escape and she followed me to my car."

"She was rather chatty. I enjoyed talking to her." That made me wonder about something. "Do spirits retain their personalities in the afterlife?"

Aunt Teresa popped into the room. "Spirits at rest resemble the people they were in life."

"Were you eavesdropping?" Victor asked.

"It's not like there's a lot for me to do," she said.

"Is Yelena's candle making you feel better?" Victor asked.

"It is," she said. "Any luck finding out who killed me?"

"No," Victor said. "But I find it hard to believe the Genevieve's death was an accident. She voted for the restrictions."

"If everyone who voted for the new laws starts dying off, that would be a clue," I muttered.

"Hopefully that won't happen." Teresa frowned. "I feel useless. Maybe it's time for me to move on."

"If you stay a ghost too long, will something bad happen?" I remembered Victor saying she'd lose her humanity and turn into a leech if no one helped her. But we'd helped her, as much as we could. We'd listened. There wasn't any danger of that now. Right?

"Being able to speak with you helped me make peace with the situation. I want the person who did this to face justice, but I'm no longer angry about being dead." She floated closer. "I've taught you everything there is to know about working with ghosts. I feel my job here is complete."

Victor sighed and then smiled. "Any time you're ready, I'll help you cross over."

Tears filled my eyes. The unfairness of this entire situation crashed down on me. "I don't want to lose you again."

"I'm not disappearing from your life. I can visit any time in spirit form. All you have to do is call out to me," she said. "Staying here is starting to feel unnatural."

"And you can be with Johnathon again," Victor said. There was no judgement in his tone, just a level of sadness.

"Victor, you know what we had was special," Teresa said. "But we weren't each other's first loves. I can say hello to Diane for you. Belinda could invite her to visit."

I sat very still trying not to intrude on their moment. Getting up and leaving the room would interrupt them. Tears welled up in my eyes as I tried not to cry.

Victor cleared his throat. "I'd like that."

"Belinda, I'm so glad I was able to see you again. And I promise this is not the end of our relationship."

The tears spilled over my lashes. "I understand. Thank you for everything you did for me. I'm sorry my mom wouldn't let me stay."

"Me too," she said. "But we have the rest of your life and my afterlife to get to know one another better."

That should have made me feel better, but it didn't.

"Victor, give me the ring for a moment so I can say goodbye," Dave said.

Victor pulled the black pearl inlaid ring off of his finger and placed it on top of Dave's back.

"There you are," Dave said. "Thank you for inviting me into your home. I've been much happier here than I was as a Familiar."

"You're most welcome, Dave. I enjoyed your company. I'm glad that you and Sadie have each other now. Make sure to take care of Victor and look out for Reed and Belinda."

"I will," Dave promised.

Victor retrieved his ring and slid it back on his finger without saying another word.

"Thank you for everything Victor," Aunt Teresa said, "I'm ready to move on."

He nodded. The glow was slight at first but increased in intensity until I had to look away. When the light receded, Aunt Teresa's ghost was gone.

Crying wasn't a rational response, since I knew I could call on her spirit and visit with her, but my tear ducts didn't seem to care. Tears flowed down my face. All of this was just too much. I wanted my simple life back. The one where I was Linda James, preschool teacher, not Belinda Harbinger ghost magnet and spirit communicator. After knowing about Mystic Hills and magic, could I really go back, just walk away from it all? I wasn't sure. As weird and frustrating as it all could be, it was a part of me now.

I needed time alone to think and deal with all of this, so I stood and walked out the kitchen door and headed for the fire escape. I ran up the steps to the widow's walk. When I reached the top, I was out of breath. I sat on the wooden terrace hugging my knees to my chest trying to make sense of the spectacular complicated mess that was my life.

The lights in the town below twinkled like nothing was wrong. It always seemed strange to me that someone you cared about could disappear and the world kept on spinning like an essential part hadn't just vanished.

"Belinda?" Reed's voice came from the fire escape.

"Up here." I sniffled.

He climbed onto the roof and sat next to me.

"I saw the light when I pulled up. Dave told me what happened. I can't explain where Teresa went, but I can tell you it's peaceful. Does that help?"

"Not really," I laughed. "None of this makes sense. I had a wonderful aunt that I loved and a mother who claims she only wanted what was best for me. It's my mom's fault I wasn't able to stay here. If she'd let me keep my memories and make my own choices Teresa might still be alive."

"You don't know that," he said.

"You're right. I don't. But I do know my mom lied to me. After college when I wanted to stay, she gave me an ultimatum, her or Mystic Hills. She swore she'd bring me back a year later and restore my memories. She didn't. She never told me."

"You remember?" Reed sounded surprised.

"Teresa hid the memories in pictures. I found them, but I didn't know how to tell you. I know we dated for a few months and then my mom showed up and forced me to leave after I'd told you I planned to stay. Sorry I ended up being one of the people who ran out on you." I couldn't see his face. I waited for him to say something, anything to indicate how he felt. Now that I knew what happened between us would he be willing to give me another chance?

"That… was a long time ago." He huffed out a breath. "I was mad for a while, but then I moved on. I'm glad you know. It felt like I was keeping a secret from you, but I couldn't figure out how to bring it up."

I swiped at the tears rolling down my face with my sleeve. "I'm mad at my mother for giving me an ultimatum. She never should've done that. I understand she was afraid of losing me, but kids move away when they grow up, and then they come home for holidays or visit on the weekends, and me living in Mystic Hills could have been like that so I don't understand why my mom was so desperate. These circular arguments keep playing in my head and I never come up with a satisfying answer."

"Do you remember everything?" he asked with a hitch in his voice.

Why did that sound like a loaded question? "Everything that happened during my past visits to Mystic Hills or everything that happened between us?"

"Both," he said.

"I have random memories from my visits. From us, I don't remember every minute we spent together, I just remember the feelings." Good God, how did I say this? "I really lo— cared about you."

"Belinda, don't."

"Don't what?" I leaned toward him. "The feelings I have—er—had for you—I know you felt the same."

He stared into my eyes and then down at my lips. I leaned closer hoping to encourage him. He closed his eyes and said, "had…the feelings I had back then…that was a long time ago." He opened his eyes and scooted away from me. "Let's just agree to leave the past in the past."

And we'd reached a new level of awkward. At least he wasn't running away from me. Time for a topic change. I cleared my throat and said, "Teresa suggested I summon your mom so your father could talk to her. You could visit too once I learn how to make it work."

"Don't tell my dad I said this, but it wouldn't be her. Spirits are like copies of the person they used to be. All the things that made them who they were in life, their likes and dislikes slowly fade away. I wouldn't want to see her if she came back."

Dang it. "Teresa made it sound like she'd be her normal self."

"As Jezelle likes to point out, I am a glass half empty kind of person, so maybe it's my perspective that skews it."

Jezelle. Crap. I'd forgotten about her and Reed. Or maybe I'd just ignored it for a moment. His bringing her up meant it was a relationship. I'd missed my chance. Time to be an adult about it.

"Now that you know I have my memories back, can we be friends?" Wow that sounded pathetic. "Let me say that another way. You seem irritated with me a lot of the time. Is there any way you can be less irritable around me?"

He chuckled. "I'll work on that, but your preschool optimism is annoying."

"My view of the world is the opposite of yours?"

"Pretty much. As far as us being friends, I don't really see the point."

Chapter 12

"Oh," was the only response I could come up with. I had a hard time taking a full breath. From the way he'd been talking I thought he'd forgiven me for leaving. I guess not.

"You came here to speak with Teresa because we thought she could tell us who pushed her down the stairs," he said. "She couldn't. We have no leads. The mayor and everyone else in power has chalked it up as an accident. There's no reason for you to stay. You should go back to your life as a preschool teacher. Play with blocks and sing songs because you aren't cut out for life here."

Was he trying to tick me off or push me

away? Idiot. "For your information I'm on summer break. I haven't cut all ties to my Outsider life. If and when I do, it will be my decision." The shock and sadness I'd felt morphed into anger. "If you don't want to be my friend then you have no business telling me what to do."

"You're reacting emotionally instead of seeing the truth. There are zero reasons for you to stay."

Wow. He'd actually made it worse. "Get your pessimistic, condescending butt off my roof before I ask Lilly to launch you across the lawn."

"I'm trying to help you."

"Help me? Really? I may not have all my memories back but I don't remember you being this much of a jerk."

"So now, I'm jerk?"

"Yes." I nodded. "Here's a preschool concept: I'm going to count to three. If you aren't out of my sight by the time I reach three we will see what Lilly is capable of. One…" I waited.

"You're serious?"

"Two." Part of me hoped he wouldn't listen.

"I'm out of here." He stood and left the

roof. I heard his footsteps ringing on the metal steps all the way down.

Just when I thought the day couldn't suck any more…I was wrong. "Lilly, can I have glass of whiskey please?" A glass appeared next to my hand. I picked it up and took a sip. The warmth of the alcohol didn't do much to thaw the cold empty feeling in my gut.

━━

I WOKE up the next morning in a foul mood. How dare Reed act like I wasn't tough enough to make it in Mystic Hills. Being an optimist didn't mean I was naive or weak. And I didn't need him as a friend. Lisa had invited me to a barbecue tomorrow. Not everyone in town was as doom and gloom as him. Having him as a friend would probably be a downer.

After a shower where I tried to find my Zen, I went down to breakfast. Dave sat on the table eating scrambled eggs while Sadie ate eggs from her dish on the floor.

"Good morning," Dave said.

"Morning." I wasn't sure there was anything good about it yet. I poured myself a cup of coffee and said, "Lilly, can I have cinnamon streusel coffee cake and bacon?" Not the healthiest breakfast, but it was my go to comfort food. A plate with a slice of cake and three strips of bacon appeared in front of me. "Thank you, Lilly."

"How are you doing after last night?" Dave asked.

"Not fabulous, but food should help."

"Victor hasn't come down yet," Dave said. "He's always an early riser. I'm afraid of what crossing Teresa over might have done to him."

"Me too. I'm not sure what we can do to help." I took a bite of coffee cake and savored the cinnamon sugar goodness. "Except give him some of this cake. It's amazing." I took a sip of coffee and then asked him a question that had been brewing in my brain. "How did Victor and my aunt become a couple?"

"He and Teresa were friends for years before they became involved. I think it caught both of them by surprise. Who knows, maybe the same thing will happen with you and Reed."

I snorted. "Not likely."

The kitchen door opened and Victor

walked in wearing the same suit he'd worn when he came to my apartment the first night we met. He set an envelope on the table and then walked past us into the living room.

"Do you want to do the honors, since I can't?" Dave said.

I opened the envelope and pulled out what looked like a wedding invitation, except it was an invitation to Teresa's funeral which was scheduled for today at noon. Victor must have made the arrangements. Good thing because in all the drama of her crossing over and Reed being a jerk, I'd forgotten her body was upstairs.

"What are Mystic Hills funerals like?"

"We'll bury her in the family crypt on the back of the property."

"I…I have no memory of a crypt."

"You wouldn't. Johnathon was interred years before you came along."

"Will there be a service?"

"If you want to say something you can. I said everything I wanted last night. Remember, she isn't really gone. You can always summon her spirit to come visit."

Reed's words from last night replayed in my head. "Someone told me visits from spirits aren't like visiting the person. He made it sound like a bad idea."

"Am I supposed to pretend I don't know you're talking about Reed?"

"Yes." I laughed.

"Fine. His opinion is just that, his opinion. I've visited with spirits before and it was like seeing old friends." Dave finished his scrambled eggs. "Speaking of him, he left in a mood last night. What happened on the roof?"

"To paraphrase, there's no reason for me to stay, and he'd like me to go away."

"Rude," Dave said. "And wrong. You're bound to Sadie and the house, so you can't leave. Plus, we'd miss you."

The lights blinked twice.

"Thanks. I'd miss all of you too. I don't know why he wants to be rid of me so badly and why he thinks it's okay to say that to my face."

Dave turned in a circle and laid down. "Maybe it's due to the glowing."

Not this again. "Don't bring it up, if you're not going to tell me what it means."

"His behavior relieves me of any guilt for sharing his secret. Plus, you have a right to know. It's a signal that your gifts are symbiotic which you already knew, but it also means you're meant to be together."

"As friends?" I asked, because he'd shot that idea out of the water.

"Yes, and as more than friends," Dave said. "Symbiotic couples usually end up as romantic couples."

I almost choked on my bacon. Once I managed to swallow and take a sip of coffee, I said, "Knowing that, he told me to go away?" I didn't get it. "I asked if we could put the past behind us. He straight up told me he didn't want to be friends."

"Maybe he decided to leave you this time, before you could leave him," Dave said.

"Maybe." I cut a piece of cake with my fork. A horrible idea occurred to me. "When I was here after I graduated college, and we dated for a short time, did I see him glow?"

"I don't think so. Most symbiotic relationships don't mature until both people are twenty-five."

"That makes me feel better."

"Here's something you won't like. Reed will be at the funeral."

"I figured. Will anyone else come?"

"No. Funerals are for family and a few

close friends."

"I should call my mom. She'll want to be here."

"I'm sorry," Dave said. "I don't believe she's invited."

That brought me up short. "What?"

"Victor is Teresa's executor and he planned the event. The only people who can attend are those he invited. I'm certain he did not include your mother."

What the heck? "Why not?"

"The last time you were here, Victor tried to intercede on your behalf, he agreed that you should be given the choice to stay. Your mother accused him of sponging off of Teresa, taking advantage of her kind nature."

"I didn't know. Aunt Teresa didn't in-clude that in my memories."

"Teresa's funeral is more about Victor and the rest of us coming to terms with our loss. Your mother let her sister go a long time ago."

I wanted to point out that Mystic Hills had shoved my mom out the door first but stating that wouldn't change the situation. I'd call mom tomorrow and hope she was okay.

━━━

HERE'S A FUN FACT, Mystic Hills residents don't use caskets. I watched as Teresa's body magically floated into the crypt which was like an open stone coffin. On another day I might have taken the time to appreciate the ornate stonework or the flowers around the crypt, but today I focused on the lid sliding closed. I'd been to funerals and seen caskets lowered into the ground, but watching her body being shut inside a stone box behind the house was far more disturbing. Victor said a few words, but I didn't hear him. After a moment of silence, the funeral was over. I wished I hadn't come. Saying goodbye to her ghost had been hard, but this felt sad and empty.

Reed took a step toward me like he meant to say something. I couldn't deal with him right now, so I turned and fled into the house. What I needed was a cup of chamomile tea and my comfy pajamas.

Fifteen minutes later I was under the covers in my bed sipping tea and eating a chocolate chip cookie. Someone knocked on my door.

"Who is it?"

"Reed."

"Not now." Under my breath I whispered. "Lilly, don't let him open the door."

The doorknob turned back and forth but the door didn't swing open.

"We need to talk," Reed said.

"Nope. I only talk to people who are my friends and apparently that doesn't include you. Go away." Was I being immature? Maybe. I didn't care. All I wanted was to finish my tea and take a nap.

I heard him walk away. "Thank you, Lilly."

I closed my eyes and drifted off. I woke to Sadie sitting on my pillow staring down at me. "Belinda, wake up."

"What?" I blinked, trying to clear my head. "What's going on?"

"You've slept half the day. I was worried about you. Come downstairs and have some dinner."

A cat was telling me I'd slept too much? That was a first. I sat up and yawned. "Maybe I should stay in bed."

"No. You need to be up and alert. I have a feeling something bad is coming our way."

"Great." I changed into jeans, a black shirt, and tennis shoes. If need be, I could run. Either towards something or away, depending on the situation.

I listened for any sounds of distress, but all I heard was Dave and Victor talking in the living room. As I came down the stairs, I realized it was Dave but I didn't recognize the other voice. When I walked into the living room, I was surprised to see the mayor sitting on our couch.

"Hello," I said.

"Good evening. I stopped by to express my condolences."

Was he the reason Sadie had a bad feeling? "Thank you. The funeral was rough."

"I understand. When I attended Mrs. Tate's funeral her children were inconsolable."

I bit down on my automatic response of, "Because they lost their money." and went with "Death is difficult for everyone."

"It is. And your actions in town after the reading of the will made the situation worse."

"Excuse me?"

"Tim told me how you accosted him on the sidewalk outside *The Perfect Fit*, showing off the new wardrobe you'd purchased with his mother's money."

I shouldn't laugh, but that's what I did. "Tim is lying. I purchased two dresses using my Outsider credit card, which I explained to him. Then he said if Sadie died, he'd get all the money back. I told him not to threaten her. He said no one would miss me if I disappeared."

"It's odd how your memories are so different."

"Would you like a copy of my receipt?" I asked. "Or a statement from my Outsider bank?"

"No. I'm sure the truth is somewhere in the middle."

"I can assure you it's not. Tim was quite drunk during our encounter, so maybe that's affecting his memory."

He gave a theatrical sigh. "If only we knew for sure that Mrs. Tate wanted you to care for her cat."

"Reed testified she did." What was this guy's angle?

"Did he? I'm not sure I remember it being that clear cut. I'll have to check the transcripts."

I walked further into the room and sat in a chair facing him. "You want something.

Instead of playing this he said, she said game, tell me why you're here."

"I can make Mr. Tate's complaints go away if you relinquish Mrs. Tate's house to me."

I pulled out my phone and hit the button to dial Nathan's number before the mayor could ask what I was doing.

"Hello?"

"Hello, Nathan, this is Belinda Harbinger. The mayor dropped by and he's asked me to give him the Tate's house. I figured you needed to weigh in on his request since I wasn't sure how the property fit into the stipend."

Nathan laughed. "You're smart. Put me on speaker phone and let me handle this."

I pressed the speaker button and smiled at the mayor like I was being helpful.

"Mayor Castor, I'm sorry to say the stipend is dependent upon the house, but Mrs. Tate owned several pieces of art you might enjoy. They weren't mentioned in the stipend and I'm sure Mrs. Tate and her family would be happy to donate them to your campaign fund since the Tate's have always backed your political aspirations."

"I feel the house should be auctioned off

for the good of town," the mayor responded.

"If that's how you truly feel, then I'll contact your lawyer and we'll work through the night, no matter how long it takes, to make it happen for you."

The mayor frowned. "On second thought, the artwork would make a suitable donation and a loving memorial in Mrs. Tate's name."

"Wonderful. Glad we could help you in your political endeavors. I'll have the paintings brought to your office first thing tomorrow. Good night." He hung up.

Mayor Castor stood. "I'll speak to Tim Tate and explain the misunderstanding. In the future I suggest you report any incidences as soon as they occur. My time is valuable. I do not appreciate being sent on a fool's errand."

"I'm sorry Tim mislead you. Would you like some tea before you go?"

"No." He straightened his tie. "I'll see myself out."

I followed him into the kitchen and put the kettle on like that had been my plan all along. After he exited, I locked the door behind him.

Dave and Sadie both hopped onto the

kitchen table.

"When Nathan said he'd work through the night with the other lawyer, I could practically see the dollar signs flashing in the mayor's mind," Dave said. "I wonder how much he charges."

"Nathan charges three hundred an hour. I imagine the mayor's lawyer charges more." My stomach growled. "I think I slept through dinner. Are you two hungry?"

"What did you have in mind?" Dave asked.

"Pepperoni pizza?" It had been almost a week since my last slice. I'm surprised my body wasn't going into withdrawal.

"Sounds good," Dave said. "I'll run up and ask Victor if he'd like to join us."

Once Dave was gone, I whispered to Sadie. "Is your bad feeling gone?"

She shook her head no.

Great. "Lilly, can we have a thin crust double pepperoni pizza please?"

The pizza appeared on the kitchen counter along with several cans of soda and paper plates. "Lilly, you're the best."

Dave returned by himself. I cut up a piece of pizza for him and Sadie. Dave and I made small talk while we ate. I had to stop myself from asking Sadie questions. I wish she'd let Dave in on her secret.

"What's on your agenda for this evening?" Dave asked.

Before I could answer a gray mist swirled into existence and took on the appearance of a man I'd never met. "What's going on?" he snapped. "Where am I?"

I set my pizza down. "Hello, I'm Belinda Harbinger, and you are?"

"James Green," He frowned. "I was eating dinner. This makes no sense."

There was no good way to tell someone this, but I tried to soften the blow. "I'm sorry, but I think you died."

"Maybe I'm having an out of body experience," he said.

"Possibly."

He blinked out of existence.

"Dave, would you tell Victor we have an I see dead people situation?"

"Who was it?" Dave asked.

"James Green."

Dave hopped off the table and darted into the living room.

"Sadie, did you know him?"

"He was on the Council of Elders with my Genevieve."

Another Council member couldn't be a coincidence.

Victor walked into the room with a scowl on his face. "James Green is dead?"

"His ghost was just here. What should I do?"

"Whenever a ghost appears you should call the authorities." He pulled out his cell phone. "You reach them by dialing zero."

I listened as he placed the call.

"Now what?" I asked when he hung up.

"You and Reed go to Mr. Green's house and help his family deal with their loss. If he's ready, you help the deceased cross over."

I so didn't want to call Reed. Not after I'd threatened to launch him from the roof. While I felt my threat had been justified, it still made things uncomfortable between us. My neck muscles tensed as I pulled out my phone and called Reed. This wasn't personal. This was business. I'd keep it professional and so would he. No big deal. After a brief and terse exchange of information, he agreed to pick me up in ten minutes.

"Victor, tell me anything you know about James," I said. "I'm tired of going into situations blind."

"He was a real estate agent. Both he and his wife were on the Council. The Greens and Teresa butted heads over the restrictions, but in the end, they came around to her side."

"How many people on the Council need to die and be replaced before the laws could be reversed?"

"I find your line of logic disturbing," Victor said. "But if the mayor could put two new people on the Council who would follow his lead, the vote would be 5 to 5. He'd only need to sway one more member to win the vote."

"Is there any point in warning the other Council members who voted against the mayor?" I asked.

"We could try," Victor said. "But we'd have to be discreet. If word made it back to the mayor and his associates we'd have fatal accidents of our own."

A car horn sounded in the driveway. "Must be Reed. I'll see you later."

I walked out to Reed's car hoping this wouldn't be too awkward. I was in the process of getting into the car when he said, "We need to talk."

Chapter 13

"Do we?" I fastened my seatbelt. "It's been a trying couple of days. Can we do our job and leave it at that?"

"Fine." Frustration radiated off of him.

What did he have to be frustrated about? I'd tried making nice and he rejected my offer. Honestly, I just wanted to help Mr. Green and get back to my pizza.

"Mr. Green was on the Council," Reed said like it was some sort of revelation.

"I know. And the mayor is now up two votes and if he knocks out another person who sided with Teresa, he'll have the numbers to change things back to the way he wants them. No restrictions. No waiting period."

"Well, yes," Reed gripped the steering wheel tighter. "It's a problem."

"I'm aware."

"We need to alert the other Council members that someone may be after them," he said like I might not have realized that fact.

"I already had this conversation with your father. He claims it's too dangerous to notify anyone. It would only lead to our own accidents."

Reed appeared shocked. "He said that?"

"Yes."

We rode in uncomfortable silence until he pulled up to a two story red house with a white wrap around porch and parked. Several people, who must be family members, paced back and forth on the porch while others hugged small children.

My stomach churned. I hadn't dealt with anyone's family before. That would make this so much worse. According to the universe, this was my job, and I could do it. I wasn't sure I agreed. Still I climbed out of the car and put one foot in front of the other. Reed followed behind me.

A police officer stopped us before we

reached the front steps. "It's not a good time to visit."

Like this was a social call. "The deceased appeared at my house. I'm Belinda Harbinger. I communicate with the dead and Reed helps them cross over."

The officer eyed me up and down and then did the same to Reed, like he didn't trust us. "The family didn't call for you. Wait in your car until they ask for your assistance."

"James appeared at my house and asked us to meet him here." How was he not understanding this situation? "I'd like to honor his final wishes."

The officer frowned. "Hold on." He walked away and spoke into a walkie talkie. A few minutes later he came back to us. "You can go in."

"Thank you." When we reached the porch, another policeman opened the door for us. "They're in the kitchen."

We walked through the foyer. I checked left and right, neither room was the kitchen, so I kept going. Farther down the hall to the right was a giant kitchen with a farmhouse table. The savory scent of steak filled the air. T-bones sat on the table, untouched. James lay sprawled on the hardwood floor, wearing a Kiss the Cook apron. Healer Bram stood off to the side talking to a police officer.

James popped up in front of me. "Thank goodness. Find my wife."

"Reed?" I held out my hand. He grabbed my forearm.

"Is your wife on the porch?" I asked.

"I don't know," James said. "Find Evie."

"Excuse me, Healer Bram? James wants to speak to his wife. Do you know where Evie is?"

"I'll locate her." He headed toward the front door.

"Someone murdered me," James image flickered.

Reed tightened his grip on my arm. "What do you mean?"

"I had a physical last week. I'm healthy as a horse."

Healer Bram came back into the kitchen. "She's not on the porch. The family will find her and bring her here."

"James claims," I didn't want to say the word murder in front of the police. "He passed his physical, so he suspects foul play."

A woman screamed and the police officer and the healer ran. We stayed rooted to the floor.

A pale wisp of a woman appeared in front of me. "James? What's going on?"

The ghosts flowed together and then separated. "Evie, I think we were poisoned."

"What? Why?" Evie asked.

"The mayor needed two more vacancies on the Council," James said. "I'm sure he's behind this."

Evie turned to me. "You can hear us?"

I nodded.

Healer Bram and the police officer came back into the room.

"Tell them we think we were poisoned," Evie said.

"Evie is here now too." I passed along her message.

"I'll do an autopsy," Healer Bram said.

"No, you will not," a man in his forties stormed into the room. "You will not defile my dad's body."

Oh, God. I clutched at my stomach. He didn't know about his mom.

Healer Bram stepped forward. "I regret to inform you that your mother has also passed away. Circumstances of multiple deaths require an autopsy to rule out foul play."

"No," the man stumbled backwards. "Mom?" He turned and fled into the hallway. "Mom?"

"This isn't fair," Evie said.

My heart ached for this family. "It's not."

"My job is to help you cross over," Reed said.

"I'm not going anywhere until we figure out who did this," James said.

"Of course," Reed nodded. "When you decide you're ready you can contact Belinda and she'll let me know."

"Thank you." Evie floated closer to her husband. "At least we have each other."

"I want the mayor to pay," James said.

"Was he here?" I asked.

"No." James said. "But we weren't on the best of terms."

"Did he threaten you?" I was grasping at straws, but it never hurt to ask.

"Not in so many words," Evie said. "But he made it known that he was angry about the restrictions."

The Green's son came back in with his wife and children. "We'd like…we'd like to talk to my parents."

I nodded. "That's why I'm here."

Two hours later when we left the Green's house, I was emotionally and physically drained. I remember walking to Reed's car, climbing in, and buckling my seat belt. The next thing I knew, Reed was gently shaking my shoulder. "Belinda, wake up."

I blinked and tuned back into reality.

"You're home," he said.

He looked as tired as I felt. I released my seatbelt. "That was exhausting."

"It was, but you did good. You really helped his family."

I was surprised by the compliment. "Thank you." I yawned. "You helped too."

"Not like you," he said. "They didn't even need me tonight, but you helped them deal with a terrible loss. You're stronger than I thought you were."

Something about that sounded insulting, but he was trying to give me a compliment. "Thanks." I exited the car and entered the house.

A shot of whiskey appeared on the table. "Thank you, Lilly. Can I have tea and wheat toast with butter instead?"

Victor, Dave, and Sadie drifted in from

the living room and joined me at the table as I ate.

"How did it go?" Victor asked.

I gave them a condensed version of what happened.

"That's terrible," Dave said.

"The mayor has his three open slots," Victor added. "I guess we'll have to wait and see how this plays out."

After I finished my food I headed up to bed. Sadie joined me a few moments later.

"Tell me your bad feeling is gone." I wasn't sure how much more I could take.

"It is. Would you like me to stay with you until you fall asleep?"

"That would be nice."

The next morning, I woke to a text from Lisa. The barbecue was canceled due to the Green's deaths. We agreed to meet for lunch one day this week. I was grateful she canceled, because I didn't have it in me to pretend to have a good time today. This gift sucked.

Reed called me strong. Was I strong enough to do this for the rest of my life? How had Teresa done it for all those years?

I went down for breakfast in my unicorn

pajamas. After last night, I might stay in my pajamas all day.

Had I known Healer Bram, Reed, and a policeman were in my kitchen, I would have put on real clothes.

They all looked at me with varying degrees of amusement. The policeman said, "My granddaughter has those pajamas."

"If any of my housemates had told me we had company I would have put on real clothes."

"And maybe combed your hair," Reed said in a teasing tone.

"Gimme a minute." I turned around and headed back upstairs where I put on jeans and a tee shirt and brushed my hair. The second time I went downstairs I made a cup of coffee and drank half of it before saying, "Lilly can we have coffee cake and bacon?"

An entire cake and a platter of bacon appeared on the kitchen table along with a stack of plates and napkins. I sat and filled my plate before glancing at the three males. "Help yourselves."

"Who's Lilly?" Healer Bram asked.

"The house."

"You named your house?" the policeman asked.

I nodded and continued eating.

After we'd all eaten, I said, "I'm capable of rational thought now. What's up?"

"The autopsies showed traces of tetrodotoxin," Healer Bram said. "It's a neurotoxin found in puffer fish."

"I'm guessing puffer fish wasn't on the menu at the Green's last night?"

"No," the police officer said. "Now we have to investigate who had access to the couple's food and their house. We hoped you could contact the Greens so we could talk to them."

I hadn't mentioned Mr. Green's suspicion of the mayor. "I can try. Do you want to do it here or at their house?"

"Let's try here," the police officer said. "Not all of my colleagues are on the same page, so I'd like to keep this quiet."

"James and Evie Green, can we speak to you?" I waited. Nothing happened. Maybe I should focus on one.

"James Green. I summon you. Please come talk to us."

James ghostly form appeared in front of me. "Come to the house," he said, and then popped out of existence.

I relayed the message.

"We'll meet you there." Healer Bram and the police officer stood and headed out the door.

Reed said, "Ready when you are."

I downed my cup of coffee and ran upstairs to brush my teeth before joining Reed in his Mustang.

"Did your dad ever help with police investigations?" I asked as we pulled out of the driveway.

"If he did, he never mentioned it."

My phone beeped, signaling I had a text message. I checked. It was from Lisa telling me she was free for lunch tomorrow. I texted back that I'd meet her at Carson's unless I was busy talking to dead people.

"Who was that?" Reed asked.

"Lisa Laddow."

"Why is she texting you?"

A small voice in my head suggested I tell him it was none of his business, but he was being polite, so I answered, "We're meeting for lunch tomorrow."

"You shouldn't trust her," he said.

"Why not?"

"Nathan said she has issues."

"I bet Nathan has never said a nice thing

about any of the women he's stopped seeing."

Reed paused like he was thinking. "You might be right."

"Nathan is a good lawyer, but I don't think he's a great guy to date."

"Huh," Reed didn't say anything else until we reached the Green's house. He parked behind Healer Bram's car and then turned to me. "Why did you say that about Nathan?"

"I think he strives to be the best lawyer he can be, and the women in his life are not a priority. If one of them demands too much time, he probably moves on."

"You've met him once. Where is this coming from?"

"Instinct, observations, experience, take your pick." With that I opened my door and headed for the house. Was Reed not able to read other people? Maybe that's what came from never sharing your feelings.

Evie popped up in front of me as I stepped on the front porch. "There you are. We need to talk."

"We do. Healer Bram and the police have questions for you."

"Let's go into the living room," she said,

and then grinned. "Kind of an ironic choice given the circumstances."

I smiled. Good to know a sense of humor could still exist in death. I headed inside and my three co-conspirators followed me.

Once we were all together, I held my hand out to Reed. "Want to listen in?"

He didn't move his hand toward mine.

The police officer said, "It would be better if you could confirm what they are saying."

He put his hand on my forearm.

"Evie what did you want to tell us?" I asked.

James popped into the living room. "We don't want to cause any trouble. Our deaths were probably an accident. We'd prefer it if you didn't investigate."

"What?" Reed said a little too loud.

"We have our kids to think about," Evie said. "If someone could get to us, they could get to our children."

I understood their concern. Still. "I'm not sure that's the best— "

Reed spoke over me, telling Healer Bram and the police officer what the Greens had said.

"Young man, I didn't give you permission to share that," Evie snapped.

"If you let whoever did this get away with it, then they'll think they can do it again," Healer Bram warned.

"We know that," James said. "But our actions might make things worse."

I repeated what James said.

"I don't have to write up everything you say in an official report," the police officer said. "No one has to know where the information came from."

Evie's form wavered. "We received a gift basket from the mayor for our anniversary. I used the olive oil from the basket in our salad dressing."

Reed repeated what she'd told us.

"Let's find that bottle," the officer said.

We entered the kitchen. I spotted the gift basket on the pantry.

"It's the lemon infused olive oil." Evie sighed. "Such a strange way to die. Death by salad dressing."

James moved closer to his wife. "There's nothing more we can tell you. Staying longer would only cause our family more heartache. I think we're ready to cross over."

Reed was standing off to the side. I held out my hand. "You're up."

This time, Reed laced his fingers through mine and held my hand. I felt a jolt of power and then Reed glowed. Warmth surrounded me. I tried to keep my eyes open to see what happened, but it was too bright. Once the light dimmed, Reed squeezed my hand before letting go. "They're gone."

"I'll pack up all the food and test it. No one has to know the Greens told us anything," Healer Bram said. "I'll write up the report and pass it on to the police."

Reed dropped me off at the house without so much as a goodbye. He seemed deep in thought, so I didn't feel snubbed, but he needed to work on his social skills.

Once inside the house, I had no idea what to do with myself. There were so many things I didn't understand. Maybe Aunt Teresa's laptop could help. I retrieved it from my room and took it to the kitchen table. Reed had mentioned a charger. Where would that be?

Sadie and Dave padded into the kitchen. "How did it go?" Dave asked.

"They passed over. It was peaceful. Do you know where the laptop charger is?

"It should be on the kitchen counter be-hind you," Dave said.

I turned and examined the countertop. There weren't any outlets or cords in sight. "Where?"

Dave hopped up onto the counter. "That's odd. There used to be a silver rec-tangular charging plate next to the coffee maker."

"Lilly, do you know where the charging plate is?" I asked.

The lights blinked once.

"I'm guessing that's a no."

The lights blinked twice. I laughed.

"Dave, does Victor have a charging station?"

"He doesn't use a laptop."

"I guess I'm headed back into town to buy a charging plate."

"Lilly could probably get one for you," Dave said.

Someone knocked on the back door. Sadie hissed.

The hair on my arms stood up. "Lilly, don't let them in," I whispered.

Whoever it was turned the doorknob back and forth. "I know you're in there," a feminine voice said.

"Who is it?" I asked.

"Tina Tate."

This couldn't be good. I walked over to the door and looked out the window. "Hello, Tina. How can I help you?"

"I need a Familiar," she said.

Crap. Had she figured out about Sadie? "What does that have to do with me?"

"I want Dave," she said. "He isn't pledged to anyone."

Dave hissed.

I turned back to Dave. "Get Victor,"

He took off like a shot.

I turned back around to face Tina. "I'm sorry. Dave isn't available."

"I'm a witch. He's a Familiar. It's my right to claim him."

I stalled for time hoping Victor would appear soon. "You don't want a Familiar. Why are you really here?"

"I'm here for a cat. You can keep one, not both."

"What is going on?" Victor dashed into the room.

I pulled him into the pantry and filled him in on the situation. "As a witch can she just take him?"

"The law would be on her side," he said.

I would not let this happen. "Victor, I need you to ask Dave to be your Familiar."

"I can't," Victor said.

"You can. Just do it. See if it works."

Both cats joined us in the pantry. "Are we hiding in here until she goes away?" Dave asked.

"No. Victor has something to ask you."

"It won't work," Victor said. "I'm not a witch."

"Just do it." I snapped. "Dave, we're trying to keep Tina from claiming you."

"Fine." Victor sighed. "Dave will you be my Familiar?"

"I would, if I could," Dave said. "But it doesn't work that way."

The air shimmered. Dave meowed and then coughed and then a man with salt and pepper hair wearing a gray suit sat on the floor in the pantry.

"Dave?" I said.

"How?" Dave asked.

"Doesn't matter. Now Tina can't take you."

I walked back into the kitchen and spoke through the door, "I'm sorry you wasted your trip out here, but Dave has already been claimed."

"You're lying," Tina said. "Open the door or I'll come back with reinforcements."

My three friends exited the pantry. Dave bent down and picked up Sadie. "Come here, girl." He rubbed her ears and she purred. "Belinda, go ahead and open the door."

"Wait," Victor whispered. "Don't tell her it's me." He dashed into the pantry and up the stairs to the third floor.

I unlocked the door and Tina Tate barged into the kitchen. "Where is he?"

"I'm right here," Dave said. "In human form, which means I've been claimed."

She looked him up and down. "Who's your witch?"

"My witch has asked that I not share his or her identity," Dave said.

"Fine." Tina took a step toward Dave. "Give me Sadie."

"Not a chance," Dave said. "The mayor ruled that Belinda is Sadie's caretaker."

Tina started reciting something. Was she casting a hex or a spell?

"Genevieve Tate," I hollered. "I summon you to come take care of your daughter."

A wispy form appeared in front of Tina

and solidified into a visible spirit. "Stop that right now, young lady."

"But, mom. She stole Sadie and took all of our money."

"No," Mrs. Tate said. "I gave her Sadie and all of *my* money because you and your brother need to learn to stand on your own two feet."

"That's not fair." Tina stomped her foot like a toddler.

"I know it may seem that way now, but later you'll thank me," Mrs. Tate said. "Why don't we go visit your brother. It's past time we had a talk and straightened all of this out."

"What about grandma's doll collection?" Tina asked. "Sadie doesn't need those."

Mrs. Tate turned to me. "Do you mind if I give her the dolls?"

"Of course not." Hopefully they weren't voodoo dolls.

"And Tim wanted Dad's phonograph and records."

Mrs. Tate sighed. "Maybe I was too hasty with my will. Belinda, do you mind if I change things around?"

"As long as I can keep Sadie and a small allowance for cat food, I'm good."

Tina appeared stunned. "But I thought— "

"You thought I took advantage of your mom and stole your inheritance," I said for her.

She nodded.

"Mrs. Tate, why don't you go spend time with your family," I said. "And let me know what you work out."

Tina left. Her mom floated out with her.

I locked the door, went into the pantry, and called out, "Victor they're gone."

He came down the stairs at a run. "How did you know that would work?"

Sadie hopped out of Dave's arms, shimmered and shifted into her human form. Instead of an orange bath robe, she wore an orange dress. "I told her."

"Sadie?" Dave looked at her in awe. Not that I could blame him. She was beautiful.

"Yes?" She moved toward him with a tentative smile on her face.

"Why didn't you tell me?" He reached out and held both of her hands.

"Genevieve kept me a secret from everyone until she passed me on to Belinda."

"That's how you knew it would work," Victor said.

I nodded. "Sorry to spring this on you, but I was afraid Tina would take Dave or Sadie."

"Thank you, both," Dave said.

"Can we go take a nap in our chair?" Sadie asked.

"Of course." Dave shifted into cat form. Sadie did the same. Together, they padded into the other room.

"That's so sweet," I said.

Victor shook his head. "This will bring nothing but trouble. I never would have asked him if I'd known it would work."

Chapter 14

"What?"

"Word will get out that Gifted people can have Familiars."

"It's not against the law, is it?"

"No, but it goes against centuries of tradition."

He was overreacting. "Tina doesn't know who his witch is, and there's no reason for her to look into it. She'll be happy that she's getting her inheritance back."

"Mrs. Tate's lawyer will have to draw up a new will," Victor said. "You need to think with your head and not your heart before you agree to give everything away."

Victor was more like Reed than I realized. "Okay, Mr. Glass Half Empty. Why don't we celebrate our small victory instead of worrying about what could happen."

"Teresa didn't worry enough and look what happened to her." Victor rubbed his temples. "I don't mean to be rude. You are so like Teresa, and I don't relish the idea of finding another body in this house."

I didn't know what to say.

"You don't understand how Mystic Hills works." Victor put his hand on my shoulder. "If you plan to stay, then you need to learn how to survive in this environment."

He wasn't wrong. "Reed said something similar, but no one has offered me an instruction manual. I'm willing to learn if you point me in the right direction."

He removed his hand from my shoulder and pointed at the pantry. "The law books upstairs would be a good place to start."

"What about Teresa's laptop?"

"I have no idea what you'd find on it, but you're welcome to look."

"Do you know where the charging plate is?"

Victor frowned and walked over to the counter and started opening drawers. He found in it the bottom one. "I moved it, since I didn't need it." He set it on the counter and headed into the living room.

I grabbed the laptop, opened it, and set it on the silver rectangle. The screen lit up, so it must be magically charging. I'd give it ten minutes and then see what I could find.

Twenty minutes later a spinning hour-glass had taken up most of the screen. Maybe that meant it was still charging.

My phone rang. "Hello?"

"What have you done?" A man yelled.

"Who is this?" I was pretty sure it was Nathan, but I wasn't going to volunteer any information because I'd done several things today he might not appreciate.

"It's Nathan. Why did you summon Genevieve Tate?"

"Her daughter was about to hex me."

"Now she wants to change her will."

"And that's a problem because?"

"Spirits have no legal standing. She claims you won't mind if we give most of her estate back to her children."

"Can we meet in person with Genevieve?"

"Who is paying my hourly rate?" he asked.

That's what this all came down to? "It will come from the estate. Happy?"

"No. This sets a dangerous precedent. Meet me at the Tate's house at seven."

Before I could respond, he hung up. This was turning out to be a lovely day.

"Lilly, can I have a large cafe mocha?"

My drink appeared on the table. I sipped the chocolate laced caffeinated beverage and reflected on the day so far. Victor was predicting doom and gloom. Nathan was worried about setting a dangerous precedent. Dave could take human form again. That was a plus. And I no longer had to keep Sadie's true identity a secret from my housemates. We weren't any closer to finding out who murdered Teresa but she was at peace now. I'd accomplished that much. Hopefully her laptop would give a clue where to look next.

My phone rang. "Hello?"

"It's Reed. Is everything okay there?"

"Mostly. Why do you ask?"

"Someone called me and suggested it would be in everyone's best interest if you left town."

"That's rude. Anyone I know?"

"Yes, which is why I'm giving you a chance to explain what happened."

"A lot happened. What parts are you interested in?"

"Fill me in on Genevieve Tate's appearance."

"The quick version is I called her spirit to keep Tina from hexing me. Mom and daughter had some quality bonding time. Now we might change the will."

A string of curse words came through the phone.

"Wow. That was colorful."

"You ignored my advice, thought like an outsider, and now everyone will think you're weak."

I gripped the phone tighter. "You weren't here. You don't know what you're talking about."

"What—"

I hung up on him. There was only so much verbal abuse I was willing to take. I texted Lisa and asked if she could meet me at Carson's for dinner because I needed to ask some questions about how Mystic Hills worked before meeting with Nathan.

THE LAPTOP DINGED. I walked to the counter and was greeted with a screen that contained several file folders labeled with initials. I clicked on the one that said GT. It contained emails from Genevieve Tate. I took the computer to the table and sat, reading through the emails. Genevieve had been opposed to the restrictions, but Teresa had been able to change her mind.

I opened another file and saw emails from the Greens. A file marked N contained conversations with Nathan. He advised her on what to change in the laws in order to get the most votes. He also billed her the full three hundred an hour. You'd think he'd give her a break considering what she was trying to do. I sifted through his emails hoping they would give me insight on who might be willing to kill over the law, besides the mayor.

Oddly enough Nathan started out for the restrictions, a week before the vote he tried to talk her out of it because it would cost certain people too much business. Aunt Teresa hadn't listened to him. In the final emails right before the vote, his tone became threatening, warning her of crossing the wrong people.

Why would Nathan have a change of heart? Maybe someone bribed him. Money seemed to trump everything for him. I'd bet someone paid him off or offered him a piece of their business.

I clicked around on her computer finding files for recipes and past emails. I was about to close the laptop when I noticed the trash can icon at the bottom. If someone had wanted to get rid of any incriminating evidence they'd probably move it to trash. I opened the trash and saw a file that said, KC. I moved it back to the desktop and opened it.

Kyle Carter had written my aunt multiple times asking that she cease and desist with her ridiculous restrictions. Each email became ruder and more threatening. His name sounded familiar. Had I met him? Wait. Was this the jerk at the mayor's office who tried to tell me I'd signed illegally for the house?

I picked up the laptop and went into the living room where Dave and Sadie were curled up in their chair. "Guys, do you know Kyle Carter?"

"Horrible man," Sadie said. "Genevieve hated him. Called him a liar and a cheat."

"Rumor has it he wants to be the next mayor," Dave said. "But I don't think he has the connections to make it happen. Why do you ask?"

"His emails to Teresa weren't nice. If he talks to everyone like that then it might not mean anything." Then again, it might.

I ARRIVED EARLY at Carson's that evening for my dinner with Lisa because I needed out of the house. Rather than sit at a table by myself, I went to the bar.

The bar tender came towards me. His kind brown eyes and genuine smile put me at ease. "Hello, what can I get for you?"

"Whiskey, neat."

He poured my drink and set it in front of me on a hunter green napkin. "You seem stressed. Want to talk about it?"

I meant to say no, but what poured out of my mouth was, "Do people in this town look down on acts of kindness?"

He drummed his fingers on the bar. "That is an interesting question."

"Why did I say that?" Had he magicked my whiskey like Jezelle?

"It's my gift. People ask me questions about things that are weighing heavily on their minds."

"Do you have answers?" I sipped my drink.

"I try. Your question is tricky. Some people view kindness as weakness. Other people, the more rationale ones who had enough hugs growing up, realize kindness makes the world a better place. Anything else you want to know?"

"Can I ask your opinion on people? There's someone I'm not sure I should trust."

"Go ahead. Everyone comes through here at one point or another."

"Kyle Carter."

He sucked in a breath. "He's known for double dealing and backstabbing."

"That's the impression he gave. What about Nathan Gunn? He's a good lawyer, but his communication skills are suspect."

He laughed and it was a nice warm sound. I felt my shoulder muscles relax.

"Nathan is one of the best lawyers in town, but his interpersonal skills aren't great. I think he puts his business investments before anything else."

"What kind of investments?"

"He and the mayor are both interested in buying up any available property."

"I've been told more property means more power."

"That's true." He held out his hand. "I'm Oliver West by the way."

I shook his hand. "Belinda Harbinger, nice to meet you."

"I knew your aunt. She was a good woman."

"Thank you. I think she made some political enemies. After the restrictions were passed, did people talk about her?"

"Some did. It seems half the town was happy with the change, and half thought the law needed to stay out of people's business."

"Where did you stand on the issue?"

"I'd rather people ask before taking my blood," he said. "I heard you had a run in with a blood-sucking bracelet."

"I did. Who told you?"

"Ann came in for lunch the day of the incident in her store. She ate at the bar and we talked about what it might mean."

Interesting. "What do you think it means?"

He grabbed a shot glass and poured himself a drink. "It means you need to be careful because your aunt's death may not have been an accident. But you knew that already, didn't you?"

I nodded. "I suspected as much."

He leaned in and spoke in a whisper. "The fact that there was no investigation means it was someone with power. You need to be careful."

"Thanks, I will."

"Making new friends?" Lisa asked as she came up behind me.

I turned and smiled. "Yes."

She pointed at Oliver. "Do not ask me what I'm thinking."

He laughed. "Fine. Enjoy your dinner, ladies. It was nice meeting you, Belinda."

"Nice meeting you, too."

The hostess seated us on the patio. After we ordered, Lisa said, "What's going on?"

I filled her in on Mrs. Tate and the possible changes to the will.

"I'm not sure a spirit can alter a will."

"I never expected to receive anything from Mrs. Tate but her cat, and I don't mind returning most of it to her children. Both

Reed and Nathan are acting like I've lost my mind."

"Legally, the estate belongs to you which means you can do what you want."

"If you were me, what would you do?"

She sipped her wine. "Mrs. Tate had a legendary temper. She may have changed her will while she was angry. That doesn't mean she wouldn't have changed it back once she calmed down. She didn't live long enough to do that."

"Someone told me the people of this town would think I was weak if I gave anything back to her family."

"That someone has a low opinion of everyone else. People might be surprised, but they won't think less of you. Good people will think more of you because you did the kind thing. I say ignore the naysayers and go with your gut."

"I don't suppose you want to join me while I try to explain the concept of kindness to Nathan tonight?"

"No. But I'll help straighten out your account if you make any changes."

Our food arrived and we made small talk while we ate. At six thirty, we paid our bills and left the restaurant. After saying our goodbyes, I climbed into the lilac Volkswagen and drove toward Mrs. Tate's house. At least I thought I did. I must have gotten turned around on all the curvy roads because I ended up on the wrong street. I missed Google Maps.

I pulled my car over in front of a gray Victorian with blue accents and pulled out my phone. Who should I call? Reed had been a jerk lately and Victor hadn't been much better. Maybe I'd just backtrack to Main Street and start over. Before I could put the car in gear, a middle-aged woman wearing jeans and a black peasant blouse came out of the house I was parked in front of and walked toward my car. She came around to the driver side, so I locked the door and rolled down the window a few inches.

"Why are you loitering in front of my house?" She acted like I was vandalizing her property.

"I was on my way to Genevieve Tate's house but I got turned around. Can you point me in the right direction?"

Her eyes narrowed. "Genevieve is dead."

Maybe introductions would clear this up. "I'm Belinda Harbinger. I speak to ghosts and spirits. Genevieve and a lawyer are expecting me at her house. If you could give me directions, I'll be on my way."

"Nothing in this world is free." She pulled a large syringe from her back pocket. "It will cost you syringe full of blood."

"Seriously?" Who carried syringes around with them?

She yanked the car door handle. "I'd be within my rights to drain you for trespassing. Consider this a small price to pay for information."

"No thanks." I put the car in reverse and backed away, forcing her to let go. Then I put it in drive and sped away. What kind of person asked to be paid in blood for directions? I made a U-turn and headed back to Main Street. On the way I spotted the street with yellow flowering trees and took the turn which led me to the Tate's house.

I pulled up to the house at five til seven, so I wasn't late, thank goodness. The house was lit up like there was a party. There were three cars in the driveway, so I parked on the street.

When I knocked on the door, Nathan opened it with an odd smile on his face. "Thank you for joining us." He led me to the dining room. The table was covered in stacks of paperwork. No one else was there, which was strange since I'd seen multiple cars out front.

"Where are the Tates?" I'd wanted to ask Tina about the creepy neighbor. Wait, the woman hadn't told me her name. That was a dead end.

"They're upstairs going through family heirlooms." He sat and gestured I should do the same. "Before we speak with them, we need to come to an understanding. You are not returning the house."

I sat and tried to project confidence. "No offense, but I can do what I want."

"No." He leaned toward me. "You can't. If you significantly alter the will, then everyone's heirs will fight for a bigger piece of the pie. A person's last will and testament is a sacred document." He smacked his palm down on the table. "You can't invalidate it."

Had he been drinking? He appeared disheveled. His hair was out of place, his tie was crooked, and his jacket was wrinkled.

My phone rang. "Excuse me." I stood and walked back out to the foyer. "Hello?"

"It's Lisa. I pulled up your account to see if I could offer more constructive advice, and there's something wrong with your first deposit."

"What do you mean?"

"Nathan took fifty percent, not fifteen."

"What? Why would he—" I heard someone walk up behind me. "No problem, Mom. I'll call you later tonight."

When I turned around, Nathan said, "Who was that?"

I shoved my phone in my pocket. "My mom. She keeps asking when I'm coming home."

"So, you're leaving Mystic Hills?"

What answer would he like better? "I have to go back when school starts." That was nice and vague.

"The good news is you can take Sadie with you, and we can have your deposits sent to your Outsider bank, although there's a fee to transfer funds to an Outsider account. The amount can vary, so don't be surprised if the stipend is less than we originally stated."

That sounded like a complete fabrication, but I went with, "I understand."

Out of the corner of my eye, I saw a handbag and a set of keys on the entry table. The Tate's were here somewhere. Mrs. Tate appeared behind Nathan. She put her fingers to her lips like she was telling me to be quiet and then she pointed toward the stairs. "Should I go find the Tate's so we can sort this all out? I know time is money for you."

"Yes. It is." He straightened his tie and patted down his jacket. His fake smile reappeared, which probably meant he thought he had the situation under control.

I walked toward the main stairs at a normal pace, even though my instincts told me to run.

"Belinda?" Nathan called out. "May I borrow your phone. I left mine at the office."

Dang it. If he checked recent calls, Lisa's number would show. If I told him no, he'd realize something was up. Could I make it up the stairs, lock myself in a room, and call for help before he caught me? I wasn't sure, so I said, "Let me call Reed first. He wanted to talk to me about keeping the house too. If you both think it's the right thing to do, then I'll listen." I hit the number for mom and hung up before it could ring. Then I hit the number for Reed.

"Hello?"

"I'm with Nathan at the Tate's house. Can you come weigh in on the estate? I'd like your advice."

"You know how I feel— "

"Great. See you in a few minutes." I hung up. "Nathan, Tina asked about a doll collection, and Tim wants some records, would that be too much trouble to write up?"

He visibly calmed. "No. That is manageable."

I held my phone out to him. "Did you need to make a call?"

"No. As long as you don't plan on giving away the house, I won't need to consult another lawyer."

Something bumped around upstairs. "Should I go check on the Tate's?"

"They're sorting through boxes. You can check on them after we go through the paperwork."

Goosebumps pebbled my arms. Why didn't he want me to speak to Tim and Tina? Had he done something to them? The bumping noises continued. Nathan shuffled papers around on the table like he didn't hear or wasn't concerned.

Genevieve appeared behind Nathan, waved her arms, and then pointed at the stairs. I needed a reason to go upstairs and check on them. "I'd rather not be here all night. I'll go upstairs and see if I can hurry them along."

"Come here." Nathan held out a pen. "I need a few signatures and then you can go."

I didn't want to go home. I wanted to check on the Tate's. This entire situation felt wrong. Nathan wouldn't try to hurt me, would he? If he was taking half my money like Lisa said, maybe he would try to get rid of me. And if the Tate's were out of the picture he could do whatever he wanted. I needed to find Tina and Tim.

"I had dinner with Lisa before coming here tonight." I edged toward the stairs. "I had several glasses of iced tea, so before I sign anything I need to use the restroom."

"Belinda," Nathan's tone took on a menacing edge. "Come here and sign the papers."

Someone knocked on the front door and I ran to answer it before Nathan could tell me not to.

Reed stood on the doorstep. "What is going on?"

I glanced behind me. "Nathan is acting weird. I think he has the Tate's locked upstairs."

"What?"

"Lisa checked the account; he's taking fifty percent. Not fifteen."

"Is that Reed?" Nathan called out.

"Yes." We walked back into the dining room.

Rather than sitting at the table, Reed leaned against the door frame like it was any other day. "What's Belinda done now?"

Nathan laughed. "I think we've salvaged the situation. She wants to give them a doll collection and records."

"Did you look at the dolls?" Reed directed the question at me. "How do you know they aren't priceless collector items?"

"I don't."

"Let's go find them so you know what they are before you agree to give them away."

"That won't be necessary," Nathan said.

"It is." Reed headed for the stairs. "Come on, Belinda. Let's make sure you aren't doing anything stupid."

Reed had better be acting, because if he thought it was okay to talk to me like this, we were going to have a problem. I followed him up the stairs. When we reached the landing, Reed called out, "Tina?"

A bumping sound came from down the hall. I ran to open the door and found Tim sorting through boxes.

Reed joined me. "Tim, are you okay?"

He turned to us with an odd look on his face. "I'm looking for something, but I'm not sure what it is." He opened a box, took out the shoe on top and tossed it over his shoulder. "That's not it." He pulled out another shoe and did the same thing. "That's not it."

"Someone put a spell on him," Reed said.

"Tim, where's Tina?"

He paused. "She's looking for her dolls."

Nathan came down the hall toward us. "I'm not proud of what I did, but Tim wouldn't see reason. He threatened to burn the house down rather than let you keep it."

"Oh," I hadn't expected that and wasn't sure I believed it. Tim may have been a jerk when he was drunk and upset, but he wanted his father's phonographs. No way he'd threaten to burn down the house. Nathan was lying.

"Where's Tina?" Reed asked.

A door opened and Tina poked her head out. "I thought I heard someone out here. Belinda, come and see my grandmother's dolls."

"Sure." Personally, I found dolls creepy, but it gave me a reason to speak to Tina alone, to see if she thought Nathan was acting strange.

We entered the room and Tina led me to a glass case featuring dolls that appeared far too realistic.

"Aren't the details exquisite?" she said.

Most of the life-sized babies' faces were scrunched up like they were crying. Some had spit up on their lips and chin. Why would anyone want those things? What could I say? I tried to be diplomatic. "I've never seen anything like them."

Still facing the dolls, Tina said, "Don't turn around if they come in the room. Nathan put a confusion spell on Tim, claiming he was unstable, but what Nathan didn't know is I was walking back into the room when he did it. I saw the whole thing.

Tim wasn't being a problem. Nathan just wanted him out of the way."

"I agree. Nathan seems off." I was glad it wasn't just me, but should I trust Tina? "I'm not sure who I can trust around here, including you, but I want to give everything back to you and Tim.

Tina's breath caught. "I'm so sorry I misjudged you."

I turned to her. "Hey, I'm a stranger who somehow managed to take your mother's estate the day she died. I understand the resentment."

The door opened. "Are we ready to go down and sign the papers now?" Nathan asked.

"Fix her brother so we can all talk like rationale human beings," I said.

"That's not a good idea," Nathan replied.

"No," Reed said. "Belinda is right. Tim needs to be in his right mind when he agrees to the new terms of the will, doesn't he?"

Nathan paused. "You're right. Why don't you three go down and we'll be right behind you."

"Do you mind if I have some movers

come tomorrow to pack up the dolls and the cases?" Tina asked.

"No," I said at the same time Nathan said, "Yes."

"As you keep reminding me Nathan, it's Belinda's house," Tina said, "so I'm going with yes."

We headed out the door and down the hall with Reed right behind us. As we walked down the staircase, Reed said, "You were right, Belinda. That's not Nathan. We need to leave. Now."

"I won't abandon my brother," Tina protested.

"Once we get out of here, we'll regroup and come back with magical reinforcements. Whoever that is tried to put a spell on me but stopped before he finished. It's like someone is controlling Nathan but he is trying to fight it."

When we hit the first floor, Reed grabbed my hand. "Come on."

We ran for the door. Tina followed. We made it outside and Reed kept running until we reached our cars.

As I climbed in, I noticed Tina having a hard time unlocking her car door. Nathan stormed out onto the porch and yelled at her from the front steps. My heart beat double time. Come on. What was taking her so long? Finally, she opened the car door, backed up across the lawn and made it to the street. I put my car in drive and headed home. Reed followed in his car. When I turned onto Main Street, I noticed he was no longer behind me. Where had he gone?

Chapter 15

Reed waited for me in the driveway when I pulled up to the house. He must know a faster way home. I parked and exited the vehicle with questions pinging around in my brain. When I reached him, I said, "Who could control Nathan like that?"

"The only people who aren't afraid of him which would mean the mayor or another lawyer."

"Do you think someone is making him steal from the stipend?"

"That part I don't know. When it comes to money he plays to win. If he thought he deserved more of the money, he'd probably find a way to take it."

"Upping his fee from fifteen percent to fifty percent is kind of hard to miss."

"If he decided to alter his percentage, he'd be sure to cover his tracks." Reed glanced around like someone might be watching us. "Let's go inside."

His phone beeped and he paused to check the text message. "Tina is going back for Tim with her husband and sister-in-law. They'll text when he's safe."

"Good." Even Nathan and his possessor probably couldn't take on three adult witches.

In the kitchen Victor, Dave, and Sadie sat at the table, playing cards.

"Dave?" Reed seemed surprised to see his friend in human form.

"Hello, Reed."

Reed tilted his head and looked at the blond woman. "Sadie?"

"Yes. Why do you two look so unsettled?"

I filled them in on our strange encounter with Nathan.

Victor stood and went to the phone. "I'm calling the police. Possession is illegal."

"We don't know who we can trust," Reed said.

"I know several policemen I'd trust with my life." Victor dialed and filled someone in on the situation, and then he listened for a long time before saying, "I see. Thank you."

He came back to the table. "They've had other instances of possession but can't figure out who is doing it."

"Where does that leave us?" I asked.

"Waiting for them to do their job," he replied.

"How does that help us now?" I dropped down in a vacant kitchen chair.

"It doesn't," Reed said. "Ask Lilly to go into lockdown mode."

"Lilly, can you keep everyone out unless we ask you to let them in?"

The lights flashed twice.

"Now we wait," Reed said.

My phone rang. I flipped it open. "Hello?"

"It's Lisa Laddow. I need you to come into the bank."

"Why?" That was a strange request. The bank wasn't open at night.

"Nathan said there were a few pages you forgot to sign when you met with him earlier tonight." Lisa seemed to be putting effort into sounding normal. "He dropped by my house and asked me to come in so we could take care of this."

"That's weird," I said.

"It is," she agreed. "See you soon."

I relayed Lisa's message. "I guess we're going to the bank."

"No," Reed said. "This could be a trap."

Was he only concerned about himself? "I realize that, but Lisa could be in danger."

"She's right," Sadie said. "Let's go."

"No," Victor said. "The police told us to sit tight."

"Belinda, I'll go with you," Dave said.

"Reed, since you're staying here, text Tina and tell her Nathan left the house."

He nodded and pulled out his phone. "Belinda, just…be careful."

"I'll try."

We headed out the door and piled into the Volkswagen. On the ride to the bank, Sadie changed back to cat form. "Nathan doesn't know about me which might give us the element of surprise."

We parked in front of the bank. The lobby was dark. We entered the building with Dave holding Sadie. The light in Lisa's office was the only one on. She sat behind her desk like nothing was wrong.

Nathan stood in front of the desk holding a pen. "I don't know what kind of joke Reed thought he was playing on me, but it wasn't funny. You're going to sign these papers so we can all get on with our lives."

"I brought Sadie," Dave said. "Do you want her paw print on anything?"

"No." Nathan looked at him like he was an idiot. "You shouldn't even be here."

"They're my moral support since you've been acting odd."

Nathan laughed. "You're the one making all of this difficult. Sign the papers to give the Tate's what they want and let's be done with this."

"I want to give it all back," I said. "Except for Sadie."

Nathan froze and then blinked like he was waking up. He printed "Not me" on an envelope in Lisa's inbox before he straightened his shoulders. "Belinda, fifteen percent of the stipend is mine, so you can't give it all to them."

"Can I give them my eighty five percent?" I asked.

Lisa placed her hand on top of what Nathan had written. "Instead of worrying about the will, we could transfer money from Belinda's account to the Tate's on a monthly basis. That way the will won't have to be changed and everyone gets what they want."

Nathan frowned and then nodded. "That works. Belinda, if you'll sign for the dolls and the records, we can all go home."

I glanced at Dave. "That sounds logical, right?"

"Yes."

I picked up the papers Nathan had set out for me to sign. It looked the same as the last contract with an addendum for giving specific items to the Tate's. I signed.

"Was that so hard?" Nathan asked while he put the papers in his briefcase and then walked out the door.

Once he was gone, I said, "That was brilliant, Lisa. Thanks for helping."

She moved her hand. "Even without this note, I knew that wasn't Nathan because he flirted with me when he asked me to come in. What's going on?"

"That is the question of the day." I pointed at the note Nathan had left. "Now that our mystery possessor has what he wanted, maybe he'll leave Nathan alone."

"Should we call the police?" Lisa asked.

"As much as I resent the guy, no one deserves to be used as a puppet."

"The police are aware," I said. "It's part of an ongoing case."

"Belinda, you should call Reed," Dave said. "He'll be worried."

I pulled out my phone, made the call, and let him know we were safe.

"Good," Reed said. "I called Tina. Tim came out of the spell. They're staying at his house."

By the time we made it home Reed was gone which made me a little sad for some reason. He'd worried about my safety tonight, which meant he cared. After giving Lilly instructions not to let anyone in without our permission, I went up to bed.

———

I WOKE to the sound of someone singing. It was a female voice, so I assumed it was Sadie. Why was she singing at...I checked the clock on my nightstand...holy crap it was nine. No wonder I felt rested. When was the last time I'd slept in? Not since arriving here.

After putting on real clothes, I headed

downstairs for breakfast. Sadie sat on the couch crocheting and singing along to the radio while Dave read the newspaper.

"Good morning," I said.

They both responded without looking up from their respective projects. The kitchen was empty. "Lilly, can I have a ham and cheese omelet and some wheat toast with butter?"

My food appeared on the table as I made myself a cup of coffee. "Lilly, you're still my favorite person."

I polished off my food and then called Tina Tate. After I explained about transferring the money to her account, she said, "Did you figure out what was wrong with Nathan last night?"

I explained our possession theory. "Do you know how someone could do it?"

"There are different possession spells of varying strengths," Tina said. "There aren't a lot of witches who can pull them off. Using those spells is frowned upon. Whoever possessed Nathan wanted you to hang onto the house to give him access to more power."

"How would that work?"

"Since no one lives there, someone could syphon power off of the house."

"Something else happened last night." I told her about my run in with the scary witch woman who wanted my blood.

"It's best if you don't stop at a witch's house, because you never know if they are old school witches who take what they want, or more evolved witches like my family. We take payment in blood for spells and hexes, but I'd never make someone give blood if they asked for directions."

"Is there a way to tell who lives in a house if I don't know the area?"

"Check the roof for weathervanes and lightning rods. witches work with elements so they'll always have at least one of each. Most gifted people wouldn't think to put a lightning rod on their roof."

Interesting information. "Thanks. I'll be sure to check for those before I park in front of anyone else's house."

After the call ended, Sadie joined me in the kitchen in human form. "You're being awfully nice to Tina. I'm not sure she deserves your kindness."

"She also didn't deserve to have her inheritance given to a complete stranger." An idea occurred to me. "Would you want to move back into your house as a human?"

"I never thought about it." Sadie leaned close and said, "Dave is thrilled to be in human form again. I prefer my other form, but I care for him so I'm making the best of it."

"I think that's how every relationship works." Although I wasn't sure what type of relationship they had. "Could you and Dave live together in your old house?"

"No. We're Familiars. We have to stay with our witches."

The house phone rang. Dave came into the kitchen. "I'll get it, if you don't mind."

"Go ahead."

He picked up the phone. "Hello. You've reached the Harbinger Residence. How may I direct your call?"

Dave held the phone out toward me. "It's Nathan for you."

Crud. I wanted to ask which Nathan but didn't want to let the bad guys know I was on to them. I took the phone. "Hello, Nathan. What's up?"

"I wanted to apologize for last night. I wasn't feeling myself."

Okay. Not sure how I should respond to that. "Are you more yourself this morning?"

"More or less," he said. "My recollection of last night is fuzzy."

Was he trying to get me to admit I knew it wasn't him? What if this still wasn't him? "Is this just a way to deny you flirted with Lisa?"

"I what?" He muttered something. "Can we meet?"

That didn't seem like a good idea. "I planned to spend most of the day at the tearoom. Why don't you meet me there? We can talk in Reed's office."

"That works. I'll see you there at noon."

I hung up and dialed Reed. "We're meeting with Nathan at noon in your office," I informed him.

"We who?" he asked.

"Me, you, and him, because I don't want to meet with him alone."

"That's smart," he said. "Since we don't know if he's still possessed. Listen, about last night, I know I sounded like a jerk. It's just...I worry about you."

How was I supposed to respond to that? "I appreciate that. See you at noon."

I arrived at the tearoom early so I could reach out to some spirits. When I walked into *Tea & Spirits* there were a dozen people spread out at the tables in groups of two or three. They all glanced up and then went back to their conversations. Good to know I wasn't an unusual sight anymore.

Jezelle nodded at me from behind the bar where she was serving Healer Bram a cup of tea. I was still ticked off at her for spiking my drink with the blabbermouth spell, but I nodded back. As I crossed the room, I noticed free floating spirits drifting in the far right corner. One floated over towards me, taking on the form of Ida.

"I have a message for you from your aunt. She's happy to be reunited with Johnathon. She says you can call her whenever you want."

"Oh," I hadn't expected that. "Thank you." Tears pricked at my eyes.

"It gets easier with time, my dear." Ida floated back over to the corner.

I hadn't expected the emotional ambush, so it took me a moment to regain control of my tear ducts. When I entered Reed's office, he glanced up.

"What's wrong?"

"Nothing," I swiped at my eyes. "These are happy tears. Aunt Teresa sent a message via one of the spirits in the tearoom. It caught me off guard."

"There are spirits out there now? Did you call them?"

"No. There's a bunch in the far corner. Maybe they popped in to visit? Is that something they do?"

"Teresa never mentioned it." He set his pen down. "Why did Nathan want to meet with you?"

I told him about the phone call and the specific wording Nathan used.

"Maybe he was trying to tell us he'd been possessed," Reed said.

Ida floated into the room followed by a male spirit.

"Hello, again," I said.

"Who are you talking to?" Reed asked.

"He can't see us," the woman said. "This is my friend Will Hanover."

"Spirits," I told Reed.

"And you didn't call them?" Reed asked.

"No." I turned to the spirits. "Ida, I thought I had to call you. Do you come here under your own power?"

Will grinned. "Sometimes we come back to socialize. You're stronger than Teresa. She couldn't see us unless she'd called us."

"Or she saw us as free floating spirits be-cause she wasn't as attuned," Ida said. "Ei-ther way, it's lovely to be able to talk to the living without being called."

An idea formed in the back of my brain. "Can you travel anywhere and see anyone?"

"For the most part."

That gave me an idea. "I don't suppose you saw who killed the Greens."

"No," Ida said. "But we'd be up for some espionage if you need help."

"What are they saying?" Reed asked.

"Don't tell him," Ida said. "We don't trust him."

"Why?"

"He doesn't trust anyone else," Ida said. "So we don't trust him."

That was twisted logic which I wasn't about to share with Reed. Even though I fantasized about letting Lilly slingshot him across the yard, deep down I knew I could trust him. If I needed him, he'd be there. He'd probably gripe the entire time, but he'd be there.

"Ida said they don't know anything that will help us." I stood. "I'm going to get a cup of tea." As I exited the room, the spirits followed. I stopped and pretended to adjust the strap on my sandal. "Ida, can you spy on the mayor and the people he works with?"

"We'd love to." She zoomed off and I continued on my way to the bar.

"One mint tea, hold the magic," Jezelle presented me with a white porcelain cup decorated with daisies.

I paused. "Can I trust you?"

She nodded and her fairy wings fluttered. "If I'd known how nice you'd turn out to be, I wouldn't have dosed you with magic."

"Is that an apology?" I asked.

She leaned on the bar and grinned. "It's as close as you're going to get."

"Works for me." I picked up my tea and sipped it. "You added the perfect amount of sugar."

"It's my gift," she said. "My cousin Bram told me how you helped the Greens children."

"That night was exhausting," I took another sip of tea. "But it felt like the right thing to do."

"Are you going to stay?" Jezelle asked.

I wasn't sure what she meant. "Here, now, or in Mystic Hills in general?"

"In Mystic Hills. Reed said you teach preschool."

"I do, and I'm not sure what I'm doing yet."

"If you go, no one fills the void to communicate with the recently deceased, but there are other preschool teachers out there."

"I thought there were others that spoke to the dead."

"None that Reed is symbiotic with," she said. "If you go, he's useless."

I couldn't help smiling. "You have no idea how ironic your word choice is."

"I tease Reed about being crabby, but he's a good man." The door opened and Jezelle stood up straight and frowned. "Unlike some people."

I turned to see Nathan headed for Reed's office. "He asked me to meet him."

"A word of advice." Jezelle touched my arm. "He can be all sorts of charming when he wants something."

I cringed. "Did you date him?"

"I've suppressed those memories," she said. "Heed my warning."

"Lisa Laddow said the same thing. You're in good company."

"We should form a support group and create public service announcements to warn other women away." She gave an evil grin. "It's my deepest desire to see him fall hard for someone who throws him away like a used Kleenex."

I laughed. "Too bad someone doesn't have a Karma gift."

Reed stuck his head out of the office doorway and waved impatiently at me.

"I'm being summoned."

"Good luck," Jezelle said.

I entered the room and didn't mention that a female spirit was floating in the corner. "Don't date him." She pointed at Nathan and then blinked out of existence. I suppressed a grin.

"Why did you want to meet with me?" I sat in the black leather chair, leaving Nathan to stand leaning against Reed's desk.

"I think you know." Nathan acted like he expected me to confess something.

"Nope." I sipped my tea and waited.

Nathan turned to Reed. "Did I seem off last night?"

Reed nodded. "At first I thought you'd been drinking."

"I had one martini. Everything went a

little fuzzy after that. I could see and hear what was going on, but I wasn't in the driver's seat and I couldn't speak."

"But you could write," I said.

He nodded. "I'm not sure who possessed me, but when I find out who did it, they will regret their actions."

"First question," I said. "Are you gifted or are you a witch?"

Gifted," Nathan said. "I can analyze situations and create logical arguments to persuade people to see my point of view."

"Who has the power to fully possess a gifted person?" I asked. "Would they use a spell or is it something they can just do?"

"It would take a powerful witch, and they would use a spell," Nathan said. "Which is why I purchased a protection charm that's supposed to ward off spells this morning." He pointed to his tie tack which was shaped like an arrow.

"Will that work?" I asked.

"For the amount I paid it should," he said. "To draw out whoever did this I want you to give the Tates their house back."

I sucked in a breath. "That's what I wanted last night, and you weren't happy about it."

"Giving the house back isn't a power move," Reed said.

"But it's believable," Nathan said. "Other people heard Belinda say she wanted to give the house back. It won't seem contrived."

"We need to let the Tates in on this," I said. "One of them could be possessed."

"Belinda, I think you'd be a good candidate for possession," Nathan said.

Chapter 16

"Excuse me?" Did he think I'd volunteer to let someone take over my body?

"Magically speaking, you're the weakest in the group," Nathan said.

I didn't appreciate his comment. "I might be the newest, but I'm not the weakest."

"Let me rephrase that so we can get past you being offended. You are the newest to magic and least likely to be able to block someone."

"That sounds better, but I'm still not a fan of this plan." If someone possessed me could I kick them out? "How do I know I can trust you? How do I know you're not setting me up for possession so someone can take over Sadie's estate?"

"My reputation is impeccable," Nathan stated like he was offended.

I laughed. "Your reputation as a lawyer is good, but your reputation as an empathetic or sympathetic human being is questionable at best. Just so you know, several people and spirits have told me not to trust you."

Nathan's jaw actually fell open. I'd never seen that before except in the movies. Red crept up his cheeks. Once he regained the power of speech he said, "What are you talking about?"

"Half the population of this town is female and you treat them like they are interchangeable instead of real people with real feelings. It doesn't paint you in a trustworthy light."

"You think the women I dated are credible witnesses? That's absurd."

I leaned toward him. "You chose them. You dated them. Did you think they were credible *before* you slept with them?"

"How did we end up on this topic?" Reed asked. "It's irrelevant. We're here to focus on the possession problem."

"You do it," I told Reed. "Set yourself up to be possessed. I believe Nathan would work to bring you back."

His eyebrows slammed together. "Are you insane?"

"It's okay for me to offer myself up to possession but it's insane for you. Why is that?"

"I didn't say it was a good idea for any-one," Reed snapped.

"I'll do it." Tina Tate stood in the door-way. "I want the house back, so whoever possesses me will get what they want. It should be easy for them to take me over since our goals are aligned." Tina smiled. "And just so you know, Nathan, the women in this town talk. If you don't clean up your act, you'll die alone without anyone to carry on your bloodline."

"I like you." I stood and walked over to her. "Want to go have lunch while these emotionally impaired males set this plan in motion?"

"I'd love to."

When we made it out onto the sidewalk, Tina chuckled. "That was fun. I've wanted to tell Nathan off for years. He dated my best friend for two months and then dropped her without so much as a phone call."

"He needs to grow up. If he wants to play the field, that's fine, but he needs to be honest and respectful."

"Where do you want to eat?" she asked.

"I've only been to Carson's. Is there a place where we could talk about the house transaction where the news will spread faster?"

"The more expensive the restaurant, the higher level the gossip. Let's go to *Chanda's*."

"One more question. Is there a spell you can buy to prevent possession or to trap someone who is trying to possess you?"

"Let's go see Ann Seacrest. I think she'll have what we need."

When we walked in the store, Ann smiled. "I thought I might be seeing you two."

"Why?"

"Nathan was in here earlier picking up an anti-spell tie tack. I heard you've been working with him to figure out the Tate's estate."

"She's giving us the house back," Tina said.

"That's wonderful." Ann pulled a pillow

of stick pins out of her display case. "These are small enough to wear without other people noticing." She lifted the collar of her blouse to show a small gold leaf stick pin. "This is a hex-shield pin."

"What do you carry that has to do with possession?" I asked.

She pointed at the pillow. "The silver circles repel. The gold squares allow you to communicate with the person while they're in possession of you, which is something only the strongest witches can do. It might convince the possessor to leave more quickly if you can tell him to get out."

I bought a silver one and Tina purchased a gold one. Ann put two silver pins in the bag she handed to me but only charged me for one. "Give one to Reed. I feel bad that I made him pay for the vampire bracelet."

TWENTY MINUTES LATER, we were in the lobby of an upscale restaurant, which featured crystal chandeliers above every table, waiting to be seated. I pretended my new green and blue asymmetrical dress was fancy enough for the occasion. I'd attached the silver pin to my bra strap because the dress didn't have a collar, but now the pin was poking me.

"Stop tugging at your dress," Tina said. "Project confidence."

"I'm confident I should have worn a different dress," I muttered.

She laughed like I'd said something funny and leaned in to whisper. "Follow my lead." In a normal voice, she said, "I can't tell you how thrilled I am about the house."

"All I ever wanted was the cat," I said. "She's such a sweet thing."

"Sadie is sweet?" She sounded genuinely surprised. "She used to shred my handbags if I left them on the floor."

"Maybe she thought they were toys? We haven't had any issues."

"I'm glad she found a good home with you. My Familiar is territorial. He wouldn't allow another animal in the house."

"Are all Familiars that way?" I asked.

"No. Their personalities differ just like people's do."

The hostess seated us. We ordered chicken Caesar salads and wine. Tina skillfully directed the conversation back to the house as often as possible.

Several women stopped by the table to ask how she was doing. Tina introduced me. Most of them seemed nice. It was hard to tell who was fake and who was real. I hoped Tina was real.

My phone buzzed with a text. I checked it and smiled. "Nathan will meet us at your house tonight at five."

Tina pulled out her phone. "Let me text my brother to make sure he can be there." Her phone buzzed with a response. "We're good to go."

We lingered over dessert to give someone more time to hear about our plan or maybe move in on Tina. As I finished off my last bite of pie, she froze for a second, and then blinked and looked around.

I pretended not to notice. "This the best apple pie I've ever eaten."

Tina's mouth opened and then closed, like the person controlling her was figuring out what strings to pull to make the puppet work. "The next time we come you should try the peach pie," she said. "It's my favorite."

When the waiter came over Tina insisted

on paying for my lunch. "It's the least I can do since you're giving us the house back."

"I'm happy to do it. Now I better get back to the tea house. I'll see you tonight."

On the walk back to *Tea & Spirits* questions ran through my mind. Who possessed Tina? Did they plan on letting her go after she signed for the house? Could someone have possessed Mrs. Tate to make her fall down the stairs? Holy Crap. Could someone have possessed Aunt Teresa to make her fall down the stairs?

My gut told me the mayor was involved, but that could be due to his scheming ways. Wait a minute. What happened to the possessor's body while they were controlling someone else? I started speed walking back to *Tea & Spirits* and once I crossed the threshold I jogged to Reed's office.

He glanced up at me from his laptop. "What now?"

"Is there a way to identify someone who is in the act of possession?"

"I don't know." He went back to his screen.

Not helpful. "Reed, this could be important. If a witch's spirit is on a walkabout, what happens to his or her body? If there are signs, like sitting and staring at nothing, we might be able to identify the bad guys."

He pushed his chair back from the desk and ran his hand through his hair. "I get it now, but I still don't have an answer."

"Who can we ask, because Mr. Evil has already taken over Tina."

"Already? Nathan texted that you weren't meeting til five." He glanced at his computer. "It's only one o'clock."

I bit down on my natural instinct to address him as Captain Obvious. "I know. Now we have time to find whoever is behind this." I pulled the extra stick pin out of my pocket. "This is an anti-possession pin for you."

"Thanks." He took the pin and tucked it in his shirt pocket.

Ida floated into the room. "I have news. The mayor and his wife had a huge fight in his office after lunch. She thinks he should give up his quest for the Tate's house since you're giving it back to the family."

"News travels fast," I said.

"What?" Reed said.

"Sorry. I'm talking to Ida. We'll relocate so you can get back to work." I followed Ida out of the office.

She drifted over to a table for two against the wall. Once we were seated, she said, "Someone who spoke to Tina at lunch called the mayor's wife and shared the news. While she had no qualms about stealing from a cat, she doesn't want to steal from Tina. The mayor was not pleased."

"Do you know what happens to a person who uses a possession spell...what happens to his body while his spirit is controlling someone else?"

Ida frowned. "Possession is despicable, unless you're trying to save someone who was knocked out in an accident, it's for lack of a stronger word, rude."

She hadn't answered my question. "How can you identify the rude person?"

"I had an uncle who used to do it as a trick at parties. His body shut down like he was sleeping, but he remained standing or sitting wherever he was. My mother warned him that one day he'd stretch the tether too far and then he'd be stuck outside of his body for good."

"That can happen?"

Ida nodded. "There are spells to stuff a spirit back where it belongs, but if no one is willing to help then the person is out of luck."

"Did your uncle listen to your mother?"

"No," Ida said. "And sure enough he drifted too far. She refused to help him back into his body until he swore never to do it again."

"Can you go back and check on the mayor to see if he's having an out of body experience?"

"I can, and I will but I bet he's paying someone else to do it. He wouldn't want to get caught with his hand in the cookie jar."

———

AT QUARTER TIL FIVE, I was freshly showered and dressed in jeans, a blouse, and sandals when Reed came into the house. The green blouse had been a strategic choice since it had a collar perfect for hiding the anti-possession pin.

"Any news from Ida about who has taken over Tina?" he asked.

"No, which means even if the mayor is behind it he's not the one in possession of Tina. Ida has been sticking to him like glue all day."

When we arrived at the Tate's house, Reed parked on the street in the same spot he did the last time. Hopefully we wouldn't leave the house running tonight.

The front door was open, so we entered and headed for the dining room to join Nathan, Tina, and Tim. Reed sat on the far side of the table by Nathan. I sat in the open spot next to Tina.

"Belinda" Tim said. "Before we start, I wanted to apologize for my behavior on Main Street. I was drunk and grieving and angry. That's no excuse, but I am sorry."

I nodded. While I accepted his apology, I'd never trust someone who threatened to hurt me or an animal.

Nathan pulled a stack of papers out of his briefcase. "This new agreement states that Belinda is returning everything but a small stipend for Sadie's care." He passed it to me. I scanned the page and saw I'd receive two hundred dollars a month for Sadie. That would be more than enough for food and any vet bills that might come up. If Sadie went to a vet. Maybe she saw a doctor in human form. This world was so complicated. "Looks good to me."

"I'd like to read it before we sign." Tina

plucked the papers from my hand. She read each page and then said, "I think we should add a clause which states if a Tate does not reside in the house it will be turned over to the mayor."

"Why would we do that?" Tim asked.

"It's what mother would have wanted," Tina said.

"That's ridiculous. We both have children who could inherit the house. It stays in the family," Tim said.

Nathan reached for the papers which Tina grudgingly released. He handed me a pen. "Sign and we can all go home."

I signed the paperwork. Tim added his signature.

Tina frowned and pushed back from the table. "I'm not signing."

"Technically, you don't need to," Nathan said. "The way I wrote up the contract, one Tate's signature is enough."

Eyes narrowed, Tina turned on him. "You think you're so smart."

"Are you feeling all right sis?" Tim asked. "You're not acting like yourself."

"I'm not?" She laughed, like he was being ridiculous. "Maybe this is the new me."

"We're all sure it's not," Nathan said. "Whoever you are, why don't you leave Tina's body. You've lost this round."

"Oh really." Tina slumped forward and then Nathan jerked backwards like he'd been shoved.

"Sorry, you're no longer welcome here," Nathan said.

Something slammed into my chest, knocking my chair back a few inches, but my anti-possession pin worked.

Tim lifted his shirt collar to show his pin. "Don't even try it."

Reed sat frozen. I realized he was wearing a different shirt than the one he'd worn this morning.

"I gave him an anti-possession pin too," I said. "You have nowhere to go."

Reed jerked backwards as the possessor called my bluff. Laughter poured out of Reed's mouth. "Someone forgot his pin."

"What's the point?" I asked. "The contract has been signed. Let Reed go."

"The point is you keep messing around where you shouldn't. Just like your aunt. Keep it up and you might have your own accident."

Anger surged inside of me. "Did you kill her?"

"Did I?" He laughed. "Maybe I did. I do what I want, and no one can stop me." He stood. "Maybe I'll climb up to the roof and have Reed jump off."

I would not let that happen. I had to distract him until I could figure something out. "You're a coward." I stood and blocked his path. "You hide behind other people's faces."

"A true genius, someone with real power, manipulates others to do their bidding." He spun in a circle and smiled. "I'm in total control. You have no power. You're just a girl with a useless gift."

Gifts. Wait a minute. "Reed, glow."

Reed convulsed and fell to the floor. Pinpricks of light shot from his body. The light wasn't very bright. I dropped to my knees and grabbed his hand. "You can do it. Glow."

Warmth flowed between us, and the light brightened. Just as quickly it dimmed.

"He can't kick me out." The possessor said, "He's not strong enough."

"He's not trying to kick you out. He's trying to cross you over."

The possessor laughed. "Not a chance."

The light faded to barely a glimmer.

Reed might not be able to cross him over, but maybe I could pull him in. I closed my eyes and imagined a waiting room with concrete walls, solid and sturdy. No doors, and no exit. Just a shoe box sized window lined with bars. I wrapped both of my hands around Reed's and pulled at the spirit.

"What are you doing?" he asked. "You're too weak to evict me."

I pulled harder, and my hands started to tingle. "I'm not trying to evict you. I'm sending you to time out."

"Let go of me." He yanked Reed's hand from mine.

Didn't matter, I was holding onto the possessor's spirit. An outline took form. "I can see you."

"Let go." His spirit glowed red.

The tingling sensation in my hands doubled and morphed into a searing burn. I gritted my teeth against the pain. It felt like I'd stuck my hand in a fire. I cried out but held on and then I shoved as hard as I could. A spirit appeared in my waiting room. It was Kyle Carter glowing orange, with black eyes but I recognized him.

"What is this?" He turned in a circle. "Let me out." His voice was his own now, thank goodness. Hearing him talk in Reed's voice had been disturbing.

"Did you kill my aunt?" I asked as I reinforced the walls with cinder blocks.

"You can't do this." He snarled and threw himself against the walls.

Apparently, I could. "Answer my question, and I'll let you out."

"You'll never prove anything," he said.

"That sounds like a confession."

"I will get out of here and I will kill you," he railed.

A wave of heat rolled over me. "Wait too long to confess, and you won't be able to get back to your body. Is this how you want to die?"

"You dare threaten me? You're nothing."

"Wrong. I'm a Harbinger. I can keep you here long enough for your connection to fade. Long enough for them to put your body in a crypt."

"Belinda?" Reed's voice sounded far away.

"It's okay," I said. The smell of something burning made me gag. What was that?

"Whatever you're doing. Stop." Reed bellowed.

"Can't." I whispered.

Something cold and wet dripped onto my arms.

"Belinda, please," Reed said. "Please. Let it go."

The please made me take notice. It made me tune into the pain I'd been ignoring. The pain that engulfed both my arms. I took one last look at Kyle Carter and then I sucked in a breath and opened my eyes.

Reed held me against his chest, just like in the jewelry store. He was glowing again, but this time he looked terrified.

"I'm back," I whispered.

"Don't try to move," Reed said. "We've called for a healer."

"What's wrong?" Why was he so freaked out?

"I performed a pain blocking spell," Tina was seated beside me. "Let me know if it starts to wear off."

"Why? What happened?"

"You helped me cross him over, or kick him out," Reed said. "Either way he's gone."

That wasn't right. I could still hear Kyle

screaming like a small insane voice in the back of my head.

"He fought hard," Reed looked away. "You took the brunt of the blast. Your arms..."

I glance down. My arms were covered with wet towels. Why were my arms covered in towels? And what was the burning smell?

Healer Bram rushed into the room, squatted down beside me, and pulled several bottles out of his bag.

"Are you going to ask me to smell those?" I tried to make a joke.

"Belinda, keep your eyes on Reed." Bram's face was devoid of any expression. "Tina, move the towels."

What were they going on about? I glanced up at Reed, but the fear on his face had me looking down at my arms, or what used to be my arms. The flesh was blistered, and burned, and blackened in places. Once I saw it, once the reality set it, panic exploded through my body. I flailed. My torso and legs responded, but my arms did nothing. They didn't even twitch.

"Sedate her," Bram ordered.

Tina poured something into my mouth. I coughed and gagged, and then a haze settled over me. I watched impartially as Bram collected blood from Reed and mixed it in the copper bowl. When he held it to my lips, I tasted cinnamon and whiskey. A wave of something calm and cool flowed over me.

"I will get out of here," Kyle yelled. "I will get out of here and I will burn you alive. Do you hear me?"

I ignored him. If I engaged with his spirit now in this weakened state, it wouldn't end well. Not that this had gone well. Still he was on hold, and I would leave him there until he confessed. He wasn't going anywhere.

"Did you hear me?" he screamed.

"Reed, talk to me. Distract me."

"Let's see. When you were nine, I taught you how to skateboard, or I tried. You fell off, a lot. We switched to bikes. You were much better at those."

"I don't remember," I said.

"Don't worry. We can make new memories."

Reed told me about time we spent together as kids. After awhile the words ran together and become distorted, but I liked listening to the sound of his voice.

"You must rest now," Bram said.

Sleep sounded good, but I didn't want to sleep on the floor at the Tate's house. "Home," I said. "Take me home."

"To your parents?" Reed asked.

"No. To Lilly." Someone lifted me, and then I was lying on something soft. Something warm and furry nestled against my legs. Must be Sadie. Home. It was good to be home.

Chapter 17

Whispers buzzed around me like annoying mosquitoes. I did my best to ignore them, to stay wrapped in a cocoon of sleep. Little by little the voices became louder. Why wouldn't they go away? All I wanted to do was sleep. Sleep and recover from...what...I couldn't remember.

The voices grew louder, crawling in around the edges of my mind, making it impossible to ignore them.

"Belinda, we need to talk. I know you can hear me."

Who was that?

The voice sounded familiar. I opened my eyes. Healer Bram sat on a stool next to my bed.

"There you are," he said. "Do you re-member what happened?"

It was a little fuzzy. "Something bad?" I croaked.

"Something unfortunate," he said, "but treatable. Can you sit up?"

I pushed with my arms, or I tried to. They responded in slow motion. My head felt fuzzy, like I was on pain killers. It took twice as long as normal but I managed to sit up with my back against the headboard.

"Good job." He offered me a glass of something pearlescent and pink. "Drink this."

I trusted him. Whatever was in the glass would make me feel better. I reached for it. My hand and my arm were bright red and the skin was peeling like I'd had the mother of all sunburns. Still, I was able to take the glass, so I drank the potion. It tasted like cin-namon. "What happened?"

"You're disoriented from the healing po-tions," he said. "What do you remember?"

Good question. What did I remember? "Something about the house, and Tina and Reed yelling at me."

"You helped Reed kick the possessor out," Bram said.

That didn't sound right. I glanced down at my arms as bits and pieces came back to me. "Touching his spirit felt like holding onto fire."

"Do you know who he was?"

I'd known the man. Who was he? One fact stood out. "He killed Teresa."

"What?" Bram sat forward. "Are you sure?"

I nodded. "He taunted me. Said I'd have an accident like her." More memories flooded back. "He said Reed wasn't strong enough. I helped." How had I helped?

"You did, and he burned your arms, but we healed them. You'll need to continue daily potions to strengthen your tendons and muscles, but in the end they will be good as new."

That part was good. "What about...?" My thought processes were fuzzy. There was something I should be concerned about. What was it?

"You have nothing to worry about. Reed contacted the police and told them about the possessor and how you evicted him."

"I'm still here," An angry voice bellowed, startling me. I flinched. His voice brought it all back. Kyle was in my waiting room, where I'd trapped him.

"What's wrong?" Bram asked.

Should I tell him about Kyle? I trusted him, but I didn't trust the police or the mayor to do the right thing if I released Kyle. "Sorry. It was a weird twinge," I said. "My head hurts."

"Finish the potion, it will help."

I downed the rest of it and handed him the glass. "Can I go back to sleep?" I needed to speak with Kyle.

"Yes. I'll send Dave in with another potion in an hour."

"Thanks."

Bram exited the room. I closed my eyes and visualized my waiting room, making certain I was on the outside of the cement box. Kyle's face appeared in the bar lined window. His outline was hazy and his eyes were dark empty sockets.

"You're weak," he said.

"Judging by appearances, so are you," I said. "I'm regaining my strength, but you'll only grow weaker. Are you ready to confess?"

"Other's will come after you," he said.

"If you keep me here and I die, they will hunt you down."

"That's the funny part. Everyone thinks I kicked you out. Reed thinks he crossed you over. No one is looking for you."

The empty sockets where his eyes should be, glowed red, but he remained silent.

"How much time do you think you have left?" I asked him.

"Belinda, what are you doing?" Sadie's voice sounded nearby. I pulled away from the waiting room and opened my eyes. Sadie sat on the bed, in cat form, studying me. "Where were you just now?"

I yawned. "Dreaming, maybe. The potions are making my head fuzzy."

"Please don't lie to me. I could feel a malevolent presence."

I trusted Sadie, so I told her about Kyle. "I know he killed Aunt Teresa."

She hissed. "You think he killed my Genevieve?"

"It's possible. If not I bet he knows who did. What should I do?"

"He's the Mayor's right hand man. Even if he confesses the police won't touch him."

"So, no justice for Genevieve, the Greens, or my aunt." That wasn't right. I checked the clock on the nightstand. "It's been almost twenty-four hours since his spirit left his body. How much longer until he can't go home?"

"I'm not sure."

I needed some advice, and there was only one person I could ask. "Aunt Teresa, can you come speak to me?"

Her spirit appeared in the room. She was more fully formed than before. I could see the wrinkles around her eyes when she smiled. Of course her smile dimmed when she took in my condition. "What happened?"

I filled her in on my injuries, my suspicions about Kyle, and his current location.

At first, she didn't respond. She shimmered and became brighter, more solid looking. "He possessed me and threw my body down the stairs?" She shook her head. "I never saw that coming. Thank you, Belinda. At least now I know how I died."

"What should I do with Kyle?"

"Genevieve Tate, can you join us please?" she called out.

She appeared next to my aunt. "Sadie, you look happy."

"I am." Sadie walked down the length of the bed.

Genevieve ran her fingers over Sadie's body. "It's lovely to see you, but I'm sure Teresa didn't call me for a social visit."

"How do you feel about a little vengeance?" Aunt Teresa asked.

"You figured out who killed us?" Genevieve said.

"Kyle Carter is in my waiting room."

"That lying, backstabbing, weasel of a man," Genevieve said. "Give him to me."

"If I let him out, won't he just go back to his body or cross over?"

"You misunderstand," Aunt Teresa said. "We don't want you to let him out. We're going to take your waiting room over to the other side. He can live out his afterlife in a cell. Because if you let him out here there will be no justice."

The screaming in the back of my head took on a fevered pitch. "He's panicking."

"Good," Genevieve said.

Spending eternity in a cell wasn't something I'd wish on anyone. "Is there another way? I'm not sure anyone deserves that."

"He killed both of us," Genevieve said. "Probably the Green's too."

"Let's take a vote," Aunt Teresa said. "James and Evie Green, we know who killed you. Come join us for some justice."

James and Evie appeared in the room. "You figured it out?" Evie said.

"Kyle Carter," Genevieve said.

"That conniving rat," James said. "Where is he?"

Evie smiled. "And what can we do to him?"

I explained the situation.

"We're going to take a vote to decide his fate," Aunt Teresa said.

"You could turn him in to the police," I said.

"Or we can keep him trapped in the waiting room and take him to the other side," Genevieve said. "He can serve his jail time over there."

Did that mean they'd eventually let him out? I was afraid to ask.

Evie drifted closer to me. "You're a good person. I can see you're conflicted. Kyle stole my children and my grandchildren from me. I can visit them in spirit form, of course, but I'll never hold them in my arms again."

"I call a vote," Aunt Teresa said. "All in favor of crossing Kyle over raise your hand."

All four ghosts raised their hands. They were avenging their own deaths, finding their own form of justice.

Kyle screamed obscenities in my head.

"We'll let you take it from here," James said. He and Evie faded and disappeared.

"Okay. How do we do this?" I asked.

"I can take possession of your waiting room," Aunt Teresa said. "But I'll be taking a part of you. You'll be in a weakened state."

I laughed. "That's where I am right now, so at least no one will be suspicious."

"Thank you, for all of your help," Aunt Teresa said. "Knowing how I died…well I'd rather be alive, but this gives me peace of mind."

"Good." A happy warmth filled my chest. I'd done it. I'd helped my aunt find closure and brought her killer to justice of a sort.

"Hold onto that happy attitude," Genevieve said. "This might hurt."

Aunt Teresa frowned. "It shouldn't be too bad because you're already on pain potions. Close your eyes."

"Promise you'll come back and visit soon?"

She nodded. "Yes."

I closed my eyes and something cold flowed over me. Goosebumps broke out all over my body until I was frozen in place. How much worse was this going to get? My heart hammered in my chest and then it felt like someone drove an icicle into my right temple. I screamed, but my mouth was frozen shut. The sound I produced was nothing compared to the screeching coming from Kyle's cage. I could see his face through the barred window. His spirit writhed like it was in agony.

Pressure built in my head and then it felt like someone yanked the icicle from my right temple which was painful and disturbing in a whole other way. Since my mouth was now unfrozen my scream echoed off the walls of the room.

I heard footsteps running toward me and then Dave and Victor were in the room shouting questions.

"Pain potion. Now." Sadie demanded.

Dave pulled a vial from his pocket and put it to my lips. I drank the contents in one long swallow and then closed my eyes, leaving Sadie to explain what happened.

Sometime later, I woke to the smell of

bacon. "You need to eat." Sadie stood next to my bed, in human form, holding a tray.

With great care I pushed myself up into a seated position. A dull pain radiated through my arms and head. I'd take that over the ice pick to the skull feeling any day.

I took the tray she held out to me and set it on my lap. Bacon, buttered wheat toast, a glass of orange juice, and a cup of coffee looked delicious. My stomach growled. "Thank you." I made fast work of my food and drank the orange juice and coffee.

"Are you in your right mind?" Sadie asked.

"Since I find that question amusing, I'm going to say yes."

"You can't tell anyone about what happened to Kyle."

"Not even Victor, Reed, and Dave?"

"Especially not them. Healer Bram and Reed believe you kicked Kyle out or crossed him over. That was an act of self-defense because possession is illegal. Damning his spirit to imprisonment on the other side is no less than he deserved but it would be seen as a crime."

Had I damned him to his own personal hell for eternity? Maybe. Did I feel bad about that? Kind of, but he had threatened to burn me alive. He was not a nice person. "What do Dave and Victor think happened when I screamed?"

"They aren't sure. I suggested it was a nightmare. You fell peacefully asleep after drinking another potion, so I don't think they'll suspect anything."

Footsteps sounded in the hallway. Dave stuck his head in the door. "You look much better today."

"Thank you. I feel better."

"Scared the life out of us last night when you screamed," Dave glanced at Sadie and then back at me. "Was it a nightmare?"

"I'm not sure." I held up my right arm. The skin was red but no longer peeling. "I think I was dreaming about the fire."

"Well, your arms look much better. Maybe we should get you a potion for a peaceful night's sleep."

"That's a good idea. Right now, all I want is a shower and some clean clothes."

Dave pulled two vials from his pocket. "Both of those are doable, after you take these. The white one is pain medication and the pink one is to strengthen your muscles and tendons."

"Thank you." I drank one after the other and my pain lessened.

"Let me know if you need anything else." Dave left the room.

"He's such a wonderful man," Sadie said in a wistful tone.

"He is," I said. "And you two make a cute couple."

She blushed and then said, "Let's get you into the shower."

Half an hour later, I was clean and somewhat presentable. Sadie helped me down the stairs to the living room. I kept a tight grip on the rail just in case Kyle had friends looking to avenge his death.

Chapter 18

My brain wouldn't stop spinning questions about Kyle and the mayor but my body felt sluggish. It was an odd combination. I sat on the couch in the living room trying to calm my anxiety. What if someone found out? I envied Sadie and Dave napping contentedly in their chair in cat form while I mentally flailed around dreaming up stressful scenarios where the mayor found out about everything and threw me in jail or worse.

I needed a distraction, so I went into the kitchen and grabbed a cookbook featuring some of Aunt Teresa's favorite cakes. Part of me wanted to bake something from scratch to honor her memory, and part of me just wanted to ask Lilly to do it since I could see

Aunt Teresa any time I wanted in spirit form. Common sense won out.

I laid the cookbook open on the page for German Chocolate cheesecake. "Lilly, can you make this, and bake it in the oven so I can smell it cooking?" Half the fun of baking was the smell.

The lights flashed twice and the smell of chocolate and cheesecake filled the air. While it cooked I made a pot of coffee.

Half an hour later when the cake was ready, Dave and Sadie joined me in the kitchen. He shifted to human form, while she hopped onto the table, flopped down, and licked her front paw.

The cake appeared on the table along with plates and forks.

"Thank you, Lilly." I cut a piece for myself and a piece for Dave. I assumed the fact that Sadie stayed in cat form meant she wasn't interested.

I took a bite of the cake and sighed in satisfaction. The German chocolate icing, chocolate cake and cheesecake base were an awesome combination.

"This is a glorious cake," Dave said. "I was a cat for so long I forgot how good it was." He pulled an orange vial from his pocket and took a sip. "Lactose tolerance spell," he explained.

"Is there a spell that sets your weight at a certain level, like you'd set a thermostat? Because I might need something like that if I keep asking Lilly to bake for me."

"That is an interesting idea," Dave said. "Not sure how it would work but I'd buy it. I've been eating more as a human because there is more variety. Does this line of thought mean you're thinking of staying?"

Was I? Mystic Hills truly was a dangerous place. I'd learned that painful lesson several times over. "Is there at least some sort of limit on the life-threatening painful accidents one citizen can have per month, because with the vampire bracelet and the burnt arms I think I've met my quota."

"You definitely have," Dave said, "In all seriousness though, when it comes to Mystic Hills, there's one thing you must remember, it doesn't have to be all or nothing. You can live in both worlds. Go teach during the school year and then come back over the summers. We'll take care of Lilly while you're gone."

The kitchen lights flashed.

"Are you saying you'd be okay with that Lilly?"

The lights flashed twice.

"Sadie what do you think?" I asked.

She stopped licking her paw. "I could go with you, or I could stay here. I'd prefer to stay. If you came home one weekend a month to maintain our bond, it shouldn't be an issue."

Could I balance a life between the real world and Mystic Hills? Was it worth it? What happened to Sadie if I chose the real world full time? "Not that I plan to do this, but what happens if I go back to my old life? Is there another witch you could bond with?"

Sadie stood and stretched. "Maybe I could bond with Reed. He stops by often enough that our connection would maintain itself, but I really hope you don't cut us out of your life."

"I don't want to." I reached out and rubbed her ears.

"Your positive perspective and your kindness are a breath of fresh air," Dave said. "Victor has barely spoken to me since I accidentally became his Familiar. He thinks I tricked him into it."

"No, that was me. It was necessary at the time to protect you from Tina."

"Tina is no longer a threat," Sadie pointed out.

"No," Dave said. "But I don't want to give up my human form. I enjoy reading books and eating different food." He reached over and ran his hand down Sadie's back. "I know you prefer this form and I appreciate all the time you spend in your human form for my benefit."

"You're welcome, my love," Sadie said.

It gave me a warm fuzzy to witness their interactions. Which reminded me of something else. "Have you ever thought it's mainly Victor and Reed that are crabby? The other people I've met haven't been nearly as gloom and doom."

"Victor and Reed are both pessimists," Dave said. "But they are good people."

"I wish they were happier people."

"They've both lost a lot in this life," Dave said. "It's made them cynical. I think you'd be good for Reed. While Victor cares for you, he thinks it would be better if you left."

That must have been what they were talking about when I overheard their conversation from the pantry. "I still need to confront my mother about her part in all of this. She never should've made me choose between her and Mystic Hills. I might be able to forgive her for that, but she didn't keep her word about bringing me back in a year. She stole my choice."

I TOOK naps on and off for the rest of the day. Healer Bram checked in on me. Thankfully nothing exciting occurred. There was no longer a mad man screaming in the back of my head, but there was a voice telling me I needed to be careful. Kyle had powerful connections in this town. The peaceful dream potion Dave gave me allowed me to sleep without focusing on that disturbing fact.

The next morning, I yearned for a fresh new perspective on life, so I put my breakfast on a tray and took it up to the roof top terrace. One of my favorite parts of summer vacation was sitting in my PJ's, drinking coffee, and watching the world go by. Today's pajamas were covered in llamas wearing sombreros. Every time I looked at the pattern it made me smile. From my vantage point, I watched people go about their daily routine. Cars came and went down the winding streets in a normal manner.

Once I finished my omelet, I realized I should have brought the laptop up here with me. Maybe Lilly could help. "Lilly, can you make my laptop appear up here? If not, that's okay." I didn't want to make her feel bad if that wasn't within her powers.

My computer appeared on the roof beside me. "Lilly, you are the best." If she could make the computer appear up here, maybe I didn't need to sit on the wooden terrace. "Can I have a small patio table and a chair?"

A small white wrought iron table and two wrought iron chairs with purple cushions appeared next to me.

"Lilly, I'm pretty sure I love you."

A battery-operated candle appeared on the table and blinked twice. I put my tray and my laptop on the table and went to work. If I decided to stay, I still wanted to teach. I opened the laptop and surfed the town internet for information on their school district. Google, it was not. After a few false starts, I found the district website. Unfortunately, it didn't include preschool information. Maybe the preschools were private instead of public. With my early childhood degree, I could teach PreK through second grade. There weren't any job openings posted. In a small town like this, people probably stayed in the same position until they retired. What if there weren't any teaching jobs? Could I work online? Not with Mystic Hills limited internet.

Lilly was amazing, but the money for the groceries she bought had to come from somewhere. How did you pay bills in Mystic Hills? Once again, I needed a dang manual or at least a brochure.

Even if I figured out the money situation there was the problem of Reed. When he wasn't being a condescending jerk, he made my heart skip a beat.

"Hello?" A masculine voice called out from the fire escape.

Think of the devil. "Up here."

Reed joined me and sat in the extra chair, like he wasn't surprised to find furniture. He pointed at my pajama bottoms. "Those aren't unicorns."

"Today, I am wearing llamas."

"Interesting choice."

"Thanks." I closed the laptop. "What's up?"

"I wanted to check in on you. My dad said you were almost good as new, but he didn't give me any details." He reached across the table and traced his finger along the exposed skin of my wrist. "Your arms," he swallowed. "I've never seen anything like that. It was horrific."

My skin tingled from his touch. "It wasn't fun."

He moved his hand away. "It was my fault. I forgot the anti-possession pin when I changed shirts after work. If I'd had it, you wouldn't have needed to save me." Guilt bled through his voice. "You wouldn't have been hurt."

"True," I desperately wanted to tell him the truth, to explain that I'd found Aunt Teresa's murderer and that he was rotting in a cell, so it was all sort of worth it. Sadie's warning stuck in my head. "We got rid of the possessor, and I'm all healed up now so it's okay."

He shook his head. "There's that annoying optimism."

"It's working in your favor, Smarty pants, so go with it."

"You're right. I'll go with it." He tapped his fingers on the table. "I'm kind of surprised we haven't heard about someone being in a coma or dying in their sleep."

"Would we hear, if it was a powerful witch, or would they close ranks and keep it to themselves?"

"Probably the latter. On to another topic, customers at *Tea & Spirits* have asked about your hours for contacting spirits. You should post a flier, so they know when to come in."

That might be one way to cover my expenses. "Not to be rude, but do people pay for readings?"

"Of course," he said.

"Good, because I'm not sure if there are any openings in the Mystic Hills school district. I checked the website…"

He looked at me like I had omelet on my face.

"What?" I wiped my mouth in case I was a mess. "Is there something on my face?"

"No."

"Back to the readings at the teahouse. Do they pay enough to cover groceries?"

"That depends on you. Teresa charged people forty bucks for twenty minutes."

"Oh." I had no idea if that was a reasonable rate. "When do people come in for readings?" I didn't want to hang around the tearoom all day if people only came in occasionally.

"It varies, but if you post hours, the regulars will show up once a week."

"Okay. I'll come in this afternoon and post a schedule."

Reed turned away from me and looked down at the street. His dark wavy hair was just long enough to be ruffled in the morning breeze. What was he thinking about?

"Since we're tossing out random questions, if I left, would you still be able to cross people over?"

He kept his eyes on the street. "I'd manage."

"You could set up office hours for ghosts," I teased. "If you glowed every day at a certain time, the ghosts could find you."

"Are you leaving?" he asked.

"I'm still working on that. Dave and Sadie said I could come back one weekend a month during the school year to maintain the Familiar bond."

"So, you'd help ghosts once a month?" Reed asked.

Crap. I hadn't thought about that. Should I lie? "I didn't take that into consideration. Does that make me an awful person?"

"No." He turned to look at me and sincerity shone from his warm brown eyes. "I keep telling you this is a dangerous place. After what happened, you know how bad it can get. I'm not sure you should stay. You're too good for this town. That was one of the reasons I liked you when we were kids. You didn't live under the same cloud we all did. You were happy and optimistic."

Did he mean when we were children or when we dated? I searched his face for some clue but didn't find one. I wasn't sure what to say, so I went with the truth. "I don't remember everything that happened here, but for whatever reason I feel drawn to you."

"It's always been there. This pull between us." He shook his head. "After you left, I told myself it was for the best because you'd see what the outside world was like and you could make up your mind about what you wanted. When you didn't come back a year later like you promised, I figured that was your answer."

I reached over and touched his hand. "If I'd known about you, I would've come back."

He gave a sad smile and pulled his hand away. "But you didn't, and we're different people now."

"Are we?" I asked. "You still glow at me. Doesn't that count for something?"

He laughed. "I can't tell you how mad that made me when you first came back. It was like my magic betrayed me."

"And now?" I tried to keep the hope out of my voice, because the odds were not in my favor.

"Now?" he sounded confused.

The answer was going to flatten me, and I knew it, but my heart held out a tiny bit of hope. One way or another I needed to hear him say it. "Now…is there any scenario where you'd give me another chance?"

His eyebrows slammed together. "How could I ever trust you again? You just told me you don't know if you're staying or coming back once a month."

He was right. He couldn't count on me

to be there for him. It wasn't fair. "I understand."

"No," He leaned closer and stared into my eyes. "You don't, because you don't remember. I do. I remember everything. I remember what it felt like to hold you in my arms. I remember your touch…your taste. I remember all of it…and I waited." He laughed. "I believed you'd come back."

Tears filled my eyes. "I would have come back— "

"But you didn't." He scooted his chair back. "And I can never trust you again. Even if you stay. And that's why you should leave." He pushed to his feet and headed for the stairs.

He wasn't wrong but that didn't make it hurt any less. I sucked in a breath and then let the tears fall. He'd never give me another chance. I'd hurt him too badly. Even if I hadn't meant to do it. The way he'd looked at me. I swiped at my eyes. The way he looked at me meant we'd been in love. And now that was gone. Which sucked.

At least now I knew where I stood. Staying here would mean watching Reed live his life with someone else. Leaving would mean never seeing him again. I wasn't sure which was worse.

———

ONCE I'D SHOWERED, and dressed, I picked up my flip phone and dialed my mom. Might as well get all the painful conversations over in one day.

My mother picked up on the third ring. "Hello, Linda."

I flinched. That no longer seemed like my name. "Hello, mom."

"You sound stressed."

"I am." This was going to suck. "I have my memories back from four years ago, when you gave me the ultimatum."

There was a beat of silence, and then she said, "I can explain."

"I sort of understand why you did it, but you promised to bring me back a year later. You didn't. That's the part I'm having trouble with."

"You were happy here. Why would I send you back to that terrible place?"

"Because it was the right thing to do. You should have let me decide. I promised Reed I'd come back. You made me a liar."

"Oh, please. You'd only dated the boy for a few months. It was a summer romance." Her tone wasn't defensive, it was patronizing. I would have preferred defensive.

"Mother, Reed and I are symbiotic. We're meant to work together. We're meant to be together."

"That's ridiculous. Teresa loved Johnathon. Her magic was symbiotic with Victors and they were just coworkers."

"Wrong. They started out that way but ended up in a relationship. They were together for years."

My mother sucked in a breath. "She never told me, not that it matters now. You can be mad at me all you want. Nothing good happens in Mystic Hills. Ever. You can't trust anyone. They're all out for themselves."

She sounded like Reed and Victor, which was odd because she'd always been a positive person. "Growing up here must have been miserable for you."

"You have no idea." She sounded close to tears. "I hate you being there. When are you coming home?"

"I don't know." I sniffled. "I haven't quit my teaching job, if that's any consolation."

"It's not." She sniffled and then laughed. "Can we talk about something else?"

"Yes, please."

She caught me up on everything they'd been doing, and I told her about Sadie, the estate, and turning everything back over to Tina and her brother. I left out the part about possession, my arms almost being burned off, and the fact that Sadie was a Familiar.

By the end of the call, I felt like my mom and I were back on track. I couldn't be mad at her for wanting to protect me. After ending the call, I lay back on my bed and stared at the ceiling. I was done with drama. I'd deal with the tea house later.

Chapter 19

It took two days for me to work up a schedule for the tearoom. Okay that was a lie. It took two days for me to feel like I could talk to Reed without arguing or tearing up. I couldn't blame him for how he felt. He was right. I had the equivalent of an unrequited crush, and he'd dealt with a broken heart. If I stayed in Mystic Hills I'd interact with him daily, so time to suck it up and act like an adult.

Armed with a schedule I'd written on lilac paper I'd found in Aunt Teresa's room, I drove to *Tea & Spirits*. When I entered the tearoom, Jezelle waved me over to the bar.

I pointed at the paper I held and then at Reed's door. I'd clear this with him first and then have a drink. Saying I needed to talk to Jezelle would give me a reason to leave his office.

As I walked across the hardwood floor, a pale spirit with indistinct features drifted towards me. Where Ida seemed full of life and humor, this person seemed faded for lack of a better term.

"Can I help you?"

"Tired," the spirit mumbled. "So tired."

Maybe it was a ghost instead of a spirit. "Would you like to cross over?"

"Scared." The word came out as a whisper.

"I'll take you to Reed. He can help."

The ghost didn't respond.

I walked slowly, not wanting to scare him off. "Follow me. It's not far. This way."

Reed glanced up when I crossed the threshold into his office and frowned. "Did you make a schedule?"

"Yes." I set it on his desk. "I also have a ghost who'd like to cross over." I sat on the black leather chair and held out my hand.

"Seriously?"

"No. I missed you and wanted to hold your hand."

He snorted and then came out from behind the desk and laced his fingers through mine.

"Are you ready?" Reed asked.

The ghost didn't answer.

"How long ago did you pass?" I asked.

"So long…" The ghost sighed. "Too long. Couldn't figure it out."

"Figure out what?" Reed asked.

"Where I'm going," the ghost said.

"You're going someplace to rest. Someplace you'll be at peace." Reed started to glow, becoming brighter and brighter. Maybe the ghost would cross over, maybe he wouldn't.

I shut my eyes. Warmth flowed over me. This connection we had was nice. If nothing else happened between us, we'd still have this.

"What are you doing here?" a familiar voice asked.

I opened my eyes. "Aunt Teresa? Did I accidentally call you?"

"No," she sounded alarmed. "You're on the other side, with me. You crossed over."

"What?" I jumped up and spun around. I was in a replica of the Reed's office and I could see and hear him below, talking to my body. It was like looking in a mirror.

"Belinda, stop fooling around," Reed said.

"I'm not fooling around," I snapped.

"He can't hear you," Aunt Teresa said. "How did this happen? What were you doing?"

I told her about the faded ghost as I watched Reed put his hand on my shoulder and shake me.

"Can I dive back in?" I asked.

"Try," Aunt Teresa said.

I focused on the scene below willing myself to drift back to my body. Didn't work. Maybe I should close my eyes. I squeezed my eyelids shut. Maybe this was like one of those freaky dreams where you knew you were asleep and you needed to wake up before a monster crashed through your bedroom door. I slowed my breathing and focused on sinking down into my body. It would be okay. I could do this.

"Belinda, you're still here," Aunt Teresa said.

My pulse kicked up a notch. "I know. I'm trying to think my way back down there. It's not working."

Reed grabbed his phone and dialed. I could hear him shouting at Healer Bram.

"He's really upset," I muttered.

"Of course he is," Aunt Teresa said. "You're his one true love."

"What?"

"You're fated to be together."

"Then why does he keep pushing me away?"

"You broke his heart," Aunt Teresa stated.

"Not on purpose."

"It's still your fault. True love would have found a way. His misery and pain are all on you."

Wait a minute. Aunt Teresa would never speak to me like that. "You're not real," I said. "None of this is real." It dawned on me. "This is a waiting room. I didn't cross over."

"It will be real if you can't find the exit." Her voice changed as she spoke. She no longer sounded like my aunt.

"Who are you? Why are you doing this?"

"Even if I can't prove it, I know you and Reed were responsible for the death of my friend. I waited and waited for his spirit to return to his body. He never came back. To-day, Reed will watch you die, just like I watched my friend die. This is vengeance."

She disappeared. Just blipped out of existence.

No. No. No. How did I get out of here? It was a waiting room. Maybe I could create a door. I reached for the wall and visualized a door. Nothing happened. Come on. Think. This was a puzzle. I could do this. Maybe the witch had blocked obvious things like doors and window, maybe I could make a hatch in the floor.

I focused on the floor below me and visualized an opening. Nothing happened. Below me, in the real office, Healer Bram dashed into the room and pulled out bottles of powder. He cut my finger and collected blood in a bowl. He added powder and the concoction swirled.

Could his potions save me? I couldn't just watch him work. I had to keep trying, so I stood and walked forward feeling the walls for any type of seam or weak spot. Nothing. There was nothing. It felt smooth like polished wood. Dizziness hit. I leaned my forehead against the wall and looked down. I saw Reed open my mouth while Healer Bram poured the potion in, massaging my throat so I would swallow.

Dizzy, so dizzy. There wasn't enough air.

I couldn't breathe. I tried to inhale but my lungs spasmed. I was choking. Choking and coughing and it felt like my chest was about to explode. The room spun as I dropped to my knees and fell forward onto the hard wood floor, vomiting the potion.

"It's going to be okay," Healer Bram said. "You're going to be fine."

My throat burned and tears streamed down my face. I was out of the waiting room and back in Reed's office. Every breath burned my lungs, but I was free. My arms gave out and I would have landed on my face if Reed hadn't caught me. He pulled me over so I was laying on my side.

"What happened?" Reed asked.

I couldn't even respond.

"Help her sit up." Healer Bram poured more powder in the bowl and grabbed my hand.

It was surreal watching him cut my finger for more blood. He'd saved me, again. He could take as much blood as he wanted. He poured another powder into the bowl and then held it to my lips. "Drink."

I sipped a little. The cool potion soothed my raw throat. The weakness in my body ebbed. After a moment I was able to hold myself up while Reed helped steady me with his arm around my shoulders. When the bowl was empty, I sighed. "Thank you."

"What happened?" Reed asked. "Where did you go?"

I recounted my visit to the waiting room and the witch's words about her friend.

"Her friend is the one who possessed Nathan, Tina, and then you?" Healer Bram asked Reed.

"I still don't know who it was," Reed looked at me. "Do you?"

"He was made of fire." That wasn't a lie. "Made him a little hard to recognize." Technically also not a lie.

"And this ghost today?" Healer Bram asked.

"That wasn't a normal ghost," Reed said. "I started to cross him over and he drifted apart. I thought maybe it was because he'd waited so long."

"I imagine the fake ghost was part of the witch's plan to make Belinda think she'd crossed over. Someone was waiting to impersonate Teresa. The ghost was part of the ruse. If she'd held you apart from your body long enough, you would have died."

"I think someone could use a ginger ale,"

Jezelle said from the doorway where she was holding three drinks on a tray.

She handed me a glass of amber fizzy liquid, passed Reed a shot of whiskey, and handed Healer Bram a cup of hot tea. "There's a lot of people out there who'd like to know what happened in here. What should I tell them?"

I glanced at Reed. "Any ideas?"

"I've got nothing." He downed his shot.

I pointed at Healer Bram. "You're up."

He sipped his tea and frowned. "You had an allergic reaction to something. They don't need any details."

Jezelle wrinkled her nose. "Someone should cast a cleaning spell."

And that's when I realized I was sitting in my own vomit. Ewwww. "Please tell me one of you has a cleaning spell for people, clothing, and floors."

"Hold still." Healer Bram retrieved a clear vial of green powder, poured some into his hand, and said words I couldn't hear before blowing on the powder.

A cool mint scented breeze flew through the room. The puddle of yuck disappeared from the floor, my clothes, and my skin.

"Much better," I said. "Thank you."

"As a healer, it's a spell I use often."

"And no one has to bleed to make it work?" I asked.

"It's a dehydrated potion which already contains blood."

"Most days I would find that disturbing but right now I'm glad it worked." I sipped my ginger ale.

"Why don't I drive you home," Healer Bram said. "I think you need to rest… again." His tone was teasing.

"I thought I'd met my quota for strange injuries, but apparently I was wrong."

"Let's start small." He stood and held his hand out to me. "Try to stand."

I grasped his hand and pushed to my feet. The room wavered a bit. I clutched at the front of the desk with my free hand. "Definitely not okay to drive."

He smiled and put his arm around my shoulders. "As I suspected. Let's go."

Bram's arm around my shoulders was warm and comforting. We exited the tea-room while people whispered and pointed. I couldn't blame them. I'd caused quite the scene.

He led me to a silver four door car. I didn't recognize the make or model, but the leather interior and wood grain dashboard told me it was expensive. Healing must pay well.

"Does everyone call you Healer Bram?"

"Not all the time. You can call me Bram if you like."

"How did you decide to become a healer?"

"It's my gift. I can diagnose medical conditions and mix spell components to heal the illness."

I looked out the window as we drove down Main Street. Once again people went about their day like everything was fine. Was it fine, or were they just pretending?

When Bram pulled up to my house and turned off the engine, I said, "Let's see if I can walk into the house under my own power."

"How about I spot you, just in case." He opened his door and came around to meet me.

I swiveled my body to the side so both of my feet were on the ground. With effort, I stood. The world went a little swimmy, so I paused and held onto the car door. This was not going as well as I'd hoped. "I could use your assistance."

"Agreed. Your body has been through a lot." He helped me down the driveway and through the door into the kitchen. "Where to now?"

"Let's be optimistic, assume I don't need bedrest, and aim for the couch."

Bram kept his arm around my shoulders and helped me navigate into the living room where Dave and Sadie were curled up in their chair.

"What's wrong?" Dave asked.

Once I was seated on the couch, I gave him a condensed version of my exciting afternoon. "And now I plan to nap on the couch."

"Don't over exert yourself," Bram said. "I'll leave you some vitamin potions on the kitchen counter. Be sure to eat before you take them. Call if you need me." His dark eyes held sincerity.

"Thank you, again."

"The next time I see you, it would be nice if you weren't in need of medical attention." He turned to Dave. "Make sure she doesn't try to climb the stairs by herself."

"I'll be on Belinda-watch until she's recovered, *again*," Dave said.

"It's not like I ask people to rip my spirit from my body," I pointed out.

"You do tend to attract trouble," Bram said. "Try to lay low for a while. I will report this incident to the police."

"Should you do that?" I wasn't so sure.

"It's standard procedure when foul play is suspected. Take care." Bram headed back into the kitchen.

When we heard his car engine start, Sadie shifted to human form. "Do you want to nap on the couch or would you like me to help you up the stairs to your room?"

Should I admit defeat?

"You look like you need sleep," Sadie said.

"Fine. I'll go to bed."

It took both Dave and Sadie to help me up the stairs. Once I was tucked underneath my covers, Sadie switched back into cat form and joined me on the bed.

"I'll check on you in a while," Dave said. "And I'll bring you something to eat and one of those vitamin potions."

"Thank you."

Sadie cuddled up against me and I drifted off to sleep.

———

"BELINDA, time to wake up and eat something," Dave said.

I yawned and opened my eyes. Dave stood there with a bowl of what my nose told me was chicken noodle soup. I pushed myself up to a seated position and accepted the tray he offered which also held a vial of the vitamin potion.

"Thanks."

"You're welcome. Send Sadie down if you need anything else."

I ate the soup, drank the vitamin potion, and tried to figure out how I felt. "I'm going to stand and attempt walk to the restroom by myself."

Sadie hopped off the bed, shifted into human form, and stayed close as I stood. The room did not go swimmy, and for that I was grateful. Walking took a little more concentration than it should but I was moving under my own power. Go me. When I emerged from the bathroom, I considered going downstairs for about five minutes before crawling back under the covers.

Sadie didn't shift and join me. She probably had things she'd rather be doing, and I felt better mentally and physically. "You don't have to chaperone me anymore."

"Are you sure?"

I nodded.

"Don't try to walk down the stairs by yourself," she said. "Call me from your doorway. I'll hear you." Sadie exited the room and I dropped off to sleep.

IT TOOK me two days to feel like myself again. Having your spirit pulled from your body was exhausting.

"Look who walked down the steps under her own power," Dave said when I came into the living room where he and Sadie were reading.

"And I'm wearing real clothes." I gestured at my oversized shirt, leggings, and tennis shoes.

"There's a debate about whether leggings count as real clothes," Dave said.

"They're a step up from pajama bottoms," I pointed out.

"True." Sadie closed her book, shifted into cat form, and stretched. "Since I know you're feeling better I'm going to take a nap."

"I'll join you for breakfast," Dave stood and followed me across the room.

"I'd like that. Maybe you can answer some questions for me." We entered the kitchen and before I could ask Lilly for breakfast, two plates of bacon, eggs, toast, and cantaloupe appeared on the table complete with silverware. Coffee cups and a carafe appeared next, along with several bottles of creamer.

"Thank you, Lilly."

"Hold on." Dave put his hand on my shoulder. "Lilly did someone tell you to serve us this food?"

The lights flashed once for no.

"Did you come up with this on your own because you're the best house ever?" I asked.

The lights flashed twice.

"Thank you." I sat down, poured myself a cup of coffee, and added French vanilla creamer.

Dave checked out his options for creamer. "I didn't know they made salted caramel creamer."

Maybe I'd try that in my second cup of coffee.

"What did you want to ask me?" Dave said as he cut his toast into triangles.

"How do we pay for groceries and water and electricity?"

"The bank pulls money from whatever account you assign to each item. Currently, Victor and I each pay one third of all the bills. Teresa left her account to you, so the money is still coming from there. I imagine you won't have to worry about paying the bills for years."

"Good to know." That took a little pressure off.

"You should ask Reed to see the books for the tearoom. Get a feel for the business."

Not a great idea. "Won't he think I'm checking up on him?"

"Technically, you're his boss." Dave looked like he was trying not to laugh.

"Why is that funny?"

He leaned in. "It's fate. No matter how many times he pushes you away, your life will always be intertwined with his."

"I never thought of it like that." I set my fork down. "How long has he been with Jezelle?" Because fate seemed to have missed that stumbling block.

"Teresa hired them around the same time. Why?"

"No. I mean how long have they been a couple?"

"Never."

I set my coffee cup down with a *thunk*. "What?"

"As far as I know, they're coworkers."

"But…he's mentioned having breakfast with her, and he repeats things she says about his personality."

"Reed is an exceedingly private person, just like his father. If they were dating there's no guarantee he'd ever mention it around me."

"Even if he isn't with Jezelle, he'd never trust me again." I told Dave about the conversation I had on the roof with Reed.

"Never, is a long time," Dave said. "Don't give up hope. Or date Healer Bram since he seems to be a good man and you suffer from terrible luck when it comes to being injured in odd ways."

I laughed. "Not a bad idea."

Victor entered the kitchen. "What are you two laughing about?"

"Dave thinks I'm prone to odd injuries."

"He's not wrong." Victor poured himself

a cup of coffee and joined us. "I'm over being mad about the fact that Dave has two feet instead of four."

"Good," I said. "I didn't mean to spring that on you, but it was an emergency."

"I'd rather no one know about this un-orthodox situation." Victor tapped his fingers on the table. "There are those who would feel threatened."

"Is it me, or do the powerful witches seem to fear anyone else gaining a little bit of power?"

"That is how the world works," Victor said. "People fight to hold onto what they have."

"The world needs to remember there is enough for everyone and we should all share."

Victor sipped his coffee. "Most people around here don't see it that way."

"Preschool rules," I said. "If everyone lived by them the world would be a much better place."

"If you teach Mystic Hills preschoolers, maybe the next generation of adults will be-have more appropriately," Dave said.

The house phone rang. Dave hopped up. "I'll get that."

Victor smiled. "Since he couldn't do it for a decade, answering the phone is a treat."

"Harbinger Residence, how may I direct your call?" He listened and then said, "I'll let her know." He hung up and then rubbed his chin. "Belinda, the mayor has invited you and a plus one to dinner at his house, tonight at six."

"Why, and do I have to go?"

"I don't know," Dave said, "and yes."

I slid down in my chair. "Would one of you like to be my plus one?"

"I nominate Reed," Victor said.

"I second," Dave said.

"Does one of you want to call him?"

"Not it." Dave shifted into a cat and ran off.

"Belinda, you should call him yourself," Victor said.

"Fine. I'll call after one more cup of coffee."

When Reed answered, I wasn't sure how to ask him. After our conversation on the roof, I didn't want to make it sound like a date. "I've been summoned to the mayor's house for dinner. You should go too."

"Why would I want to do that?"

"Because you're my friend. Misery loves company. I need backup. Take your pick."

"Fine. Do I have to wear a suit?"

"I don't know. Dave took the call and didn't ask for any details."

"Figure it out and get back to me so we don't show up underdressed." He hung up.

I picked up the phone and paused. "Lilly, do you know the mayor's number, at his office?"

A drawer opened. I checked the contents and found a small business phone book. After looking up the mayor's number, I called and spoke to his secretary. She said the mayor and his wife dress for dinner, and then she hung up on me.

I checked with Dave and Sadie, they confirmed that dress for dinner meant a suit or a dress. I called Reed to share the joyous news.

"Great," he said. "Do you want to meet there or ride together?"

"Considering I don't know where the mayor lives…"

"Fine. See you at quarter til six."

Okay that was taken care of. What should I wear? I had the little black dress I'd purchased from *The Perfect Fit*. Was that appropriate? There was one way to find out. I grabbed my keys and headed to Main Street. When I walked into The Perfect Fit, Ethan took one look at my over-sized shirt and leggings and said, "Oh, Belinda. No."

I rolled my eyes. "I'm dressed for comfort, not fashion. I need your help. I've been invited to dinner at the mayor's house and I'm not sure what to wear."

"That's exciting."

"More like intimidating. I'm supposed to dress for dinner, and I don't know what that means."

"It means a dress, and I have just the thing to accentuate your figure." He grinned. "That's my new line when people come in. What do you think?"

"Much better than listing their imperfections," I said.

"And if people want to know why I choose an item, then I can explain." He walked over to a rack of dresses and selected one in navy, and another in red. Both had asymmetrical lines and were made of a silky material. "What color do you prefer?"

"I love red but not for this dinner."

"You can never go wrong with navy. It's classic."

I tried on several navy dresses, modeling them for Ethan. "They are all flattering," he said, "but you need something with a little more oomph."

"Is that a fashion term?"

"Yes, it means slightly sexy but classy." He sorted through the racks and found a navy dress and a black one with lower necklines which would show a small amount of cleavage. "Try these."

In the dressing room, I tried on the navy dress and smiled. It showed a little skin and made me feel good about my figure. For comparison's sake, I tried on the black one, and decided I needed them both. The black one I'd keep for a special occasion. I changed back into my clothes and exited the dressing room.

After paying for the dresses and chatting with Ethan, I considered walking down to *Tea and Spirits*, but decided to go home instead because I didn't want to give Reed an opportunity to back out before dinner.

Chapter 20

Sadie clapped her hands when I came downstairs at five thirty. "You look amazing."

"Thank you." I'd put effort into my hair and makeup. It was nice someone noticed.

Dave chuckled. "Ten bucks says Reed is rude to you on purpose because you look so good."

"We're supposed to be on the same side tonight," I said. "Hopefully he'll remember that." I was nervous about the dinner already and didn't need added drama.

"Any strange magical dining customs I should know about?"

"Just the usual," Dave said. "Don't chew

with your mouth open. Don't put your elbows on the table."

The sound of the mustang coming down the driveway made my stomach flip. This was not a date. I needed to remember that. It was more like a business dinner.

Honk, honk.

The fact that he honked for me rather than coming to the door proved this wasn't a date. Darn it. "Wish me luck."

"No." Dave stood. "He needs to come to the door. You're going to dinner for goodness sake."

I was torn. In principle I agreed with Dave but making Reed crabby would only make my night worse. "He's attending as a favor to me, so I shouldn't make him wait."

Pretending I wasn't nervous, I exited the house and walked to the passenger side of Reed's car. To my surprise, there was already someone sitting in what I thought would be my spot. Jezelle looked other worldly in a green dress that hugged her body like a bandage. She grinned at me and then looked behind me like she expected to see someone else. When she didn't, she frowned.

Why would he bring Jezelle? It didn't

make sense. Unless ...Reed had miscon-strued the invitation. Rather than being my plus one, he'd brought a date. My face burned. How could I recover from this? I held up one finger and pointed back toward the house and then dashed back inside and into the living room.

"Dave, you have to pretend to be my date."

"What? Why?"

"Reed brought Jezelle. I can't go as the third wheel."

"Why would he do that?" Sadie asked.

"I don't know." I'd gone out of my way to make it not sound like a date, maybe I'd done too good of a job.

I heard the kitchen door open and the sound of high heeled shoes crossing the floor coming toward us. Jezelle joined us in the living room. "When you asked Reed to go to dinner tonight, you meant as your date, didn't you?"

Should I lie? "Not a real date, just as my plus one. Like a business dinner. I guess I didn't make that clear."

"I can go with Belinda," Dave stood. "Give me a moment to change."

"No," Jezelle said. "That won't work. The mayor is expecting two people for dinner, not four."

Dang it. "I could call the mayor and explain the mix up. He could add two more place settings to the table."

"That would be rude," Jezelle sighed. "I've never had dinner at the mayor's house. I bought a new dress."

"Take Jezelle as your plus one," Dave said. "Tell Reed he misunderstood the invitation and send him home. You'd probably have a better time with her anyway."

"It's not like Reed wanted to come in the first place," I said. "Jezelle, what do you think?"

"I'm not sure."

The sound of the kitchen door opening and footsteps meant Reed was about to join the fun. He entered the living room in a black suit that emphasized his broad shoulders and narrow waist. "What are you doing? We're going to be late."

"Apparently I wasn't clear earlier." I said. "I asked you as my plus one. The mayor is only expecting two people."

His eyes narrowed. "How was I supposed to know that's what you meant?"

"We don't have time to play the blame game. Either you or Jezelle can come with me.

Reed crossed the room and touched Jezelle's bare shoulder. "Do you want to go?"

She nodded. "If you don't mind."

"You know me, I'd rather have pizza and beer." He grinned and ran his fingers down her arm. "Call me later with the details." And then he left without acknowledging my existence. It stung. It shouldn't have, but it did. I'd just have to put on my big girl panties and deal with Reed dating Jezelle. It's not like I had a choice. A small part of me may have hoped Reed would find me attractive in my new dress. Total fantasy, I know.

"Okay," I said. "Let's go have dinner."

On the drive to the mayor's house, Jezelle said, "You should know when it comes to social situations with Reed you have to spell things out for him. His parents didn't socialize a lot so he doesn't always know what you're talking about."

"I will keep that in mind." Now what should I say? "I love your dress. Did you buy it at the Perfect Fit?"

"Yes. I love that store. Ethan is always so complimentary."

Of course, he was. From what I could see in her form fitting dress, Jezelle's figure was probably symmetrical and perfect in every way. It would be ridiculous and immature to dislike her for that, so I squashed down those feelings and said, "I bet your dress doesn't have pockets."

She laughed. "No, but I'm pretty happy with it."

We discussed dresses and shoes for the rest of the drive. She was funny and easy to talk to. I could see why Reed liked her. By the time we reached our destination, I was convinced I'd made the best choice for my dinner date.

The mayor's home was a huge two story farmhouse with a wraparound porch on the first and second floor. I'd never seen anything like it. "Impressive."

"I've always wanted to see the inside."

I parked in the driveway and we walked down the sidewalk and up the steps to the front door. Before I could knock, the mayor opened the door.

"Thank you for coming this evening, Belinda."

"Thank you for inviting me."

His gaze traveled to my untraditional dinner date. "Jezelle, what a lovely surprise. I thought we'd have to put up with Reed, and he is not a sparkling conversationalist. Come in."

He stepped back and swung the door wide. We entered a house worthy of a photo shoot. The foyer opened into a great room decorated in creams and browns with gold and copper accents. The effect was modern, warm, comfortable, and luxurious.

"We're having drinks on the back porch before dinner." The mayor led us past a cream colored sofa that I'd be afraid to sit on, and past a curio cabinet filled with what appeared to be dolls made of animal bones. What was up with that? The dolls were slightly less creepy than Tina's grandmother's baby dolls because at least these bone dolls didn't look like they could come back to life at any moment. Then again what did I know.

I was grateful when we reached the seemingly normal screened in back porch.

A golden skinned woman with silver hair and dark eyes glanced up from the bar cart when we entered. The black silk sheath she wore floated over her skin. Her appearance and her manner seemed effortless.

"Belinda and Jezelle, this is my wife, Penny."

"Welcome to our home," Penny said. "Would you like a cocktail before dinner?"

"Yes," I said.

Jezelle approached the cart. "Don't tell me. Gin and tonic with lime?"

"How did you … oh, you're the drink fairy, aren't you?" Penny said with a laugh.

Jezelle stiffened slightly and then she nodded. "That's me. Although technically, I'm the drink half-fairy."

"What a wonderful gift," Penny said. "You know exactly what someone needs to make them happy."

"I enjoy it," Jezelle said.

Penny poured the drinks and gestured that we should take one. I picked mine up but didn't drink right away. Call me paranoid, but I wanted the mayor or his wife to take the first sip.

The mayor finished half of his in one swallow. "Booze should be served in larger glasses."

"The glass is refillable, dear." Penny took

a step toward me. "Belinda, I've heard good things about you. Healer Bram said you've done a wonderful job helping families communicate with their loved ones who've passed on."

"Thank you," I said. "The learning curve has been interesting."

"I can imagine," Penny said. "What is your gift in the outside world?"

What an odd way to phrase it. "I teach preschool."

"Is that like baby-sitting?" Penny asked.

The mayor's wife appeared to be one of those women who was skilled at casting insults while pretending she hadn't said anything negative. This should be a fun evening. "No. I teach pre-reading and pre-math skills to children, so they'll be more successful in kindergarten."

"Shouldn't their parent's take care of that?" she asked.

"In a perfect world they would, but not all parents have the time or the ability to help their children learn."

"What a shame," the mayor chimed in. "If you stay in Mystic Hills would you like to continue teaching?"

"Yes." Was this the part where he offered me a job to stay, or the part where he told me I should leave if I wanted to teach? I sipped my drink and waited to see how this would play out.

Chapter 21

"If you stay," the mayor said. "I'm sure we can find a place for you in our educational system."

Nice, vague comment. "That's good to know."

The savory smell of roasted meat drifted into the room. "It smells like dinner is ready." Penny said. "Feel free to bring your drinks. We can refill them in the dining room."

The white oak dining room table was set with cream-colored dishes. The copper edged napkins were folded into fans and the water glasses had copper rims.

We took our seats and a waiter served us steak, white asparagus, and salad. He offered us water or tea. Once everyone had their drinks, the mayor raised his glass. "A toast to good company and good food."

We all raised our glasses and drank. I cut into my steak, took a bite and was completely underwhelmed. The meat was seared to perfection but tasted bland, like someone forgot to season it. Jezelle glanced around the table like she was looking for something. I'd bet she was looking for salt. There wasn't any on the table and our hosts seemed perfectly happy with their meals so I guess we'd have to deal with it.

The mayor had asked us probing questions earlier, I decided to return the favor. "What made you want to become mayor?"

He paused and then smiled. "No one has ever asked me that. As witches we wield more power than the gifted. More power means more responsibility. I believe I'm one of the few witches responsible enough to wield power for the good of all."

There were so many things I wanted to say about my aunt and the restrictions, or about my run in with the vampire bracelet, but now wasn't the time. The mayor had invited me into his home to share a meal. I needed to respect that but I couldn't quite let it go.

"I know my aunt's views differed from your own, and sometimes in life you have to agree to disagree. That's part of being an adult. I'm still learning about Mystic Hills. Is there anything, as a newcomer you think I should be aware of?"

"I thought Reed would've told you everything you needed to know."

I snorted, and Jezelle laughed.

"Reed isn't cooperative when it comes to sharing information about this world," I said.

"And he's quite the cynic," Jezelle added. "His explanations are always from the glass half empty perspective."

The mayor set his knife down next to his plate. "I appreciate your forthright nature, so I will answer in kind. Witches use their magic to keep this town running. Everything from your house to your phone is powered through the personal sacrifice of witches. The gifted are an important part of our community, but they don't give as much of themselves as we do. That's why some witches believe they can demand blood whenever they want. I'd prefer if donations were given in a more civilized manner, but not everyone agrees."

"Why not ask every citizen to give a pint of blood a month. You'd have a ready supply of blood which you could distribute to the witches."

The mayor's wife laughed. "Can you imagine, if you suggested such a thing?"

"We have never demanded that citizens give blood," the mayor said.

"Everyone pays taxes in blood. If people donated blood a few more times a year, then maybe my aunt's husband wouldn't have been bled out."

Penny's knife scraped across her plate. "It's rude to discuss such things at dinner. I'll assume you're unaware since you're an outsider. Let's change the subject to something more pleasant."

It took effort not to lash out at her, and there wasn't a chance I'd apologize, so I nodded and took a drink of my iced tea.

"We're thinking of stocking a new honey wine that Lisa Laddow brought in for us to sample," Jezelle said.

"Sounds interesting," the mayor said. "Is the wine local?"

"Yes. Her friend runs a bee farm. She started making wine a few years ago."

Jezelle carried the conversation. She managed to involve the rest of us by asking questions. By the time dessert was served, the tension had left the room.

"I hope you like peach pie," Penny said. "I bought one from *Chanda's*. It's my favorite."

The waiter cleared our dishes.

I blinked and paused. "I'm having the strangest sense of Deja vu right now. Someone else told me peach was their favorite pie, but I can't remember who."

"It's a popular flavor," the mayor said.

"I've always been torn between triple berry and apple," I said. "But there is no such thing as bad pie."

"Wrong," Jezelle said. "If anyone offers you rhubarb pie, run. My friend told me it tasted like strawberry. That was a vicious lie."

"It was that bad?" I asked.

She nodded. "It was the only time in my life I've ever wanted to spit out pie."

We all laughed. The waiter served the pie with a small dish of vanilla ice cream. I took a bite and swooned. "Penny, you're right. This is the best pie I've ever tasted."

She beamed.

Once everyone finished their dessert, the mayor said, "Belinda thank you for coming this evening. There are those in this community who would paint me as a villain. As you said earlier, we don't have to agree on everything to respect one another. We can agree to disagree. I wanted to make you aware that I'll be calling a new vote on the restriction your aunt championed, not to erase her good intentions, but as a peacekeeper. There are powerful witches in this community who believe might makes right and they are the type who would grab a citizen off the street and think nothing of draining them. I'm going to propose that involuntary donations be limited to a non-life threatening amount."

"I see." I blinked my eyes rapidly to fight off angry tears. "I appreciate you making me aware of the impending vote. I wish there was another way to satisfy the population without changing the law."

He frowned. "If it's any consolation, we're leaving the hex waiting period in place. Those who complained about lack of sales have made up their losses by selling a wider variety of potions and charms."

"That does make it better, actually." Not all of her work would be undone.

"Good."

The mayor sipped his gin and tonic. "If I share something with you about an on-going investigation, will you vow to keep the information to yourselves?"

"I'm not good at keeping secrets," Jezelle said. "Maybe I should visit the powder room."

"As you wish," the mayor said.

Penny stood. "I'll show you where it is."

Both women left the room. The mayor raised his eyebrows at me. "Belinda, are you going to flee, or do you want to know what's really happening in this town?"

"I desperately want to know, but I'll also want to share with Reed and my house-mates. Can I do that?"

"No. Give me your word you'll keep this information to yourself, or we're done here."

It's not like I couldn't keep a secret, it's that I didn't like keeping information from people I cared about. "My friends and family won't be endangered by this knowledge?"

"No."

"Okay, then."

"Repeat after me, I will not divulge this information until given permission to do so."

"Is that a spell?"

"It's a vow. Vows in Mystic Hills carry weight. If you break a vow, there are consequences."

Maybe I should go to the bathroom. "What type of consequences?"

"Imprisonment for five days without food or water," he said. "Are you still in?"

Was this a trap? There was only one way to find out. "I will not divulge this information until given permission to do so."

"You're aware that Nathan and several others in this town have been the victims of possession."

I nodded.

"A member of my staff was responsible for these crimes. Apparently, he had political aspirations to unseat me in the next election and he was trying to gain power by taking the Tate's house. Evidence has come to light that he was responsible for your aunt's death."

Was he going to tell me the truth or a political lie? "What kind of evidence?"

"Possession spells require uncommon ingredients which are perishable and only last a few days. He purchased those specific ingredients the day before each death. We believe he was responsible for Mrs. Tate's death as well."

Funny how he hadn't given me a name yet. "What about the Greens?"

"You're aware of the toxin placed in the olive oil gift basket I sent them?"

"Yes."

"He purchased the gift basket for me. I believe he put the toxin in the olive oil in an attempt to frame me for their murders."

This all seemed a little too convenient. "Where did the toxin come from?"

"We're still investigating where, but we found what was left of the poison at his residence."

I couldn't admit that I knew who it was, so I went with, "Have you arrested him?"

"We intended to arrest him and charge him with murder, but before we could complete the case, he died." He stared at me like he expected a confession.

"How?" I asked.

"You should know." He leaned toward

me, keeping his eyes laser focused on mine. "You were there."

Uh-oh. "The possessor we kicked out?"

The mayor shook his head. "Not kicked out. Crossed over. You met him the day you came to sign citizenship papers in my office."

I wanted to push away from the table, but I held my ground. "I remember him. He was not a pleasant man."

The mayor smiled. "No. He was not. Kyle Carter was an over-confidant fool who possessed the one man in this town who could separate his spirit from his body permanently."

"That wasn't our intent." I couldn't appear too calm. "He threatened to throw Reed off the roof. We just wanted him out of Reed. We never meant to kill anyone."

He continued to stare at me.

I looked down at my hands. "What happens now?"

"Nothing," the mayor said. "It was self-defense. You and Reed performed a service by ridding the community of a ruthless witch."

"Will you release this information to the public?"

"No. The matter has been dealt with. There's no reason to alarm the population."

"Are you aware that Kyle had an accomplice?"

"Are you referring to the witch who pulled your spirit from your body?"

"Yes."

"I read the police report. Healer Bram didn't indicate you knew the identity of the attacker."

"No, but they were close to Kyle." That had to narrow it down.

"The police are looking into it, but this type of crime doesn't leave behind specific clues. That type of spell uses common ingredients with long shelf lives, so there is no trail to follow."

"That's too bad. Can I tell Victor and Dave we think Teresa was killed while possessed? They deserve some sort of closure."

"Do you want to spend five days in jail without food or water?" he asked.

"No."

"Then keep your vow."

"I will, but why did you share this with me?"

"Because you are tenacious, like your aunt. I knew you'd keep digging until you found an answer. And now, you owe me. In the future I'll call upon you for your support."

Reed was right. The mayor hadn't told me out of the goodness of his heart. He expected something in return. It was time for me to learn how to play this game. "Thank you for telling me."

"You're welcome." He gave a slow grin. "Now that I think about it you owe me two favors. This dinner invitation implies that you are aligned with my team, so Kyle's friend or any other member of my contingency should leave you alone."

"I didn't realize that." I grinned. "Considering Kyle's friend was scary strong I appreciate the implied protection."

"All done?" Penny asked from the doorway.

"Yes," The mayor said.

"Jezelle is waiting for you by the front door," Penny said.

"Thank you for inviting me to dinner." I stood. "It was an interesting and illuminating evening."

"I'm glad you enjoyed it." The mayor said. "I'll walk you out."

———

ONCE WE WERE in the car with the doors locked, I said, "That was intense."

"Was what you learned worth the vow?" Jezelle asked.

"Yes." And I couldn't say much more than that because I believed he'd follow through on his threat. I put the car in drive and realized I didn't know where Jezelle lived. "You'll have to give me directions to your house."

"You can drop me at *Tea & Spirits.* I left my car there."

I headed into town toward Main Street. "What do you think about the mayor changing the restrictions?"

"The witches have always done what they wanted," Jezelle said. "Every gifted person in town has someone in their family tree who was drained and found dead. It's a few generations back for my family. For other people it's more recent. It's always been a scary fact of life."

"Why not set up a blood bank?" It made perfect sense.

"Because they want us to be afraid," Jezelle said. "They want us to know they have the power to take our lives. They want us to know we are the inferior species."

"I have so many responses to that statement and none of them are appropriate for polite company."

Jezelle laughed.

We pulled onto Main Street and the car bumped up and down on the cobblestones. "If someone had a spell that made your car ride smoothly over these cobblestones, I'd buy it."

"A spell like that would be a guaranteed money maker." She pointed at her car on the right side of the street. "That's my blue Honda."

I pulled in next to her car. "I had fun tonight. We should do dinner under less stressful circumstance."

"I'd like that," Jezelle said. "And thanks for picking me over Reed."

"Any time," I said, which made her laugh.

I waited while she climbed into her car and pulled out of her spot before I headed home. All three of my housemates waited for me in the living room. Dave and Sadie were curled up in their chair. Victor sat on the couch. I joined him and shared what I could.

"I guess we should be grateful he's leaving the hex restriction in place," Victor said.

"Only because it doesn't affect the bottom line, not because it's the right thing to do," Dave said.

"On that frustrating note, I'm going up to bed. Good night."

A chorus of goodnight's followed me up the stairs. As I changed into pajamas and climbed into bed, I realized something. The mayor had acted in kindness. He didn't have to tell me about the new vote or why he wanted the change. He didn't have to serve me dinner. He certainly didn't have to tell me about Kyle Carter. When it came down to it, he might be a decent yet scheming human being. What type of favors would he want from me in the future? It might be best not to think about it. For now I'd enjoy the fact that Kyle's friend shouldn't come after me.

The best part of the evening had been spending time with Jezelle. I liked her as much as Lisa and Tina. Maybe we could form a book club or something where we'd meet and go out to dinner on a regular basis.

Uh-oh. I was making plans like I intended to stay. My mother would not be pleased. Dang it. I should go home for a weekend so I could remember what normal life was like. Then again, I was on my summer vacation. I'd found Aunt Teresa's killer and justice was definitely being served. Maybe now I could focus on enjoying my time here.

With the self-cleaning, cooking, and grocery shopping house this was like an all-inclusive resort. A resort where someone might try to drain your blood, but still, I needed to enjoy the positive aspects of the situation. Reed's face flashed in my mind. I wasn't sure if he went into the positive or negative column. I couldn't undo the past, but maybe I could mend fences and build a friendship with him.

It's not like he was the only guy in town. Bram was charming and handy to have around. Maybe I'd call and ask him to lunch so I could get to know him while I wasn't suffering from some life-threatening injury. Then again, I didn't need a guy to enjoy my time here. It might be best to hang out with friends, especially if I didn't plan on staying. Which I might not. Magic could become boring, just like anything else if you're exposed to it day after day. What is that saying…familiarity breeds contempt? Like a new toy it might lose its shine after a few months. I'd have to wait and see.

Double Trouble in Mystic Hills

BOOK TWO, CHAPTER ONE

Three days later…

───

"Belinda, wake up."

"What?" I opened my eyes and saw Sadie, in cat form, sitting on my nightstand.

"Good morning. Reed brought donuts for breakfast and he insists you join him."

"Really?" I yawned. "Why?"

"I don't know. He's all smiles this morning."

"That's odd." I climbed out of bed. "Is anyone else here?" If not, I planned to greet him in my sloth pajamas, just to see the expression on his face.

"Just him."

I brushed my teeth and my hair and went downstairs.

Reed looked up from his glazed donut and narrowed his eyes while he studied my outfit. "Are those sloths wearing berets?"

"Yes. They are obviously Parisian sloths."

He shook his head and took another bite of his donut.

"To what do I owe the honor of your presence?" I made myself a cup of coffee, joined him at the farmhouse style table, and selected a chocolate cake donut. Yum.

"I thought about what you asked me," he said. "I think we should start over."

I almost choked on my donut. Reed was willing to give me another chance. I never believed he'd—

"There's no reason we can't be friends," he said.

"Friends?" I said and then tried to cover my awkwardness with, "I'd like that."

"Good. Someone may have mentioned that I have a pessimistic view on life and I should try harder when it comes to people. You're the experiment in progress."

"I'm honored."

"You should be. Tell me what happened at the mayor's house."

"Jezelle didn't share?"

"She told me she fled the room because she's not good at keeping secrets."

In between bites of donut, I told him what I could.

"You're holding something back," he said.

"Of course, I am. Unlike Jezelle, I took a vow, and I don't want to go to jail for five days without food and water."

His eyebrows came together. "I can't believe he threatened you with that."

I wiped icing off my fingers. "It's an effective deterrent."

"Let's play charades. I could guess what he said."

"Nope." I believed the mayor would follow through on his threat.

"Chicken," he teased.

I laughed. "Bock bock bock."

"What does that mean?"

"It's what a chicken says, bock, bock, bock."

"No. A chicken says cock-a-doodle-doo."

I shook my head. "Wrong. That's a rooster. How can you not know your farm animal sounds? What kind of preschool did you go to?"

We laughed and talked through a few more donuts. It felt nice. I could enjoy Reed's company as a friend.

The house phone rang. I waited for Dave to rush in and grab it. When he didn't appear, I answered it. "Hello?"

"Belinda, this is Bram. Is Victor home?"

"Yes."

"Good. Reed is acting odd and I'm hoping his father can help."

What was he talking about? "Reed's already here. He's happily eating donuts."

There was a pause, then Bram said, "That's impossible. Reed is in the car with me."

I glanced at the dark haired, dark eyed man seated at my table. "Then there must be two of them," I said, sort of joking.

"I have no idea what's going on. I'm coming over. Tell him I have some questions about the possession case. Don't let him leave."

"Okay. We'll be here." Had Bram been drinking?

I hung up the phone and said, "Lilly, can we have bacon?" Because no one walked away from bacon.

A plate of crispy crunchy savory yummi-ness appeared on the table. I sat and grabbed a piece. "That was Healer Bram. He wants to talk to us."

"Do you have a thing for him?" Reed asked.

I almost choked on my bacon. "What? Why would you ask me that?" Better yet, why would he care? Especially if he wasn't Reed.

"Jezelle thinks he likes you, so it could be a good thing."

"He's saved my life multiple times, so I'm fond of him." That was a nice safe answer.

The back door opened, and Dave came in. "Good morning." He walked over to the table and grabbed a piece of bacon.

"Donut?" Reed gestured towards the box.

"Donuts satisfy human cravings. Bacon works for cats and humans."

"Where's Sadie?" I asked.

"She's sleeping in a sunbeam. I think I'll join her." He snagged another piece of bacon as he walked off.

"I should go." Reed stood.

"Bram said the questions will only take a few minutes."

I heard a car coming down the driveway. "That's probably him." I walked over to open the door while simultaneously blocking the exit. Not that Reed couldn't pick me up and move me out of the way if he wanted, but I was banking on him going with the flow.

Bram came down the sidewalk with another Reed behind him, a Reed who emitted waves of anger and fury. Despite my best intention to play it cool, I made a sound of surprise somewhere between a gasp and a yelp and backed away from the door.

"What's wrong?" Happy Reed came toward me.

"I'm not sure."

Bram opened the door and stepped in with Angry Reed on his heels.

Happy Reed froze. "Is this a joke?"

"You tell me," Angry Reed stalked toward us. "Who are you?"

"Reed Clay. Who are you?"

"I'm Reed." He reached out and shoved Happy Reed.

"None of that." Bram pulled a glass bottle from his pocket. "Calm down or I'll knock you both out."

"Belinda, what did you do?" Angry Reed turned his glare on me.

"I didn't do anything." Jerk. "Just so you know, I like Happy Reed better."

"Thank you," the more pleasant of the two said.

"Belinda, you may have hit on something. I'm going to perform some tests, but I think both of these men are Reed."

"What?" The Reeds yelled in unison.

"I think your personality has been split into your light side and dark side."

"What?" I said.

"Come stand by me," Happy Reed said. "I don't trust that guy."

"Belinda, get away from him. Go play with blocks or something."

"Can we keep the happy one, and banish the crabby one to the void?" I asked.

Angry Reed's face turned the color of a tomato.

"Just joking," I said.

Happy Reed grabbed my forearm and shoved me behind him. "I don't think he has a sense of humor."

"Belinda, are you all right?" Sadie entered the room in cat form. "I sensed a threat."

"We have a situation," I said.

She glanced back and forth between the two Reeds and came to sit by my feet. "Positive and Negative Reeds?"

"Something like that," Bram blinked at Sadie. "You're a Familiar?"

"I'll explain later," I said. "Can you fix them?"

"I believe I can, but they're going to have to work with me. Happy Reed, why don't you go into the living room while I work with Angry Reed for a moment."

"Don't call me that," Angry Reed snarled.

"How about Rabid Reed?" Sadie said.

Reed took a step toward Sadie. "Cat, I will drop kick you through the wall— "

Sadie shifted into her human form and made herself as tall as Reed. "Never threaten me or mine again, young man. I've worked with generations of witches, and I will turn you into a cockroach. Do you understand?"

No one spoke. Angry Reed paled. "I'm sorry, Sadie. I didn't mean that. Something's wrong with me."

"Sit." Sadie pointed at the kitchen chair. Reed sat.

"Perhaps a sedative?" Sadie turned to Bram.

"A sedative might be a good idea," Reed agreed.

Bram pulled a small bottle full of blue liquid from his bag and passed it to Reed. "Drink half."

Reed drank half of it and sighed. "That's better. Being angry all the time is exhausting."

Sadie shrunk down to her normal human size and then changed back into her cat form. "Reed, I apologize for my rude joke during your time of distress. I didn't realize how serious the situation was. Belinda, Positive Reed, come with me."

We followed Sadie into the living room. I sat on the couch and whispered, "Sadie, that was awesome."

"I may have over-reacted." Sadie hopped up onto the couch next to me. "And now Bram knows about me."

"He's honorable," Positive Reed said. "He'll keep your secret. On another note, am I that much of a jerk?"

"No," I said. "You can be cranky but you're not aggressive."

"Cranky," he smiled. "That's a preschool term, isn't it?"

I nodded. "In class we have a cranky corner. Kids who feel overwhelmed can go hug teddy bears or curl up in a bean bag chair until their cranky mood passes."

"No wonder you like being a preschool teacher." He smiled at me, and my heart fluttered.

Dave and Victor came down the stairs into the living room.

"What did we miss?" Victor said.

I caught them up on the morning so far.

"There are two Reeds?" Victor said.

"Surprise," Positive Reed said. "You're the father of twins."

Victor walked into the kitchen and then came back into the living room. "I see what you mean. Any idea how this happened?"

"Not a clue," Positive Reed said. "I haven't felt this good in years."

"Belinda, can you come in here?" Bram called out.

"I don't want to," I responded.

Bram laughed. "Please. I need your help."

"Fine." I walked into the kitchen and saw Negative Reed with his head down on the table. "Is he okay?"

"He drank the rest of the potion because he was afraid he'd hurt someone. Can you find Jezelle for me? She's the last person he had contact with."

I pulled out my cell phone and dialed Jezelle. She answered on the second ring. "Hello?"

"It's Belinda. When did you last see Reed?"

"About an hour ago. Why?"

"This is going to sound weird, but there are two Reeds now."

"Is one happy and one angry?" she asked.

"Yes. How'd you know?"

"This morning, I told him he was acting like two different people."

"Any idea how this happened?"

"Meet me at *Tea & Spirits*. There's something you need to see."

━━━

━━━

Want to know what happens next in the Mystic Hills Series? Check out Double Trouble in Mystic Hills:

About the Author

Chris Cannon is a speech therapist by day and the award-winning author of the Going Down In Flames series, the Boyfriend Chronicles, the Dating Dilemma series, and The Crossroads Chronicles by night. She lives in Southern Illinois with her husband and several furry beasts. She believes coffee is the Elixir of Life. Most evenings after work, you can find her sipping coffee while writing fire-breathing urban fantasies, sweet snarky romantic comedies, or paranormal cozy mysteries. You can find her online at www.chriscannonauthor.com.

Ingram Content Group UK Ltd.
Milton Keynes UK
UKHW011029300323
419408UK00004B/336